NO ONE
HEARS
BUT HIM

TAYLOR CALDWELL

NO ONE HEARS BUT HIM

FAWCETT CREST • NEW YORK

NO ONE HEARS BUT HIM

THIS BOOK CONTAINS THE COMPLETE TEXT OF
THE ORIGINAL HARDCOVER EDITION.

Published by Fawcett Crest Books, a unit of CBS Publications, the Consumer Publishing Division of CBS Inc., by arrangement with Doubleday and Company.

ISBN: 0-449-24030-4

Printed in the United States of America

21   20   19   18   17   16   15   14   13   12

*Dedicated with all veneration to the
Blessed Mother of the Man who Listens*

NO ONE
HEARS
BUT HIM

Many years have passed since old John Godfrey, the mysterious lawyer, built his Sanctuary in a great city for the hopeless, the grieving, the despairing, the churchless, the cynical, the defeated, the dying and the bereaved, the betrayers of men and the betrayed, the burdened and the old, the young and the lost.

Here, in the Sanctuary, waits the Man who Listens, who waits and listens endlessly and patiently to the anguished stories told to him in a blue and marble silence. There is no experience that he has never heard before. There is no grief with which he is not familiar. There is no crime against God or man that he has not seen with his own eyes. He has heard the blasphemies of the self-congratulatory. He has heard the cry of all parents and all children. He has listened to all prayers and all excuses. The experiences of all men are his own. Nothing disturbs him except hatred and violence. He knows them, too.

He does not confine himself to the Sanctuary built by the devoted John Godfrey so many years ago. He can be found anywhere in the world—if he is sought for and if his advice is desired. He will never turn away from any man, no matter how depraved. There is no one he has ever rejected. His patience is never at an end, his love is never exhausted. He will listen to anyone, for he has all the time in the world.

The Sanctuary waits for everyone, but especially for those who have never sought the Man who Listens anywhere else. It stands in the midst of several beautiful acres of parklike land in the heart of the great city, surrounded by apartment houses, theaters, shops, business buildings. It is a simple marble building containing but two rooms, one for waiting, and one in which the Listener waits. Nothing has been added to it over the years but one white marble tablet in the wall of the waiting room: *"I can do all things in Him Who strengthens me."* And a fountain or two on the green lawns.

Here come the sheep whose shepherds cannot find them or who have no faith in the shepherds or have never known them. Sometimes the shepherds come also, to learn what they have forgotten. Some come to the man in anger and disgust and outrage, denouncing him for "medievalism." Some come with rejection and contempt, exclaiming that this is an Enlightened and Modern Age and that there is no need for a man who listens—except a psychiatrist. Some come assured that the man within the sanctuary is a clergyman, a doctor, a social worker, a teacher, or just simply one who will listen in a world that has forgotten how to listen to anyone—so busy is it talking to itself, and talking only incoherences, irrelevances, theories and endless blasphemies, and all the bloodless violent trivialities which cannot satisfy the soul.

Some come with absolute disbelief and leave with the same incredulity.

But almost all, as they talk to the man, find an answer to their agonies and despairs, their sins and their sufferings. The world never gave them an answer, nor their schools, nor their pleasures, nor their affluence, nor their little satisfactions, for the world has no answer to the most terrible need of the human spirit: Someone to listen. Someone to be truly involved, truly compassionate, truly loving, truly faithful, truly understanding.

For all the talk of "love" there is in the world today the fact remains that never has the world been so absolutely loveless, hard of heart, murderous, cruel, rejecting, contemptuous, and indifferent. Never have so many been betrayed as they are now being betrayed. Never have so many been lost as they are now lost. Never has the heart of man been so faithless as the heart of modern man, for all the babble of "involvement" and "concern for humanity." Never has death menaced so many and never has freedom been so little, no, not ever before in the dreadful history of the world. We are no longer disturbed by massacres; we do not hear the man who implores our help on our very doorstep. We turn away from it all, as the skies continually darken and the Apocalypse approaches. We are busy—with nothing. We talk—of nothing. Our neighbor, our brother, cries to us for help and we do not care. Worse, we do not even listen to him in our busy, busy, unremarkable, and unimportant lives. Even worse, we do not listen to ourselves and are never aware of what we are saying all the days we live.

Hatred, not love, permeates the spirits of all mankind today. The triumph of evil is almost consummated in a world that has despised the good for "scientific truths" which are the scientific errors of tomorrow. Relativism has replaced eternal and absolute verity. Our children, in our secular schools, are not taught reverence, faith, duty, responsibility, pride in accomplishment, respect for authority. They are not taught these things because their parents do not wish them to be taught. This was so yesterday and now today we have a young generation that has never learned restraint, good will, authentic peace, tranquillity, faithfulness, and virtue. These young people are the truly lost. Only the Man who Listens can rescue them now. Who will bring them to Him? These are the deprived in truth, though they do not want for bread or shelter or comfort. We have given them "love" but not love. We have given them slogans and jargons but no living word. We have left them desolated, and so they are violent and Godless, with no respect for themselves and their country and their neighbors.

But still the man waits to listen, to admonish, to teach, to love, to advise.

As He waits for you. Will He answer you when you cry to Him? He has never failed yet. He requires only one thing: That you listen, too.

This book is deliberately designed to anger many. It is the hope of the author that the anger will induce you to "listen," also, or at least to inspire thought, before it is too late.

TAYLOR CALDWELL

SOUL ONE: The Watchman

"Watchman! What of the night?"
ISAIAH 21:11

Fred Carlson had had an excellent lunch with his prospective employers. They had parted from him with expressions of great cordiality, for they respected good and dedicated and intelligent men. His Bachelor of Arts degree, his postgraduate work in government and in applied science, had impressed them favorably, though they were somewhat amused and puzzled about the reasons he had chosen his particular present work in his home city. As they were such smooth and alert and sophisticated men he had not told them the truth; he had let them believe he had had a period of romanticism in his life, but now it was time to get up and out. They could forgive his romanticism; all young men were romantic, they said indulgently, and he was only thirty-two, though a married man with two young children. "Some of us even wanted to be soldiers!" one of the gentlemen had said. "Or railroad engineers in the old style, or firemen." He let Fred imply that he, Fred, had let it go on a little too long, however, and Fred had colored. He did not like that particular gentleman and it was he who had prevented Fred from telling the truth. He feared to be thought sentimental or a little lacking in ambition, all great crimes and unworthy of a man in his thirties.

They had offered to assign someone to drive him about the city until he had to go to the airport, catch his plane, and go home. But Fred liked to walk. He had colored again when they had laughed affectionately. "I'll walk everywhere I can," he said. "Just tell me of particular points of interest."

"Well, we have a fine museum of science, right in your real line, and a historical museum, right in your line from your studies in government, and an art gallery, which would interest you, too. They're all here, within fifteen minutes' walk of each other. But we'll send someone to your hotel to pick you up for the airport."

He had three hours. It was a fine autumn day, the sort he

13

liked, winey and smoky and brilliant with sun. He began to walk. It was really a handsome city, though only half the size of his own. The buildings were brighter and of lighter stone and brick, and the city had a southern air, though it was not really in the South. The streets were wider, and cleaner, and the people very energetic. Connie would like it; they would live in the suburbs, the one the company particularly advocated for its organization men. He had seen that suburb this morning, briefly; his own city had no such pretty suburb as this, and so close to all the center of city life. The houses were very attractive and cost much less than his own house, which he would now immediately put on the market. The school nearby had been unusually pleasant and modern, and soon his first child would be going there. In short, everything was fine, including the fact that his income would be twice what he was already earning, not to mention bonuses, stock benefits, expansive vacations with pay, excellent pension arrangements, sick insurance, dependents' insurance, allowances for illness, and a dozen other agreeable things not to be thought of in his present work.

"I've been a fool," he said to himself as he strolled down the main street and looked at the windows of the shops glittering in the sun. "I'm glad I didn't wait too long."

It was too nice outside to think of visiting any points of interest, so he strolled casually along, carrying his coat on his arm and thinking how enjoyable life would be in this city. The vague depression he was beginning to feel was, of course, only loneliness and a desire to get back home to his family. Besides, he had never been away from home before with an idea of leaving it permanently. He was a gregarious man, he told himself. He'd soon make many friends among all those congenial men he had met today. Connie, too, would soon find church groups to belong to, and his children would soon be absorbed with new playmates and new activities. And then the winters here were short, unlike those at home, which were hell on a man who had to walk a lot. But I won't be walking like that any longer, he thought, though I've not been walking so much these past three years or so.

It was strange how each city had its individual odor. His own smelled of dust and rubber and steel and electricity—yes, electricity, and it wasn't his imagination. But this city smelled of pale stone and clean pavements—he knew all about pavements!—and penetrating warmth and, funny, sort of like fruit. He decided he liked it.

The traffic was very brisk, he noticed with an experienced

eye, and the people appeared less sullen than in his own city and less belligerent, though there were crowds of them as every city was crowded in these days. The traffic was less frantic, the pedestrians less rude. All in all, it was "easier." He saw a patrolman standing on the corner, alertly watching, and he involuntarily, and out of habit, went up to him at once.

"Hello," he said, "I'm a stranger in town and—"

The policeman was young but he turned at once and Fred saw on his face what he always saw on the faces of the police at home: sharp wariness, quick suspicion, all unconscious but dismally there.

He was a little shocked, for he had thought this city unlike his own. He said quickly, "I'm a cop, myself. Made sergeant only three years ago. Fred Carlson's the name. I'm from——." He held out his hand. The young policeman was still wary, but he took Fred's hand quickly and as quickly let it go. "Sergeant?" he repeated. Fred took out his badge and his card and showed it to the policeman as politely as he wished ordinary citizens would so identify themselves. The policeman examined the offered credentials with a thoroughness which had not been necessary ten years ago, and studied the photograph. Then he handed them back, gave a boyish salute, and smiled.

"What you doing here, Sarge? Looking for a criminal?"

"No." Fred hesitated. He said, "Looking for another job. I've got it, right here."

"Police work?"

"No. I'm going into private industry with the Clinton Research Associates."

The young policeman eyed him curiously, but made no comment.

"A man has to think of his future," said Fred.

"Oh."

"Besides, being a cop these days isn't what it once was—what's your name? Jack Sullivan. A real cop's name. No, it isn't what it was, and what I thought it'd be."

Jack Sullivan's eyes narrowed. "Some have to be cops," he said. "That's how I figured it. It's the only thing I ever wanted to do."

"Same here," said Fred. They looked at each other, then Jack Sullivan said, "I've got to go along on my beat." He began to walk away, after the briefest salute, but Fred went after him and strolled along with him. He hadn't liked the

15

expression in the blue and intelligent eyes. "But where does it get you?" he said.

"Somebody has to keep law and order," said the young policeman. He glanced sharply at Fred's unhappy face. "That's what some of us are made for, but I guess you, Sergeant, were made for something else."

Was I? Fred asked himself. But it was too late to think of that now. He said, "How's crime in this town, Jack?"

"Hell," said Jack with eloquent brevity.

"It's that way all over the country these days, isn't it? I wonder why; everybody wonders why."

"We lost four of our best men last month," said Jack, and his young face darkened. "Ten last year. Are people getting to be some kind of nuts? And now everybody's talking of civilian review boards. That's the time," said Jack with passion, "when we'll go on strike and let the criminals take over for a while and blackjack some sense into the people!"

"I know what you mean," said Fred, depressed. " 'Police brutality.' All the sweet little criminals howling about it when you've caught them red-handed. Then the social workers and the do-gooders and the kissers and the cooers come into it, and the damned old judges who want to be re-elected and have soft hearts and soft heads and no sense of public responsibility. We've become a nation of psychopathic sentimentalists with no respect for authority and decency, and no dignity. Worse, we're a nation of criminals."

"That's right," said Jack Sullivan, with a suddenly wooden face. "I guess that's why you're getting out, isn't it, Sarge? So you can forget all about it?"

He looked fully at Sergeant Fred Carlson and there was no expression in his eyes. He saw a tall young man, lean and strong and hard, with a fair complexion, light brown eyes and light hair and an air of resolution and tautness and authority. Jack pursed his lips.

"I wouldn't say that," said Fred. "But I was thinking of the future, Jack. What future is there in police work?"

"Sarge," said the policeman with an elaborate politeness which was like an insult, "I wouldn't know. I'm just a dumb cop or I wouldn't be spending my life trying to uphold something everybody laughs at. Just a dumb cop. I've got to be on my way."

The dismissal was all too evident. Fred Carlson, Sergeant, was no longer important. He was only another civilian who didn't understand police work. He was left standing on the sidewalk, watching the straight young back of the policeman moving rapidly away from him. Finally he turned about and walked slowly on, his head bent. He forced himself to think of the bright new future in this city, the appreciation for all his work, the doubled salary, the security, and, damn it, the end of fear and the end of the feeling of enraged helplessness and bitter hopelessness, and the end of contempt.

Connie was a patrolman's daughter. Her father had been killed only a year ago on his beat by criminals, who, subsequently caught, were released on a technicality. She knew what it meant to be a cop. She was afraid for her husband, though his patrolling days were over and so he was in less danger. Less danger—but not much. He had had many bad moments since he had made sergeant, some of them even worse than when he had been only a rookie. He had never told Connie of how close to death he had come only a month ago; it would only frighten her. She lived in fear for him. But she was a policeman's daughter and to her police work was the most important thing in the world. "Like a soldier," she said, "guarding the city." Connie was quite poetic sometimes. But there was no poetry to police work, only threat and violence from the lawless, only dirty, grinding work and poor pay—and, always, the new contempt and derision. That was the worst.

"Damn, damn, damn," Fred muttered in fury.

He came to an intersection with a red light, and stopped. A car passed before him. On its bumper was a big red and white sticker: SUPPORT YOUR LOCAL POLICE! What a laugh. "Support your local police!" He laughed. A man standing beside him laughed too. "That's a joke, isn't it?" he asked Fred.

Fred looked at him somberly. "Yes. A joke," he replied. The man did not like the look in his eyes. He hurried away. Another solid citizen, commented Sergeant Fred Carlson to himself, a reader of some screaming newspapers that were always howling about "police brutality." A man who believed the sons of bitches who were saying, in these days, that men became policemen because they were too stupid and too indolent to be anything else, and because they were natural sadists. No wonder such "citizens" were no longer safe on the streets of their cities; no wonder their children were threatened every hour of every day and that old shopkeepers were shot behind their wooden counters and women scurried in the darkness for fear of their lives and houses were burglarized in broad daylight and women raped in their suburban or apartment homes. No wonder terror stalked the countryside and the towns, defiant and brazen and red with murder.

17

Chaos was everywhere, because the lawless and the psychopaths were no longer what they truly were: criminals. Now they were "mentally disturbed cases," or "victims of broken homes," or the "culturally deprived and disadvantaged and underprivileged."

And the people expect every decent, hard-working brave cop to be a drooling psychiatric social worker and not a guardian of the law and a protector of the public! thought Fred with intense old bitterness. Damn, damn, damn!

He felt the familiar despair and frustrated anger again, and the outrage. Slobs, he thought. We've become a nation of slobs, simpering with fake good will, and dangerous and dreamy-eyed and soft and lachrymose, mouthing every sick platitude the sly and crafty enemies of society can think up, for their ultimate ends. We've become womanish and—what do they call it in their jargon? Scared. Everything is scary, now, from a threat of war to a TV show. What kind of a people are we?

Slobs. Effeminate slobs! Transvestites in more ways than one!

He thought of the last time, a month ago, when he had attended the Communion Breakfast of the Holy Name Society, of which he was a member. He had seen old grizzled retired cops there, manly old fellows whom none would ever mistake for old women. They had strong and resolute faces, these men who had guarded the public safety and weal for over fifty years, who had demanded and had received respect from the people. They had been the terror of criminals. "Tell me, Tim," Fred had asked one of them during the breakfast. "Why is it that people don't respect cops any longer?"

"It's the wimen," said Tim in his rough brogue. "We got afraid of the wimen and their big mouths and their pokin' their noses in politics and such. We let them make wimen of our bhoys, too, God have mercy on our souls!"

Fred asked another old retired patrolman the same question. "Well, I tell you, Sarge," the old man had answered. "It's the gineril breakdown in religion and public morals, and who's to blame? Over the past forty years I seen it for meself. I ain't sayin' things wasn't tough for people in the old days; they was. But people were workin' too long and too hard to listen to pussy-footers and their soft-headed tripe, and they laid a heavy hand on their kids, too, and dragged them off to church. But now my grandchildren laugh at religion and go their ways, and who did it? I don't know, son, I don't know. I think it's too many women in things and wantin' too much

18

for their kids before they've earned it. That makes 'em weak and whimperin' and no muscle in their bodies or their souls."

"Well," said Fred, with gratitude, "my Connie slams the kids if they get out of line, and she's right. No 'democracy' in our household, and diapers having an 'equal voice.' What do kids know?"

"Nothin'," replied the old man promptly. "But you'd think, listenin' to the women and the women teachers, that every time a kid opens his fool mouth he was sayin' Holy Writ, instead of s——. And so the kids think they own the world. I tell you, Fred, one of these days there's goin' to be a real shakin'-out and it can't come too soon."

"They call 'em kids when they're old enough to be married and have families of their own," said still another old policeman. "On one hand they tell you that the kids are more mature these days, and know more than we did at their age, and on the other hand they call 'em 'babies,' and cry their fool eyes out when some young hussy has a bastard and says she 'didn't know,' and what the hell didn't they know, with everythin' out plain in the newspapers and magazines and advertisements and TV? They just figure some one'll bail them out of their mess instead of throwin' them into jail as they used to, when they rolled in the hay."

Permissiveness, thought Fred. What was it Lenin had written? Debase the morals of a people and they will have no courage to resist. Well, the morals of the American people had been debased as far as was possible, now! A faithless and adulterous generation. They were ripe for harsh totalitarianism, and the whip. Inevitably they would get them.

He had been walking very fast and now stopped, in the warmth of the autumnal day, to wipe his face. He saw that at his left hand there rose a gentle swell of green land, in the very midst of the city, with brilliant gold and red trees in clusters here and there, and flower beds filled with bright autumn flowers. At the top of the rise was a single white building, classical, with a red roof and bronze doors shining in the sun. It was a beautiful small park, Fred thought, and wonderfully well-kept. He saw fountains and marble benches in the shade of the trees, and squirrels romping on the grass, and children playing here and there while their mothers watched them from the cool shadows.

A little church up there, a museum? Fred began to walk slowly up one of the gravel paths, his interest excited. The white walls in the distance gleamed in the shining light. He had never seen anything so handsome and so peaceful. He saw a young mother sitting under a great red oak, watching her little boy feeding a squirrel. She had a beautiful face and large black eyes and a mass of black silken hair falling almost to her shoulders. She smiled at Fred and he stopped. He touched his hat.

"Pardon me," he said. "I'm a stranger in town. What is that building up there?"

In a clear and very sweet voice she told him the history of the building and old John Godfrey, and he listened with deep interest.

"The man who listens, eh?" he said. "A doctor, a psychiatrist, a social worker, a lawyer?"

The girl smiled and her face became vivid with light. "Oh, no," she said. "That's what some people think, but it isn't so."

"Well, who?"

The girl was suddenly grave. She studied Fred. "You could find out for yourself," she said. "No one seems to tell anyone else."

"Did you ever see him?"

Her voice was very quiet. "Yes." She hesitated. "You see, four years ago I—well, I was pretty desperate. I was going to kill myself—"

"You?" He was incredulous. "And leave your husband and little boy?"

"We didn't have him, then, Tom and me. If it hadn't been for that—that man—up there, little Tom wouldn't be here now, and I wouldn't, and what would have happened to my husband I hate to think. And where I'd have been—well, I hate to think of it now." She studied Fred again, very acutely. "Why don't you go and talk to him, yourself? If you have any troubles?"

"I haven't any troubles," said the reticent police sergeant. "At least, not any I can't manage myself."

"How lucky you are," said the girl, and her eyes were very sober. She called to her little boy and Fred sauntered upward toward the building. How lucky he was! He was leaving the hopeless and heartbreaking rat race of police work and making a future for himself and his family in a job that would be respected by everybody. Yes, he was very lucky to be getting out in time before it was too late. It was only the thought of selling the first home he had ever really had that was making him feel depressed, and the idea of leaving familiar places and old friends. Yes, that was all. In a couple of months he would be happy again, or at least contented, for who could be happy in this world?

20

He stopped on the wide low step to read the arching golden words above the marvelously carved bronze doors: *THE MAN WHO LISTENS*. I could tell you a lot, brother, thought Fred with such powerful bitterness that he was astonished. I certainly could! But, would you listen to me? Or would you purr like these neuter-gender counselors and soothe me with foolish words and platitudes? Or would you tell me I was doing exactly right—when I know damn well I'm not!

He was struck by the treacherous vehemence of his own thoughts. Why, of course he was right! Why had he thought for even a second that he was not? What hidden thing in himself had betrayed him? He was so disturbed that he felt hate for the man within this white sanctuary, the cooing, murmurous liar who probably had no manliness but only that nauseating, and emasculated "good-will" that was replacing Christian righteousness these days. He probably stroked the cheeks and the arms of the piteous wretches who came to him for advice in their desperate misery, and bleated psychiatric jargon and told them that "society" had mistreated them and that they had his "compassion."

Compassion, hell! thought Fred Carlson. What people need these days is real understanding, the kind that told them, as God told Job, to gird up their loins and be men, and not "scared" pseudo-men. Brother! he thought, staring at the bronze doors, I bet you never heard a real man's complaints in your life! I'd like to tell you! Not a doctor, a psychiatrist, a social worker or a lawyer, that girl had said. Then, he must be a clergyman, one of the glossy New Breed full of sophistication and concern over "modern, complex problems," and "our duties to the world," and with never a word about a man's stern duties to his God and the imperative to be a man and not a woman in trousers!

Fury made Fred Carlson push open the doors so strongly that he was almost catapulted into the cool dim waiting room beyond. He exclaimed, "Excuse me!" But there was only an old man there, in the midst of glass tables and pleasant lamps and comfortable chairs. The old man smiled at him. He had a very brown face webbed with years and a shock of virile white hair, and his whole appearance, and his clothes, revealed him as a countryman.

"Boy! You sure got troubles!" said the old man, with a deeper smile. "Runnin' in like that!"

Fred's new hat had fallen almost over his nose in his rush.

He pushed it back. "No," he said. "I haven't any troubles. I'm a stranger in town."

"That's what we all are, son," said the old man. "Strangers in town. Always was, always will be. I remember somethin' I heard once—my wife was a great reader and liked poetry. 'Strangers meeting in an alien land, at the gates of hell.' Never thought much of that until lately, but now I know what it means. Yes sir, I sure do."

Fred was so interested by this that he found himself sitting down and taking off his hat. The old man was studying him with tired but very sharp eyes. "You said you ain't got no troubles? Son, if that's so, then you ain't got much sense, either, or much feelin'. When somebody tells me they're awful happy, I think, 'You're either a liar or a fool.' 'T'ain't possible to live in this world and be happy, after you're about three years old."

"And that's why you're here?"

"That's right. I come to the end of the road and don't know what to do. I hear that man in there can give me some good advice. Nobody else can!"

He must be at least seventy, thought Fred, and he's worked hard all his life, as my father and my grandfather did. He's worked on the land and from the look of his hands he's still working on it. He had a lonely look. He was probably a widower, too.

"I hope that man will help you," said Fred, politely.

He heard the chime of a soft bell and the old man stood up. "That's for me," he said. He paused and stared down acutely at Fred. "Son, you'd better talk to him, yourself. You look as if you need it. I can smell trouble, the same as I can smell snow and rain before they come."

He went toward the far door, shaking his head. Fred fumed. He saw the door close behind the old man without a sound. He sat back in his chair. It was pleasant in here, and cool, and as good a place as any to rest before going back to the hotel. Fred picked up a current magazine and began to turn the large picture-pages. There was a huge colored spread here of a certain famous evangelist with a fervid and excited face, wind-blown hair, and upraised hands, addressing a vast outdoor audience. Under the picture, which was a double-fold, there was a caption:

"Watchman! What of the night?"

Fred's restless hands stopped. He stared at the printed words, which seemed to leap at him. "Watchman! What of the night?"

From the Bible, of course. He remembered that, vaguely, from long ago. In the ancient days the watchman patrolled the walls of the city, and the gates, with his lantern at midnight and his sword at his side and his alarm trumpet. Under a great golden moon or under dim stars he pursued his slow and resolute way, guarding the city while it slept, his eyes seeking enemies and criminals, murderers and thieves. That was his duty, his sacred duty. Without the watchman the city would fall—

Fred hurled the magazine vindictively across the room, and his great rage returned. Oh, he'd mention that to the soothing and sanctimonious liar in there! He'd ask him what he thought of a nation that attacked its watchmen and jeered at them and accused them of "police brutality." What do you think of a city, he'd say, that despises its watchmen so much that it won't pay them a living wage and fulminates against them and catcalls at them derisively? Why, I'd say: Well, I'm leaving my post and I just hope to hell the vandals will murder you in your sweaty beds and burn your houses down around your ears! That's all you deserve. Take your measly handful of dollars and stick it! Let your civilian review boards patrol your city and kiss every murdering son-of-a-bitch they find in the dark! We cops have had it.

He sat and brooded in his rage and indignation. Then he heard the chiming of the bell. He looked up. That call was for him. He jumped to his feet and went to the farther door, his mind boiling with furious questions and furious answers. He flung open the door and charged inside, full of hate and bitterness.

He did not know what he had expected, but certainly not this blue and white calm, this windowless peace, that distant blue-shrouded alcove and the white chair with its blue cushions. He had half-thought to see a serious middle-aged clergyman at a desk, with files of "cases" behind him, a pad and a pen before him. He had expected a rich greeting, "Good afternoon, won't you sit down and tell me what is troubling you?"

Fred was surprised and the heat in his mind calmed a little. There was no one here but himself. Had the man left after the last visitor? Fred looked about him, seeing softly lighted walls and hearing the faintest whisper of fresh air-conditioning. There was a scent of fern in the air, like the fragrance of a deep forest.

"Anyone here?" he asked tentatively.

No one answered him. He put his coat over the chair and

laid his hat on the floor. Then he sat down and stared at the blue velvet draperies. It was very strange, but they seemed to hide someone who was very much at hand, and who was listening. Fred leaned forward a little and said with abruptness, "I'm a cop."

There was no answer. Fred laughed a little. "A retiring cop. I'm getting out. Do I need to tell you why? It's very simple. I'm tired of being ashamed of my job, of having to apologize for it, to a bunch of fools who think cops are stupid or sadists, and love to shoot and to club for the sheer hell of it. Well, they've driven me out into their own ranks, and when I see a cop on the street after today I'll think, 'You poor, unappreciated slob! One of these days some punk is going to shove a knife into your ribs or blow your brains out, and then your wife can leave your kids and get a job for herself, for there won't be enough money to let her stay at home. There won't be any justice for you, either, or any public tears. The judges will fall on the neck of your murderer and sob about his "broken home" and how he was "deprived," and your murderer will be sent to a nice cozy jail for a couple of years or to a country-club sort of psychiatric hospital, and everyone will be sure he has been abused. You were using "police brutality," weren't you? Sure you were! You were protecting your city and your life. You slob!' "

"Watchman! What of the night?"

"What?" exclaimed Fred. "Oh. That stupid question. I'll tell you. When the night comes, and it sure as hell is coming, the cities will be chaotic with murderers and looters and that is all they deserve. Talk of alarms! I'll be glad to see it, I tell you, I'll be glad to see it. I'll be the first to laugh at the shocked and frightened faces. Women and kids murdered in the streets? Stores looted? Churches burned? Men scurrying along walls like mice, and whimpering? Who cares?"

His voice, almost violent, rang back from the walls like challenging echoes.

"You don't think so, eh? You think men are getting more and more civilized, do you? 'The perfectibility of man!' You know what I think of that———! I don't give a damn if you are a clergyman; you might as well hear a few brutal words from a 'brutal' cop, probably for the first time in your life.

"The only way the majority of men can be kept in line is by fear of the law or by the fear of God—"

He stopped. "The fear of God," he repeated, slowly. "And where is that now in America today, or anywhere else in the world? And what have some of you clergymen done to put

24

the fear of God into people? Nothing. You deplore what you call 'force,' whether it be the authority of parents, the law, or of Divine Justice. You believe in persuasion and education and enlightenment. So did other men, in the past, and they found out, as we'll find out, that they are only words and maudlin ones at that.

"Let me tell you of a few things I've seen for myself in my own city. There isn't a day but what some cop doesn't bring in a punk caught stealing or manhandling or killing. And then when the punk is brought to trial the social workers swarm in and the crying parents, and it turns out that the cop was wrong and the punk was only abused and 'never had a chance in life.' The judge listens. Does he turn to the parents of the punk and say, 'It is you who should be punished or executed, for you did this to your son and to your country and you are the real criminals.' No, he doesn't say that. He wipes away a tear, himself, and he sharply questions the cop and half the time he doesn't believe the slob who had risked his life to defend the law and society. Sometimes he even reprimands him. And the punk goes free and ends up committing another theft or another murder. Then people ask, 'Where are our police? All they are doing is handing out traffic tickets.'

"I'll tell you where the cops are! They are patrolling their beats by day and patrolling them by night, and they know it is useless. The people won't back them up. In fact, the people are their enemies. The watchman, the 'fuzz' as they call him, is desperately serving the very men and women who are busy destroying his authority and condemning him, and releasing murderers and thieves on themselves again. All in the name of 'brotherly love!' for God's sake! They don't understand any longer that millions of people are natural-born Cains, and must be 'cast out,' as the Bible calls it, and ostracized from society, and not 'rehabilitated' until they show repentance—and I've been a cop for years and I never saw a criminal repent. The only thing the criminal fears is stern justice.

"The fear of God. It's been replaced, nowadays, by what they call 'love.' You must love every punk and every scoundrel you encounter. They'll ask you, making big eyes, 'Am I my brother's keeper?' They don't know, or have forgotten, that it was the murderer, Cain, who asked that question. And when Cain asked it God didn't say, 'Sure, you are your brother's keeper!' He only said, 'Your brother's blood cries up from the ground *against* you.' And for that Cain was marked and exiled, and became the father of all the criminals

25

who have ever lived in the world since that time. But now we don't mark them and exile them! We give them 'love.' And they come back again and again into the same courts and are hugged by the same social workers—and they prance out to do the same job over and over again.

"I've noticed, and every other cop has noticed it, too, that the majority of the crimes are committed by released criminals, over and over again. We can look at a job and almost always we can name the man who did it. But bring him in again, and we are faced with all kinds of hampering restrictions handed down by courts. Confessions are rarely accepted by judges any longer; they believe that all confessions are 'forced' and false, and were extracted under 'police brutality.' Even when the criminal looks the judge in the face and tells him the truth the judge beams down at him compassionately. And it's hard to get a decent, self-respecting jury nowadays to bring in the right verdict. They've all been corrupted by this Godless 'love' you hear and read about everywhere."

"The fear of God is the beginning of wisdom."

"That's right!" said Fred. Then he halted. Had he heard that from the man behind the curtain or had he only been thinking it? A faint confusion fell over his mind. It was this silent place where a man's thoughts seemed to be external to him and not internal. "Anyway, it's right," he said, "whether I heard you say it or I only thought it.

"Do you know something? All this love you hear about these days is unclean. That's what it is: unclean. You look at the people mouthing it and you get the sensation of moral and spiritual uncleanliness—unnatural, indecent. Like—well, like the 'love' between homosexuals and other perverts. It may be 'love,' but I don't call it that! And I don't call all this pervasive 'love' in the national atmosphere real love, either. It's repulsive; it's disgusting. It's unmanly. It's dangerous. Have pity on the unfortunate, yes, the truly unfortunate, like the sick and diseased and crippled or handicapped and the old, and those who are truly victims of their wonderful fellowmen. But not on the criminals, the misfits, the perverted, and the habitual thieves. No, not on them, these real enemies of society. They chose to be what they are. I was raised in the slums, myself. My father was a laborer. I don't remember eating well the greater part of my childhood.

"But I sure as hell was afraid of the old man! He was the boss of the family. He sent us to school and to Mass, and God help us if we failed in either school or in catechism! He

26

taught us to be clean, mentally and physically, even if we were crowded four to a dark little bedroom. One step out of line, and we smarted for it for days.

"None of us became criminals, though we were what they now call 'disadvantaged.' My brother is a lawyer. My two sisters married good, God-fearing men. And we sent ourselves to school and to college, working on vacations and at night and on weekends, to finance ourselves. No one paid for us, and we're proud of it.

"But next door to us lived another family of six people. The husband and father worked with my own dad. But what a difference! The kids raced the streets. They were expelled over and over. They were delinquents before they were in their teens. They never went to church. They ended up thieves, and one is a murderer, and one is a convicted child-molester. Their father never beat the hell out of them, never disciplined them. He'd talk to my dad about 'loving your kids,' but if ever a man hated his children he did! How do I know? The police records show it. The man let them do as they wanted to, and gave them as much as he could and asked nothing in return, and never even mentioned to them what it means to be a good citizen and a good American. They had no duty except to gratify themselves at the expense of society. If that isn't hate I'd like to know what it is.

"One of them killed a cop. And he tried to kill me."

Fred shuddered, as he remembered that night only a month ago. He said, "We got an alarm that a jewelry shop was being looted. This was one of a series. I went out with four of my men. We cornered the three thieves, but not before one of them shot at us, killed one of my best kids and almost got me. They'll be coming to trial, soon. The soft-headed judge has already appointed one of the city's big lawyers for them. If they get five years each, even the murderer, I'll be surprised. For the murderer has already said that his confession was 'extracted under police brutality.' And we caught him with the gun still smoking in his hand! I know that lawyer. He boasts he always gets his clients off. He'll do it this time, too. The social workers are already busy. They've made full dossiers about the criminals, all about how they were 'culturally deprived and disadvantaged' and all the other measly words, the unclean words."

He struck the arm of his chair with a fist. "And when these criminals commit the same crimes again, people will write to the newspapers and ask, 'Where are our police?'"

The man behind the curtain did not speak.

Fred said, "All my life I wanted to be a cop. My father had great respect for the police, and he taught us that respect, too. He said he'd always wanted to be a policeman, himself. To him there wasn't a better occupation than being a guardian of the city, and the city's peace and safety. Why, it was the most important thing in the world to him. And it was to me. I'd walk with the young and the old cops on the beat and talk to them by the hour. They were proud to be policemen then. People admired and respected them. A mother had only to say, 'I'll tell Mr. Mullaney on you the next time I see him,' and the kid behaved. The cop was lawful authority, next to God, Himself, and must be obeyed and honored. The priests told us that, too.

"But nobody tells us that, now. The kids jeer at the police and taunt them and dance just out of reach. They're the 'fuzz.' They're the contemptible members of society.

"So, I know it's useless. I'm getting out. I'm leaving police work. I want to live a little before the inevitable fall of my country. I'm getting out."

"Watchman! What of the night?"

Fred nodded grimly. "Yes, what of it? And all the watchmen will be killed or disgraced or disarmed. I don't want to be one of them. Don't tell me, as the chief did last week, that the local police are the only defense the people have, not only against criminals, but against tyrants themselves. I know he's right. But I'm sick of derision and contempt; I'm sick of the miserable pay for risking my life and trying to uphold law and order against all the stupid will of the people who prefer chaos and tyranny. Let them have it, I say. In the meantime I want to live a little, myself, respected and reasonably secure against being murdered."

"What of the night?"

"Well, what of it? It's coming, of that we can be damned sure. And I'm leaving the walls and the gates of the city and my lonely lantern and my weapons and my trumpet. Let some other poor slob take them—if he wants to—and get killed in the doing of his duty."

He suddenly saw the face of the young patrolman, Jack Sullivan, and the peculiar look in his eyes. "Me, I'm only a dumb cop." And then he had walked away.

"A dumb cop," muttered Fred Carlson. "A watchman in the night."

He looked at the curtain again. "Where shall we go to be safe?" he asked. "Soon there won't be any safety in the world for anyone—"

28

"Watchman!"

"Don't call me that!" he shouted with anger. "I'm finished with it, I tell you! I'm not your watchman any more!"

He jumped to his feet and confronted the silent curtain with crushing rage. "You can't say anything, can you? You're one of them, aren't you, whimpering over all the criminals and thieves and misfits and pouring love on them? What do you care about the decent people, the little kids, the helpless women, the hard-working citizens? Tell me, what do you care?"

He saw the button beside the curtain, and he struck it with his fist, cursing under his breath.

The curtains silently parted and in the light they revealed he saw the man who had listened so silently to him.

"Oh, my God," he muttered, and fell back.

He sat down and pressed his hands to his eyes. He felt the light that surrounded the man. He felt his silent rebuke, and heard his questions. It seemed that he sat for a long time in the chair, his eyes hidden, and with a thin trembling running along his nerves.

At last he dropped his hands and he and the man regarded each other in the intense quiet.

"I know what you're really saying," said the policeman. "You are reminding me that you never left the walls and the gates of the city and never will. You won't deliver the people up to their tyrants and their murderers and leave them hopeless. You'll patrol all the time with your light, and you won't sleep. You'll sound the alarm; you're always sounding the alarm, aren't you?

"I suppose it doesn't matter that in these days the people laugh at you, too, and make fun of your fellow watchmen in the night. You know that the night's rushing in on us, just as I do. Somebody's got to be around, to guard the people—

"Somebody. I suppose you mean that's me, too?"

He shook his head. "I'm remembering something. When it was a choice between you and a criminal the people chose the criminal. They always do; it never fails. But you didn't hold that against them. You've been watching all through the night, and you'll be on hand when the last night comes."

Fred Carlson stood up and approached the man slowly. He knelt before him and blessed himself and bowed his head.

"Watchman," he said, "you're not going to be alone. I'm going to be right there with you. Patrolling the walls and the gates of the city."

SOUL TWO: *The Sadducee*

"A Mighty Fortress Is Our God"

"**I**s that all you can tell me?" asked the desolate woman.

What is it you want me to say to you? The man commented to himself. Do you want old-fashioned and sentimental cant in which I don't believe and which is absurd in these enlightened and sophisticated days? I am no parson, dear lady, full of soothing platitudes and maudlin aphorisms. I am a teacher, a leader, a guide to my congregation. Do you expect me to soothe you with evangelical hysteria or invoke some tribal god? The Catholics are not the only ones who have gone in for "aggiornamento." We have been evolving that since Luther. Now religion is intellectual and must appeal to the intellectual, and to modern reason.

He, Dr. Edwin Pfeiffer, looked down from the top floor of the smooth and gleaming apartment house and saw the bright turbulence of the trees in the spring wind. That confounded "Sanctuary" down there! He could see the red roof of the low white building in its masses of foliage and flowers; lovely red tulips, really, and all that golden forsythia and those bursts of lilacs and mock orange blossoms. A silly old hymn came to him from his childhood, in his minister-father's church: "The Old Time Religion!" He saw his father's parishioners, simple men and women, singing heartily and fervently, the men in their Sunday suits, the women in cheap cotton dresses and hatted and gloved. They loved the foolish and passionate old hymns which appealed to the emotions and not to the mind, but after all, they were emotional people who believed simply and accepted things simply, and had a—wholesome?—fear of the Devil and all his works. Dr. Pfeiffer sighed and smiled. Yes, they accepted all things, including their hard lot, meekly. But their sons and daughters, thank Heaven, believed in the perfectibility of man's nature and in changing society to fit new wants and demands, in order to satisfy modern man's felt needs for comfort and sat-

30

isfaction, and some of the joys of the material world. Those poor undemanding people of his father's day! They had nothing much of worldly pleasure and satisfaction, except their religion which, while teaching them ancient religious values also kept them too industrious and too docile in the face of social injustices.

He saw their faces suddenly, calm, kind, strong, and peaceful. Sudden uneasiness came to him. He scratched his chin thoughtfully. Why did he not see such faces in his own church in these days? Why had he not seen them for years? Well, men were more aware now, more seeking. Was that not desirable?

"Nothing at all?" said the woman behind him, who was seated on a long sleek sofa in her elegant living room. But Dr. Pfeiffer did not hear her. Ethics, reason, civilized behavior: That is what we teach these days in the place of the unthinking emotionalism of the past. Man advancing mentally and spiritually to a state of supra-manhood, under the guidance of the Teacher, an evolving supra-Christ. Chardin. He really liked Chardin. Now, there had been a priest, a true mystic with a vision of the Fulfilled World, here on earth. An intellectual. But all his old fellow priests were adamantine against him, and the Hierarchy did not permit his books to be published during his lifetime. What bigotry, really. In these modern days! Pastel statues and bleeding hearts! Didn't they realize—?

He heard a faint sound behind him, and turned, glazed with his thoughts. He said, with real distress—and did not know how helpless he sounded—"Dear Susan."

"You have nothing to say to me," she said, behind her hands. "Nothing but words without comfort or consolation."

He was shocked. He had talked with her for over an hour, as one reasonable and intelligent person to another, giving her fortitude and strength. She had only stared at him with desperate hunger. What did she want? What, in Heaven's name, did she *want*? He had known Susan Goodwin for over fifteen years, and her late husband, Frederick. She was a member of his congregation. (One didn't speak of "parishes" these days, as if one were a shaggy shepherd in charge of a mass of unthinking sheep.) She had always impressed him as the true modern woman, suave, urbane, polished, poised, intellectual. He knew the story behind the Goodwins. They had been intelligent and educated young people if frightfully poor. Then, about twelve years ago Frederick had unexpectedly inherited what would be considered a fortune even in

31

these days, from a relative he hardly had known. Two years after that, at the age of thirty-four and thirty-two, respectively, they had had their first and only child—after a marriage of ten years. The boy was now how old? Ten, of course. Not yet confirmed. He had baptized the child, himself, Charles Frederick Goodwin. A fine boy. Unfortunate about the father, who had died of a heart attack five years ago. Susan had only her son, now, to whom she was devoted. It was not likely that she would marry again; she had been shattered when her husband had died. And, at forty-two, even if she remarried, she would hardly have more children. Unfortunate, unfortunate. But, after all, one must have fortitude and strength of character and not turn, in such absolute despair, to sentimentality and one must never demand from a spiritual adviser what he could not give in all honesty—but what did she *want?*

"Only ten years old," said Susan, from behind the hands pressed against her face and her eyes. "And now he must die, if not tomorrow, then within a year at the most."

"We mustn't give up hope," said Dr. Pfeiffer, glancing furtively at his handsome watch. "They are doing some excellent work on leukemia, you know. They are keeping children alive far longer than it was possible to do a few years ago. And any day, now, there may be a breakthrough. There is always hope."

But Susan said, "He's had three transfusions this week. He may never come home from the hospital." She dropped her hands. Her face, her usually composed and faintly smiling face, was ravished with grief and suffering so that she seemed much older than her actual age. Her light chestnut hair was disordered as if she had repeatedly plunged her fingers through it; her slender body had taken on an appearance of emaciation since her child's disease had been diagnosed only a month ago. An acute case. But her eyes—and somehow this heartened the minister—were tearless. He did detest unrestrained tears in the face of fate and before inexorable facts. That was for peasants and not civilized ladies.

He went to her and sat down beside her gravely, a tall and well-built man in a fine secular suit, with a florid and alert face and keen dark eyes and dark waving hair. It did not offend him too much when some young and irreverent people declared he looked like a film star. He was proud of his sonorous voice, and his presence. He said, "Susan, things have to be faced with courage, you know. There are some things that

32

can't be—wished—away, no matter how desirable that could be. Fortitude. Resignation—"

"Resignation, to my child's meaningless death?" Her blue eyes flared on him now with total anguish. "Why does he need to die? Why, why?"

"I don't know," said Dr. Pfeiffer with genuine distress. "These things happen all the time, unreasonable, inexplicable things. We can only face them as strong human beings, not permitting ourselves to dissolve into mindless despair. That isn't worthy of humanity. There isn't an hour that someone doesn't cry out, 'Why, why?' We—"

"Yes, why?" asked Susan.

"I don't know," he repeated, feeling a flushed uneasiness again, and a little pang of resentment at her childish demand. "But one must be realistic—"

"You don't know," said Susan, and the blue eyes were bitter. "And you a minister!"

He was vexed but he was also full of pity. He wished, for the first time, that cant would come to him and he could say in honesty, "It is all God's mysterious will, and His ways are not our ways, and someday we will understand, if not here, then beyond the grave." But he was an honest man. No more than anyone else did he really know what lay beyond the grave, if anything. The Resurrection of Christ, of course, was only symbolic. The *Spirit* of Christ, of course, had survived His death, and had persisted through the ages and, it was to be hoped, would always persist. Just as the *spirit* of man—the reasonable, civilized, enlightened spirit—would survive through offspring into all the future generations. One looked for immortality through one's children. In the meantime, before death, one lived an orderly and reasonably disciplined life seasoned with some legitimate pleasures and joy in mere existence, and did as little harm as possible to others. —It was the *heritage* of man which survived, the heritage of an historical being, his influence on his present. What more could an intellectual being ask or desire?

All else was conjecture and in this scientific age one did not conjecture much.

It was not the first time that he had seen despair and agony on a human face. He had given his consolations: courage, fortitude, bravery. Time will heal. Life goes on. Day by day the torment will lessen, believe me. One has to live and endure. One must take up again, and rise from the place where anguish had hurled us. That is Expected of Man. And the fu-

33

ture will hold new pleasures and consolations again—just wait and see.

Some, of course, were unreasonable creatures. Two men and one woman had committed suicide in the past year or so, all from his congregation. They had no patience to wait for the healing succor of time and renewed life. He had never forgiven them for being so emotional and so distracting to his orderly existence and his reason. But of course, poor things, they had been psychologically sick, and therefore to be pitied. If they had only taken his advice and had gone for therapy to a psychiatrist who would have explained that their terrible anguish had its roots in some childhood frustration, and that they must Understand Themselves and their Inner Conflicts if they were to go on serenely again! But they had not taken his advice, in their sick turbulence and mental disturbance. They had just killed themselves. Sad, and a little disgusting, but still sad. He hoped Susan Goodwin was not of their kind. No, she was a sensible lady.

He cleared his throat. "May I suggest something, Susan? You know Dr. Snowberry, the psychiatrist. Do go to him at once. I will make an appointment for you, if you wish; he is a member of my congregation. He will explain to you that your—your misery and rejection—are rooted in your earlier frustrations, when you and Frederick were very poor. Or that, as a deprived child, you were deeply rebellious against circumstances and would not accept it. He—"

"A *psychiatrist*, when my child is dying?" Susan's voice was almost a scream.

"I know, I know. It sounds heartless, doesn't it? But believe me, Susan, I know what I am talking about; experience, you know. You are still a young woman—"

She looked at him and her eyes were blue ice. "Please go, Dr. Pfeiffer," she said. She wrung her hands together; she was still tearless. "Please go."

Now he felt a stir of anger. What did she *want?* Everything he had said to her over this hour had been met with hostility and despairing derision—most unreasonable. She was like those simple women in his father's parish—congregation. She wanted maudlin answers to things for which there were no answers. Didn't she? He stood up stiffly.

"I'll visit Charles in the hospital tomorrow, Susan."

"No! Don't! You have no more to say to Charles than you have to me! Will you tell him, Dr. Pfeiffer, to be brave, that little boy? To Face Facts and Accept Things in a Civilized Manner? You'll give him a stone, too, instead of bread?"

How the platitudes rushed up even in modern people! In extremity they didn't want realistic answers and courage. They wanted to be consoled— Again the sick uneasiness came to the minister, and renewed resentment. He would speak of this in his next sermon. His sermons were always published in the biggest newspaper in the city the Monday after Sunday, and were greatly admired for their style and intellectual content and calm understanding. Sometimes dailies in other cities picked them up, too.

"You are a fraud," said Susan Goodwin. "You are a false shepherd."

"Because I won't lie to you?" he said. "Susan!"

She did not speak to him again. In fact, she left the room. The maid came with his hat and topcoat. He was outraged. He had been dismissed like an importunate salesman. He went out into the brisk and glittering spring air. A beautiful day. He inhaled deeply. Why was it sometimes impossible for men to enjoy the immediate, the present, all that a man possessed? Why was he always straining after—what was he straining after, when some calamity overtook him? Superstition. Lies. It was impossible for most men to accept the Symbolic. Very primitive. Life had such delights, so many innocent joys, so many means to satisfaction in work and simple living. Yet still, after the Enlightenment, men strained after misty and unsubstantial and mythical follies. I'm not a witch doctor, said Dr. Edwin Pfeiffer to himself, as he enjoyed the sunshine and the bright wind and the scent of the awakened earth. I have no incantations, no incense. My duty, as a minister, is to preach disciplines and virtue and good sense to my congregation, and fortitude. All else must be left to— He looked at the great blue arch over the heaving riot of the city. To What? Of course, there was the Unknowable, the forever Unknowable to man. And there were, of course, the parables of Jesus, tailored to a simple people in a simple time. But all was Symbolic. Doctrine was well enough for the Medieval Age, but not for today. Of course, some ministers talked of Divine Authority, and Tradition. Divine Authority was well enough in an atavistic era, but not today! Not in the Enlightened Day! The Scriptures were not superstition, of course. But they were only guidelines for civilized behavior; at the worst they were poetic myths. Man's fate was in the present; his destiny was in his children. The Protestant Reformation in its true essence was Protest—against obscurantism and absurd supernaturalism, Protest against Myths of the night and affirmation of the broad daylight of reason. Protest against social injustices. Catholics spoke of Grace, but what was Grace except an awareness of daily duties and responsibility for one's fellowman and obedience to civil authority? And the need just to be a man?

The day was so lovely that Dr. Pfeiffer did not go at once to the parking lot of the luxurious apartment house. He decided to walk a little. He was still resentful against Susan Goodwin. What did she *want?* His church was ready to give her everything, his beautiful modern church with the symbolic Cross rearing hugely over the modern steeple. The cross of life. One had to carry it with fortitude, accepting human existence. To lay it down and wail was unworthy of a man. Was not upright man enough, the Rational Animal? Beauty is all we know, said Dr. Pfeiffer to himself, and in some peculiar fashion he was comforted. All we know, and all we need to know. Keats, yes. It was comforting in a way, to know that we cannot know— If there was an *imperative* to *know* how disorderly life would be, how distracting and tumultuous! Man would have no time left to do his Duty in this world; he would be too involved in abstractions and vehemences and controversies. He would no longer be the one Hero in this world. He would be caught up in the chaotic supernatural world, a sort of spiritist. Madness. Unreality.

Why had Susan Goodwin been so hostile when he had mentioned Dr. Snowberry? A sick woman. A sad woman, and unfortunate, too. Full of hostilities. Aberrations. It was regrettable about little Charles, of course. He was only ten, and the only child. But Such Things Happened. It was really too bad that Susan had told her boy that he would soon die. Cruel, cruel. She should have spared him that; she should have told him brightly that he would be home soon, and well. It would have been a compassionate lie. But lies had their place also.

Lies. Lies.

I told her only the truth, said Dr. Pfeiffer to himself. Why will not men accept the truth? And then—it was absurd—he thought of Pontius Pilate and his cynical remark: "What is truth?"

The thought was so disturbing that he stopped and meditated. He saw gravel before him, a gravel path. Aimlessly, he looked up. He was on a path leading to that confounded "Sanctuary." It was a scandal. Fundamentalism. A clergyman there, howling about the Old Time Religion to the unfortunates, the churchless, who came running to him in their despair. He had signed a petition to have the "Sanctuary" turned over to the city for The Children, or a school. A scandal, in this day and age. Who was the clergyman who lurked behind the blue curtain? A howler. A Disgrace. A charlatan, a liar.

"What is truth?" said Pontius Pilate, and washed his hands.

Well, said Dr. Pfeiffer to himself, I won't wash my hands! It is time for that screamer to be confronted and be shamed. I'm tired of him and all that has been written about him. Supernaturalism! Miracles! Disgusting. The refuge of people like Susan Goodwin, the people who will not face Reality, when Reality was all that was. He saw his father's face, that simple face, and he felt a rush of pure rage. He was a little shocked by that rage; he had not thought himself so vulnerable to past indignities, past simplicities, past meek acceptances. And faith. He heard his father's voice, "A Mighty Fortress is Our God!" He had never liked his father, actually. An Unlearned Man. "Our Lord," his father had once said, "was never graduated from the best universities. He knew only truth." But what could one expect from a "minister" who had entered a seminary with only an elementary school education?

He walked slowly but determinedly up the gravel path. He saw the fountains and the grottoes, and the long green patience of the lawns and the massed trees. Beautiful, beautiful, he thought reluctantly. But why is it not used as a public park, and for Senior Citizens who could sit on those marble benches and— Stare? Stare at what, at the end of their lives? Well, anyway, they could look at the flowers, couldn't they, and be happy that they had given their knowledge to their children and their grandchildren? It was restful. Then he thought, I am only fifty! I am not old, I don't stare at the ages! He stopped and wondered at the faint nausea in himself. He felt around for his box of digestive tablets. Acid indigestion. He slipped a tablet on his tongue and let it dissolve. He wondered if he did have ulcers after all. He smiled a little. Most of his congregation appeared to have ulcers these days. The stress of modern life, of course. The hurry and the turmoil. So much demanded of everybody in this modern life. So much to do.

Do what? asked the incorrigible new voice in his mind. What are they doing half so well as their fathers and their grandfathers did? What have they given to their fellows? They have endless leisure—but what do they give? Community activities? What are they? Their fathers gave work and friendship and kindness, personal kindness and personal re-

37

sponsibility and true brotherhood as one man to another. What do your people give these days, of themselves, of true love? They sign checks and talk politics and join Social Welfare organizations, and feel very righteous. The righteousness of the Pharisee.

We live in an Urban Age, commented Dr. Pfeiffer's mind.

And what is that? asked that protesting voice. There was always an Urban Age, from Chaldea to Alexandria to Jerusalem, to Athens to Rome, to Paris to New York. What is so "new" about an Urban Age? What have you discovered that is so unique? The desolation of abomination. The weary land.

I should have known better than to go to that disturbed and rebellious young woman, thought Dr. Pfeiffer. He walked up the path, and his face was flushed angrily. He had a Duty to Do. He paused at the bronze doors and again reluctantly admired them. No money had been spared here! Lavish. It should have gone to the United Community Fund. Or in taxes. All this was tax-exempt, of course. A scandal. This wonderful marble, this peaceful stretch of land in the very midst of the city: It should be a public park and not administered by private individuals. *THE MAN WHO LISTENS.* He saw the gold characters above the doors. A screamer, a clergyman who disgraced his calling. Dr. Pfeiffer angrily pushed open the doors and peered inside. He knew! The waiting room was filled with shapeless humans, if you could call them that. Old people. No, there were the young here also, waiting silently. Why were the confident young here, the astute and knowledgeable young, who had been taught well? What problems did they have, these girls and boys, that could not be solved by such as himself or an excellent psychiatrist? People demanded too much these days. They had everything, therefore they had no problems in this affluent society which did so much to make them happy. He wanted to shout to the youths and the girls in the waiting room: What can possibly disturb you in this age?

He sat down in a comfortable chair and looked with annoyance at his fellow waiters. Then his eye was caught by a marble tablet in the marble wall: *"I can do all things in Him Who strengthens me."*

A nice sentiment, but unrealistic. One had to rely on the good offices of government and good will on the part of government, and not haphazard charity. Or individual effort. That was nice for the past but not for These Days. Society must move as One to alleviate misery. Society had the answers to all things if only people like Susan Goodwin

38

would listen, the miserable and rebellious people like Susan Goodwin who demanded answers where there were no answers but reason.

He watched with detached interest as chimes sounded and one by one the superstitious and the maudlin rose and went behind a door at the back of the room. There was no sound. All sound seemed suspended in this gracious sweet air with its hint of fresh fern. He heard no traffic, no voices. Of course, it was all sound-conditioned. He picked up a magazine from one of the tables and became absorbed in international news. For the first time he thought, as he scanned the pages: Why is there so much turmoil in these days when everything is planned and there is so much freedom and so many enthusiastic emerging nations? Men did not have to struggle for existence now as their fathers had struggled. Concern for everybody was rife in the government and among all peoples. Foreign aid. Public assistance. Social Responsibility. The Peace Corps. What was once the province only of religion had extended to secular life and everyone was involved in mankind. The Secular Missions. It was wonderful, really. Then, why was there so much mental misery and frustration? We need, said Dr. Pfeiffer to himself, a crash program for psychiatrists. International psychiatrists administering to the needs of all the nations. Not religious missions, which are old-fashioned and which do not meet the demands of modern society and modern truth.

"What is truth?" said Pontius Pilate, and washed his hands.

Dr. Pfeiffer suddenly saw the vast and polished spread of his congregation before him on Sunday mornings. Nice people, well-dressed, quiet, attentive, hushed and listening. People with folded hands, listening courteously. To his lectures. People who contributed adequately to the various demands of organized charity, people who were interested in the works of the church.

Were they? Those three suicides. The defections. The suddenly ironic eyes of young people, the questing eyes of the middle-aged and the old. The suddenly averted heads. Boredom? That was ridiculous. He was known for his stimulating sermons—no, lectures. There was always at least one reporter there for the local papers and even for the ones in distant cities. They wrote busily on their small pads. He had so much to give—

Do you? asked the incorrigible voice. What did you give today to Susan Goodwin? I gave her the truth, he replied.

"What is truth?" asked Pontius Pilate, and washed his hands.

I am no parson, he said.

What are you? asked the voice.

I am a civilized and reasonable human being, acquainted with reality, he said.

And what does that mean? asked the voice.

It means, he said to that terrible voice, Charity.

Oh? said the voice. Do you not mean: *"Odium humani generis?"*

He was horrified. Hatred for the human race? No! Above all things, no! He loved reason and good will and good behavior and righteous conduct and enlightenment for everybody. Brotherhood. He detested disheveled emotions and superstition and obscurantism. All could be explained by—

What? asked the voice.

He heard his father's choir singing with deep passion: "A Mighty Fortress Is Our God!"

Oh, simple faith, undemanding faith, childish faith! Total faith.

What other is there? asked the voice.

Damn Susan Goodwin! She had disturbed his thoughts, his reason, his discipline. He stood up, disgusted, prepared to leave. He heard a chiming, and he saw that he was alone. Therefore, the clergyman inside there had struck a bell for him. He was suddenly confused. An irrelevant thought came to him: "Ask not for whom the bell tolls. It tolls for thee."

The sound of the chimes seemed to be echoing in himself, a somber and dolorous murmuring and an ominous one full of reproach. You are a man without conviction, said the voice, and therefore you are impotent in the face of tragedy. You do not even know you, yourself, are tragic, you false shepherd.

Never, in all his fifty years, had such a frightful voice come to him from the very depths of his—what? He had lived rightfully and virtuously; why should there be this dreadful disturbance in him, this reproach? He was no—sinner. Sinner! What an anachronistic word! There was no sin. Now a deeper rage came to him, revolted. His father had unendingly talked of "sin." He felt hatred for his father. He said to himself, I always hated him, that ignorant man.

He went to the far door and thrust it open with utmost anger. It closed behind him silently. He was not surprised at what he saw in this other room, for it had been described to him. But he glared furiously at the thick blue curtain that covered the tall wide alcove. Howler! Fundamentalist fool! He was an embarrassment to the clergy of the city. Dr. Pfeiffer went to the chair and stood behind it, clenching his hand over the back.

"I'm Dr. Edwin Pfeiffer," he said in a harsh but controlled voice. "You probably can see me from a peephole or something and it's possible you recognize me and know my church. I've come to have a decent man-to-man talk with you, a fellow-clergyman, and to ask you to stop this nonsense. Do you know what you are doing to your fellow-clergymen? You are holding us up to ridicule and shame. Haven't you any self-respect at all? These aren't the Dark Ages, you know, and the days of circuit riders and Holy Rollers and evangelism. Most of us don't think much of the Council of Trent. You've heard of the Council of Trent, haven't you?"

He smiled with a cool sneer. The man behind the curtain did not answer him. So, he was embarrassed, was he?

"We no longer believe in *Sola Scriptura,* except as parables to point a simple tale, and of course we—we—don't believe in the twin 'sources of truth,' Scripture and tradition. Not any longer. It's not that we denigrate the idea of Divine Authority, no. Rather, we believe that man has now so advanced intellectually that he can discard his mystical crutches and stand alone, as a Rational Creature. I am not denying the Divine Source; that would be absurd. But the Divine Source, as we are now all agreed—except the Roman Catholics—is in man and not external to him in some silly golden streets of heaven presided over by a patriarch. We look, not to some supranatural future, but to the world and the perfectibility of man, for this is all we can know and it is surely the noblest object of man's striving."

His voice rolled sonorously back to him from the marble walls and he was pleased at the sound. He hoped that he had made his point though he doubted that the idiot behind those curtains had understood one word. At the very least he ought to feel damned uncomfortable.

Again the minister felt angry and affronted, and outraged that he had even come to this place to confront the unlettered clergyman in this room.

"I've heard a great deal about you! Do you know what you are doing? You are misleading the people! You deceive them with lying promises of what does not and cannot exist and never did. You speak to them of 'miracles,' and you are alleged to have performed them. Do you know what blasphemy is? If you do, then you must realize you are blasphemous as

41

well as sanctimonious. Life itself is a miracle; we don't need anything else, and there was never anything else. You have probably absorbed a little psychiatry and understand psychosomatic medicine to some extent. Through these things you have, no doubt, been able to misguide the ignorant and the mindless and the hysterical. That is inexcusable in these days. You must stop this deceit, this superstition, this encouraging of the darkest aspect of the human—mind."

He heard himself speak with heat, and he reflected on what he had said so eloquently. Then it came to him that somewhere, at some time, men had said this very thing to—someone? He could not remember. But he felt a hard sickness in his chest, a curious sensation that he had betrayed—But whom had he betrayed, and why this strange sense of haunting familiarity, a kind of memory of something that had happened long ago?

Don't you remember? asked that new voice in him. Surely you remember?

"In less enlightened days," said Dr. Pfeiffer, vaguely fearful of that voice in himself and repulsed by it, "men like you would have been driven from the religious community. In less enlightened and more barbarous days you'd have been cruci—"

Something struck at his heart like a gigantic fist, and he stepped back involuntarily from the chair. But he was not a man to let fantasy and strange fears possess him. After a moment he went on: "You are irrelevant, in these times. I dislike calling any man a fraud, but I'm afraid you are. I ask you now to leave this place and let it be closed. Send the churchless back to us, where they belong. Let them come to us if they are in need—"

Such as Susan Goodwin? asked the inner voice.

"People should not be encouraged to have atavistic needs," said the minister. "But you are encouraging them with lying hopes beyond reality. That way lies madness. Men no longer live in a simplistic era; we are very complex in the world now. But when a man is led to believe simply and literally—the things which are only symbolic and meant only to be symbolic—then he encounters confusion when confronted with reality, for he sees reality not clearly any longer but distorted and smeared. He can even, in his attempt to adjust these irreconcilable things, become fanatical, and there is no place any longer for the fanatic, except, of course, the madhouse. Christianity is a truly *sane* religion—"

And what do you know of it? asked the inner voice, but

now it appeared that it was external also and full of powerful sternness.

"The Social Gospel," said the minister, hurrying his words to drown out his most irrational fear, "has not exactly replaced the Four Gospels. It has only made them more meaningful for Our Times." He was exasperated both with the nameless thing in himself and with the silent man behind the curtain. "Have you ever heard of Paul Tillich? No? Then I advise you to read him. He speaks of the irrelevances in old interpretations. But you would not agree with him, I'm sure. And there are others like him, whom I admire very much; they divorced ethics from mysticism and placed them firmly in the frame of reference of modern life and modern demands. Secular ethics—the very base of good government and good will and responsibility. It's not that I am a secularist minister, but I do understand that the secular and spiritual realms are the same and not divided by supernaturalism. We aren't medievalists any longer, you know. Or, do you know?"

The man had the wit not to answer, for, of course, he did not understand.

"Are you there?" asked Dr. Pfeiffer, the thought coming to him that no one was there at all. Was that a movement of assent behind the curtain or a mere stirring of the air-conditioning? Then he became convinced that he was not alone; there was a sense of a powerful presence in the room, a listening presence. It seemed to have focused itself upon him.

"Well, if you are really there, I beg you not to deceive the simple any longer. It's really dangerous these days—" He stopped. The ghastly sense of reliving something, or of rehearing something, which he could not remember, came back to him like a long echo over a range of mountains, over a range of time. "Dangerous, these days," he repeated. "It disturbs the people; it makes them discontented, makes them look for contentment and hope where there are no contentment and hope. Superstition, in short.

"Today I visited a lady whose son will soon die very cruelly, I'm afraid. Her young son. I always thought she was a sensible young woman, totally rational and perceptive, aware of the inexorable when it happened. It's an awful thing to have to accept, I know, the death of her son, her only son—"

Her only son, said the new voice and again it appeared to be external also.

"Yes, yes. Her only son. I went to console her, after she had called me. I'm her minister; she is a member of my congregation. What could I tell her? I could tell her only the truth, that she must accept what can't be changed, and go on with her life. After all, this is the twentieth century. But she became—almost violent. She was bitter, she, a young and intelligent woman! It was incredible. She seemed to be demanding something of me—"

What? asked the voice.

"I don't know!" he exclaimed. "Or, I should say that it wasn't possible for me to give it to her, for it would have been cant, and absurd. I couldn't say to her: 'It is God's Will, and He knows what is just and for the best.' For, how can we be sure of that? Who has ever declared it to be so?"

Who? echoed the voice.

He shook his head with an almost despairing impatience. "She wanted pious platitudes from me, and assurances that her son would not be lost to her but would be restored to her in some pastel heaven. If I had said that, to a normally intelligent young woman, I'd have been ashamed of myself, and later she would have been amused. I'm a compassionate man. But I couldn't lie to her and tell her things in which I don't personally believe. I think she even wanted a miracle—prayer, you know, kneeling together—"

Yes? said that questioning and ridiculous thing in himself. He shook his head over and over.

"My God!" he cried. "I wish that I could have lied to her! I honestly wish it! If it would have brought her comfort, any comfort at all, when she thinks of the approaching death of her only child! Some pietistic nonsense, such as my father could pour out at the slightest provocation. Such as—"

He stopped, for the inner voice appeared to become totally external now.

" 'I am the Resurrection and the Life?' "

What was it that Paul of Tarsus had said? If Christ indeed had not risen then our faith is in vain. Dr. Pfeiffer started. Why should he have remembered that now? He had forgotten, in his pity for Susan Goodwin, why he had come here at all. He must remember and stop imagining nonsense. Why, damn it, he was like some petitioner himself, in this shameful place! He said firmly, "I'm off the subject, I'm afraid. You really must close up shop, you know, for the sake of all of us."

"The cock crowed thrice."

He could not believe it. His ears rang with the appalling words. Yet, surely, no one but himself had spoken. Now the words of betrayal, of most deathly betrayal, had begun to ring on his heart as well as on his ears. Hypnotism, he thought wildly, self-hypnotism, in this confounded silent place. He moved step by step away from the silent blue curtain.

"Who do you say I am?"

He stopped abruptly. No, no one had spoken. He was imagining it all. Then an emotion ran through him like the utmost despair, a sense of deprivation and desolation beyond anything he could have imagined.

He cried, "My God, my God, I wish I knew! I only wish I knew!"

He lost all pride, all dignity, all that he admired in civilized man. He approached the curtain again, forgetting that he was self-hypnotized, forgetting that all this was fantasy. He saw the button near the curtain and the little sign informing him that if he wished to see the man who had listened to him he had only to press that button.

He hesitated. He was all painful and burning confusion, all inner dishevelment, all distraction. Never, in all his life, had he ever experienced this. His hand plunged to the button and struck it and the curtains rolled aside.

He saw the man who had heard him in the glow of the pure bright light. He saw the Reality of the ages, and all that he had denied while believing he had accepted. He flung up his arm at last to conceal that face and those accusing eyes, those most pitying eyes. And from behind the childish sheltering of his arm he spoke.

"No, I never denied you because I never truly believed in you. You were a beautiful Symbol to me. I was never confronted by you before. Was that because I never looked for you? Because I was convinced there was nothing to find but a code of ethics, spoken in majestic language, but only a secular code and not a way of spiritual life?

"I denied you because I denied myself and all that I instinctively knew. I was ashamed of you in my heart—because I was ashamed of myself. I believed that only that which could be explained had verity, that only rational explanations were worthy of a man. I denied your authority because there was no real authority in me, and because of the lack of personal authority, based on your own, my people look at me denyingly—and I have nothing to offer them. Is that why their eyes are often ironical and bored or desperate? Yet, my church is so fashionable!"

He dropped his arm and looked pleadingly at the man.

"So fashionable," he repeated, and laughed bitterly. "Why

did they come at all, then, when I had nothing to offer them? Are they not as guilty as I?"

The man did not answer him. He only waited as he had waited through the centuries.

"No," said Dr. Pfeiffer, "only I am guilty. Today I was called a false shepherd. It's quite true. I am also a stupid shepherd. No. I was never a shepherd at all, not once since I was ordained. A woman who is about to lose her only son held out her hands to me today and I had nothing to give her, nothing of consolation to offer, for there was nothing in me and nothing of consolation. It was not my son who was dying, therefore I was not intimately concerned." He stopped and stared at the man. "It was your mother's son who was about to die, and there was none of his friends to comfort her; they ran from her, just as I ran from Susan Goodwin, the mother. They had one excuse, cowardice. My only excuse, which is the worst of all, is that I had no answer to a mother's grief. It is the very worst, for I had no faith. No faith, not even in a Symbol."

He went to the chair for he felt exhausted. He sat down and the man and himself regarded each other in a long silence.

He said, "I not only betrayed you. I betrayed my people, and yours. I never once said, as Peter said, that you are the Lord. To me you were a disembodied Idea, a diffusion of good will, and peace, a beautiful Idea—but only an Idea. Why, then, did I become a clergyman?"

He threw out his hands. "I don't know. Before God, I don't know. But I'm not the only one. So few of us know, or are even aware that there is something we do not know. We are just Guides, just Leaders, just learned discussers, just erudite—fools. Theological fools who don't believe in theology, and regard it as only an intellectual exercise. Prophets of Freud, by God! And prophets of fraud. We say we have the water of life, but our vats are dry, and we eulogize the dust. We speak only of the world and never question the stars, for the world is all we know—and all we want to know. Our little bright corner is enough for us, and there we can sit and talk our blasphemous and urbane nonsense, and utter our words of peace in a world where there is no peace, and offer up well-rehearsed prayers which are empty of content, as we are empty of content. Who shall forgive us?"

The man regarded him gently. The minister said, "Who can forgive us?"

There was such anguish in him, such total belief, and such

sorrow. "Yes," he said, "though the cock crowed three times you will forgive me. You have already forgiven me. I will take up the rod and the staff you gave me but which I rejected. I will find the flock you entrusted to me and I will bring them to you. I will say to them, 'Here is the Way and the Truth and the Life, and there is none other, world without end.' For now I know."

He slipped from the chair and knelt humbly before the man and bowed his head.

"There is a mother waiting, whose son is going to die. Walk with me, and let me tell her your truth—that there is no death, and that you are the Everlasting Life and her son will be restored to her. As you were restored to your mother."

He stood up and smiled at the man. "Indeed, indeed, 'A Mighty Fortress Is Our God,' in which we are safe and in which we are protected. Forever."

SOUL THREE: The Afflicted

"I know that my Redeemer Liveth."
JOB 19:25

"I didn't come here for counsel," said Francis Stoddard to the hidden man behind the blue curtain. "I've had plenty of that stupidity. When I lost my business fifteen years ago, you should have heard all my self-appointed advisers! I should have listened to them; I shouldn't have done this, I should have done that, if I'd only watched my step here, or been plenty smart there—it wouldn't have happened to me. Then when I made my comeback, they were almost offended. I hadn't asked their advice; I'd done it all myself. When I was down, they could feel superior and pity me—and avoid me, too, afraid I'd ask them for money. My best friend—he'd suddenly cross the street when he saw me coming. You'd have thought I'd taken something from him, personally, when I began my fight up again and paid off all my debts and became richer than he is. They were all the same. Did one of them help to keep me in the clubs I once belonged to, when I was in debt? No. Did they come to the house when I was threatened with foreclosure and advance me the money I wouldn't have accepted anyway? No. You'd have thought Agnes and I were lepers or something.

"Then, when I came back they were either offended or ashamed. They needn't have worried. We never saw them again. I made sure of that. Agnes called them 'Job's Comforters.' I don't know what she meant; I must look it up sometime. If there is any 'sometime' ahead for me, which I hope there wont' be.

"Then, we lost our daughter, our only child." His voice became hoarse and slow. "On the day before she was to be married. Nineteen years old. The prettiest girl in our community. That was soon after I lost my business. We thought we'd have a little joy in Pat. But I suppose Agnes' God couldn't stand that, either. She was all we had. Beautiful girl, honors at college. Going to marry a young man who was all I'd ever

48

have chosen for my daughter. I ought to tell you a little more about Pat, but I suppose Agnes told you, when she was here a couple of weeks ago, and why the hell she came to you I don't know.

"Pat never caused us a moment's anxiety or misery in all her nineteen years. That was twelve years ago—when she was killed in a senseless automobile accident, with the boy she was to marry. It didn't matter to him that I was a bankrupt, trying to get on my feet again. A fine boy. He was almost worthy of Pat. She was like a blaze of light in the house. I never saw anyone more alive than my daughter. My Pat. When she left a room it seemed to be darker. When you heard her voice, well, it was like hearing someone bringing you good news. She enjoyed everything; she loved everybody. She could even make me laugh, in those terrible days when we didn't know if we could keep the house the next month. There was nothing she couldn't do. She could paint and sing. She was going to teach for a while, even after she was married. She was full of plans—"

The man broke off. Twelve years ago. It was only yesterday, when all that light and love and joy and hope had been instantaneously blotted out, to leave only a black hole in his life. He remembered her when she had modeled her wedding dress for him—thin white stuff like mist, and the long lace mantilla which Agnes had worn at her own wedding. He remembered the bright fluff of her hair about her shining face and the deep blue of her eyes and the long whiteness of her neck. He had felt—though no one believed him now, except Agnes—a sudden horrible clenching of his heart when he had seen her dressed like that, an awful premonition as if he had seen her in her death clothes. (She had actually been buried in her wedding dress, complete with veil and with a bride's bouquet in her silent hands.) No, no one believed it, after he had told it later.

"She looked like Agnes, standing and whirling and curtsying before me," he said to the man behind the blue curtain. "And then she must have seen my face, for she ran up to me and kissed me and said, 'Daddy, I'll never really leave you, never.' But she did, she did. She left the next day, and we'll never see her again. I don't care what the priest tried to tell us. Pat is gone. Twelve years. She's all dust now, our little girl, all empty bones and worm-eaten lace and satin. Sometimes, thinking of it, I can't stand it."

He put his thin hands over his thin face and pressed them, and when he removed them his dry flesh was red and seemed

49

as sore as if scoured by new tears. But he had long forgotten how to cry. He hadn't cried since he was a child. He couldn't cry now, though the very last was on him and his life had come to an end.

"I said to Agnes," he continued, in his curiously toneless voice which was the very echo of despair, "that we'd reached the end now. I didn't want to live. I wanted to go to some quiet place and lie down and die. Then the comforters came again. The priest—at least he's Agnes' priest. With his, 'I am the Resurrection and the Life—' I don't want Pat 'resurrected,' damn it! I want my sweet real Pat, in her own body, with her teasing and her running and her shouting on the stairs, and sunburned in her white shorts, and her hair tousled, and the way she would whirl around on her bicycle and play with the dog—rolling over and over on the grass with him. That's the girl I want back, not some transcendental angel with wings, not real, not warm and human. As if I ever believed in that crap, anyway.

"Yes, the comforters came again, the ones with their sound money in the banks and in investments and not in a shattered business, the ones with sons and daughters at home. People whose houses weren't threatened, and a whole lifetime of work. People who were safe. I could see their self-righteousness. All this tragedy hadn't happened to them— because they were better people than Agnes and me! I could see it on their faces, their smugness, and even under their soothing words. Why, I heard one man, another best friend, actually say to some other people when he didn't know I was near him, 'Poor old Frank. Well, I guess my wife and I live right, that's all.' And that meant that in some way Agnes and I had offended their supercilious God and were being punished by Him! If that's the kind of God He is, their God, who the hell wants Him? If He afflicts senselessly, the way we were afflicted, then He either doesn't exist or Agnes and I are better people than He is. We wouldn't treat our worst enemy as He has treated us."

He leaned forward in the white marble chair, broken like a dried branch, for he was very thin now and his brown hair had turned very gray over the past three months, and his eyes moved in their sockets like dead and lifeless mud, dully, sightlessly.

"The comforters! 'Perhaps it is all for the best. God knows. His ways are mysterious. The Lord giveth and the Lord taketh away. Blessed be the Name of the Lord!' What kind of nonsense is that? 'Blessed be the Name of the Lord,' because He let Pat and that boy be killed by a drunken criminal! The comforters! Why did they come? There wasn't any real pity in them. They were complacent. Agnes says they weren't, but I've dealt long enough with people to know what they were. For death had passed by their houses and hadn't come in; death had ridden on the highways with their sons and their daughters, and he hadn't put his hand on them. Death didn't stand on their doorsteps; he didn't afflict them with—disease. Oh, my God!" cried Francis Stoddard. "Oh, my God! Why did it all happen to us? Our only child, our only child. Oh, my God! There isn't any way out now for me. I've known that for three months."

Again he put his hands over his face. The horrors of his life seemed to be crowding about him, like unclean black monsters, slimy and violent; he had overcome them, but now it was nothing. They had returned to exult over him.

He said, "The comforters. Financial disaster hadn't struck at them, depriving them of a whole life's work, threatening them with disgrace and penury and total loss. As if that wasn't enough to kill a man. Then—Pat.

"It's easy enough to comfort people like me when you can go home and sleep peacefully, and talk to your children. And under all that comfort—well, old Frank was being punished for something or other by an obscene God, or at the very least he wasn't much good or he wouldn't have gotten himself in that spot, losing his business which had been his father's business, too. Old Frank wasn't very bright, at that. Poor Agnes, to be married to a failure. Yes, it was too bad about Pat—but those things happen every day.

"They didn't happen to my dear old friends. They still don't happen. They go on with their placid, rich, comfortable lives, serene and self-congratulatory, making plans for their children, playing with their grandchildren. My God!" cried Francis Stoddard, moving furiously in his chair, "I'd like to see them suffer a little what Agnes and I have suffered, not only the financial failure—and my Pat—but almost from the very minute I was born!"

His gaunt face became shrunken with terrible resentment and anger. "I wasn't born in this country," he said. "I was born in one of the old wretched countries. And my real name isn't Stoddard, either. It was one of those names Americans call 'unpronounceable.' My father changed it, not because he was ashamed of it, but because it stigmatized him as a 'Polack.' It made things tougher for him, if possible. He came with a pack on his back, all he owned. My mother carried

51

some old blankets. Pa had wanted her to leave them behind, but she said—and she was a wise woman, my mother—'Who knows? We might need them.' And we did, for five starving, wretched years when my father worked for twelve dollars a week in a ditch or laboring in a factory. That was before the First World War. I was only a baby. My parents left the old country because they felt, in their peasants' blood, that something terrible was going to happen to them if they didn't leave at once. It did—to their families."

He paused, then he smiled with infinite disgust and anguish. "Agnes tells me that the Holy Family ran away like that, for approximately the same reasons. I suppose I remember that from parochial school, in a miserable part of the city—another city than this. I didn't pay much attention. I soon didn't believe in a merciful God when I saw the mercilessness of the life my parents led. They had four more children besides me. They all died of tuberculosis and semi-starvation. And, I'd see my mother—I always see my mother like that—on her knees, meek as milk, praying her Rosary and telling about the will of God. The will of God, for Christ's sake! Four little children dead because their parents couldn't afford enough food for them or a decent place to live! No matter how hard my father worked, and he worked twelve hours a day six full days a week, and he was stooped like an old man at thirty and broken down, he couldn't make enough money to keep his family clothed and adequately sheltered and fed. The parish—and it was as poor as we were—helped to bury my brothers and sisters."

He paused. His face changed a little, then it became hard as steel again, and engraved with agony. He pushed the thought of the parishioners from him.

"I was the only one left. My father wanted to be a 'real' American. His boy was going to have an education, if it killed him, my father. My father was a proud man, even if he was only a 'Polack.' A good, God-fearing, devout man, trusting in the God who killed his children. Yes, I was going to have an education. My father looked for a way, but he didn't find it for many years. His factory, the last one, manufactured windshield wipers, among other things. He invented a better one, simpler, more efficient. We became moderately rich, and I went to college. But I'd put in four years of hard work in a factory before that. I was a full-grown man by then. Besides the years of grinding factory work I had worked after hours in high school. My hands—look at them—are callused and bent and twisted, from all the work I did. And the dirt is in my soul, if I have one, and the cold and the misery and the contempt and hunger. They say you forget. You never forget. I'll never forget the months of pain my mother suffered before she died, the result of privation and the lack of money to have a doctor when she first became sick with cancer."

His mouth parted in a gasp of torment. "My mother died before she could enjoy my father's success. My father couldn't get over it. 'Maria never had it,' he'd say. But—it was God's will! My father died two years after I was graduated from college and took over his little factory. He wasn't really alive after my mother died—"

Francis Stoddard stared bleakly at the blue curtain. He had come here only because Agnes had begged him to come. He had come because he refused to see a priest or talk with him. The only time he had ever come into contact with priests, after his rejection of God as a young boy, was when he had married Agnes and Pat had been baptized and confirmed. The priests! What did they know of a man's bitterness and striving and hopelessness and terror, face to face with a dangerous and merciless world? Except, perhaps, for Father Nowaczysk, another "Polack" with tragic eyes, who had also been born in the "old country." He, Francis Stoddard, refused to remember that old priest who had buried both his parents, and to whom he had refused to listen, turning away in despair and disgust.

Agnes had talked of the "comforter" here. Another one of Job's pals! A priest. Another one who would talk of "God's will." Another one, perhaps, who would hint, as Job's friends had hinted, that his afflictions were, in some way, a punishment on him for his "sins."

"Why did you go to him, my darling?" he had asked Agnes, terrified that she knew the dreadful truth.

She had smiled at him tenderly. "Well, you wouldn't listen to the priest of our parish—"

"About what?" He had pounced on her, the fear gripping him, the awful, sweating fear.

"Well." She had looked at him, denying the truth he feared she knew, but which the doctors had told him she did not. "You won't talk to Father— I thought you might— Why did I go to him? I thought I'd ask him—about you, Frank."

"And what did he say?"

Her pale lips had trembled. "Everything," she said.

"You saw him?"

She had sighed. "Yes, I saw him. Oh, yes."

"And what did he say—about me?"

"He—well, he seemed to want to talk to you—about so many things. Frank, you've been so wretched so long. Frank, go to him for my sake, to please me."

He wouldn't be able to talk to her much longer. For her sake, to please her, he had come to this stupid place, and was now talking to the man coyly hidden behind that blue curtain—for Christ's sake!—and he was talking as he had never talked to anyone before except Agnes. He couldn't understand it. He was a reticent man, taciturn like all Poles, reserved and proud. No, he couldn't understand it. He had just gotten started— Besides, it was so quiet here, so white and blue, so soundless. But the moment the priest there behind the curtain began his sanctimonious homilies he, Frank Stoddard, nee Stypscynzki, would laugh in his face and walk out. He would go home to Agnes— Oh, God, Oh, my God!

Because he had so much self-control he could bring his mind back to the moment. "Why should a man have to change his name to be accepted by people no better than himself, and perhaps not as good? Why should he be despised because of his race, or the accent in his voice—by ignoramuses who can hardly speak their own native language in decent syntax and in adequate communication? Why should he cringe because he had not been born where his peers—God help us!—had been born?

"I suppose you are an American priest, American born. Were you ever despised because of your parentage, your people, who were probably much more intelligent and more honorable people than your neighbors? Do you know what it is like to be jeered at on the street and called 'Polack,' or 'Polski?' Did you ever think twice before speaking so that your accent wouldn't offend people who didn't have a tenth of the native vocabulary that you had? Did you ever see the sneers on the faces of fools because of your pronunciation, or the 'old country' lilt when you spoke? Do you know what it is like to labor among brutes who mimic you or shut you out or treat you as if you were a swine or a yellow dog? Do you know what the laughter of animals is like? It makes you feel like an animal, yourself.

"That is only part of the misery I went through when I was a child in America. Once hoodlums broke the two windows in the little shack we lived in and the landlord held my father responsible—he was Polish, himself. And, by the way, do you know what it is like to have a richer member of your own people, your own race, imitate the contempt of others when speaking to your parents, or to you? 'Dumb Polack.' That was the very least of the epithets, from people who had been born here—and damn it, aren't we all Europeans? Even if we've lived here for twenty generations? At least my people weren't deported here from the British gutters and from the prisons!

"Oh, God. It doesn't matter now. I don't know why I've even mentioned it to you, who wouldn't understand anyway. Even when I was graduated from college, even when I went into my father's little factory, even when I married an 'American' girl—I never gained any assurance. I was always an outsider. I always will be. The bitterness is too deep. You don't forget things you suffered when you were young. Your parents tell you of the great men of your race—but who cares among people who don't even know the great men of the past in their own country?

"Yes, it's part of the misery I've had to carry. Perhaps I'm more sensitive than most. I know my race is almost accepted in Detroit and Chicago; we've given a few mayors here and there, and Congressmen, and a Senator or two. But everyone always looks so surprised, and considers them an exception, for God's sake. Oh, it doesn't matter."

But his face showed that it mattered, and that he would never forget. The sore was only one sore, however, in the enormous wound that was his heart now. And the wound was killing him, he who had been so brave and proud and defiant and strong for too many of his years. There came a time when a man thought he deserved some peace—but it was taken away.

I shouldn't have told him of Pat, he thought. He is probably only thinking that, after all, it was twelve years ago, and "time heals all wounds." The cant. Time doesn't heal. You do go on, but you go on crippled. And this time I won't even go on—

"I've told you I failed in my business. You don't need the details. I was just trying to expand too fast; it was all in the air, expansion. Then I got down to bedrock. I hired some good mechanical engineers. We improved the windshield wipers, and diversified. I came back. But I won't, and can't, forget my 'comforters' who had found my failure a sort of vindication of their own virtue, their own smartness. Never mind."

The cool sweetness of the room flowed all about him. "I think," he said, "that's all. I promised my wife to see you, to tell you some of my damned troubles. That's all."

But he had not spoken of the worst at all. He had spoken of it to only three doctors and to no one else, for fear of Agnes knowing. Now it seemed to him that he could actually see the wound that was spreading and bleeding in him. But to speak of it would be to reveal it to this silent and indifferent man behind the curtain. Not to speak of it made it easier to bear. Not to speak of it guarded Agnes from the knowing. Not to speak of it would prevent that stranger from trying to prevent what he, Frank Stypscynzki, intended to do tonight, tomorrow, or at least in the next month. Even thinking of it now was like a desperate relief in him, such as a prisoner, condemned to death on the scaffold next week, kills himself tonight to escape his executioners, his ceremonial, sadistic executioners. To die privately, to die alone—that retained a man's dignity. His affairs were in order—

Are they?

He almost jumped from the chair, and his agonized heart struck against his chest. Then he fell back. He hadn't heard the man speak. It was only his imagination. He heard himself saying, hurriedly, stammering, "There comes a time in many men's lives, as it has in mine, when you just can't go on living. You can't endure it. It's a—it's a kind of horror. Your mind—it won't accept the fact that you may actually be alive. It refuses to think of it. It won't have it. You've had enough. You've lost nearly everything—and now you're faced with losing the last, and the best of it. How can you live?"

Agnes, forgive me, but how can I live? How can I live, watching you, waiting? Agnes, my darling, my gentle darling, you who have such faith in a God that doesn't exist. Would you have such faith if I let you wait? But I can't wait.

He heard himself, out of his agony, saying the words he had sworn he would never say here or anywhere else: "I am a potential murderer and suicide. No, not potential. I am going to kill my wife, then kill myself, very soon."

He heard his voice, numbly, his calm, indifferent voice, his traitor's voice. He jumped to his feet. That horrified listener there, the man who never spoke, would call the police! He would have him followed. He would tell Agnes. He would have him, the treacherous stupid fool, arrested, thrown into an insane asylum—and Agnes would die alone in all the torture of her disease, protected from him, the husband who had intended not to let her know that torture, nor his own. Then they would both lie, side by side, near Pat, and all the monstrous abomination of living would be behind them forever and it would be almost as good as if they had never

56

been born. "In the grave there is no remembrance." Not to remember all the terrible years of youth, the struggles of maturity, the stunning agony of loss, the final end of torment—yes, it would be almost as good as if it had never happened.

Now he would leave before the man could rush from behind that curtain or out of that door, and call those who would insist that Frank Stypscynzki endure to the end a life that should never have been lived. But the curtain did not stir, there was no movement behind it. He was probably waiting, the smart operator, for him to reveal his name.

But I know you.

"No," said Francis Stoddard. "You don't know me. There are half a dozen manufacturers in this town like myself. Besides, I don't live here. You don't know me and I don't know you."

But I know you.

He pressed his hands to his temples. No, no, he said to himself, no one spoke. I must be going out of my mind.

"Don't interfere, in the Name of God, if you believe in Him. The only thing that has kept me alive is Agnes. We've been married thirty-two years. I had no one before I married her; I have no one now. I never did find life worth living, except when I married Agnes, and then when Pat was born. All the years I worked—I now see they weren't worth the living. It was all useless; it doesn't have any meaning. I have money and a good business. What is the use of it when Agnes is dying and nothing will save her? How can I live when she dies? Just going on working, piling up money, expanding—for what? I don't need it; I won't need it when Agnes dies. I won't want it. I'm fifty-nine years old, nearly sixty.

"The doctors have told me Agnes has inoperable cancer, a terrible thing that didn't show itself until it was too late. There is nothing they can do for her. In about a month she'll begin to have pain. Within a few weeks it will be unbearable. Then she will die in blood and suffering, screaming for them to kill her. She will beg me to kill her. You don't know what wonderful eyes she has, such good sweet eyes. They'll be like the eyes of a tortured dog—don't you know that? She won't even be Agnes any longer. She'll be like someone—on—on a rack, shrieking to be killed, to be put out of her misery.

"How can I stand that? How can I sit by and watch her suffer, drugged, half-dead even before she is dead? And when she's dead—how can I live? What for?"

57

He did not know how beseeching his voice was, how broken and desperate.

"I couldn't have stood all those years after Pat died, if it hadn't been for Agnes. It was Agnes who kept me alive. It was Agnes who never complained or was frightened when the going was tough fifteen—twelve years ago. It wouldn't have mattered if we'd been reduced to one room, she said, as long as we had each other. It was Agnes who could laugh during the worst days, and hold my hand and be cheerful about tomorrow. She—Agnes—is my whole life. There was nothing before her. There won't be anything after her. Have a little mercy and try to understand and let me go and forget I was ever here."

He moved toward the curtain, his hands held out like a beggar. "Don't you understand? We've kept it all from Agnes; I made them promise. She doesn't know. And when I—when I do what I must do—she'll never know in this life or in any other. She'll never know the pain—"

It had been three months since the sun had winked out, since the days had not been numbered, since the nights had not been hours of sleep except when stunned by sedatives, since the weeks had been without light and there had been no voices at all but a crushing silence, since all had been like an awful dream from which he could not awaken, since everything that moved in the world had become totally unreal, shadowy, without significance, since every moment had been like a moment, renewed, of continual death. The very taste, smell, sight of life had been a cemetery full of the dead, moving spasmodically and without volition. He had known death for three months, in all his body, his vague thoughts, his sudden frenzies, his gasping nights, his blind days, his longing to believe in God so that he could hate Him.

"What is wrong, darling?" Agnes had asked him with anxiety. "You look very sick. You hardly sleep at night."

"Nothing, nothing," he had replied. "You mustn't worry. There's just something at the plant—"

"There usually is," she had said with a smile. "You've gone through it dozens of times. Well. Maybe you need a tonic. The tonic the doctor gave me three months ago has really helped me, and you remember how thin I was getting, and tired."

But she was daily becoming more thin and tired. She was only lying to him now so that he would not worry about her. Soon, the pain would begin, the remorseless killing pain, which would not kill cleanly and mercifully, at once. But he would not let it happen to her.

Who has given you the power of life or death over another, or yourself?

In his extremity he no longer wondered if he heard or was imagining he had heard. He said, "I did, for I have the power of will and decision, and that is reserved for man, and I am a man. Don't tell me of morality or immorality, or sin, or punishment. They don't exist. I didn't choose to be born. I can choose when to die."

Agnes, then, should have that right for herself. You should not abrogate it. She may prefer to live as long as possible—with you. How do you know what pain she can bear, that brave and loving woman? Is she a mindless and suffering animal which you have the right to exterminate? She would never forgive you.

"She would never know, because 'in the grave there is no rememberance.' "

Who has told you that?

He stood before the curtain and raised his hand as if to strike it in his anguish.

"My reason tells me."

And who has told you that your wife does not know that she will soon die?

The appalling question—or thought—was like an explosion of fire in his mind, roaring and leaping. He cried, "She doesn't know! No one told her. She couldn't possibly know."

The white room was very still. Did Agnes know? No, no. He thought about it frantically. He began to recall small things which he had hardly noticed at the time. Agnes reading, then letting the book lie in her lap, while she looked into space, her eyes very still and dreaming. Agnes at Mass every morning, in spite of her silent weariness. Agnes suddenly touching his hand and smiling, as if pleading for something. (He thought she was trying to "encourage" him about some problem "at the plant.") Agnes kneeling by her bedside not only before sleeping, but sometimes in the darkest hours of the morning. (He thought she was praying as middle-aged women often prayed during sleeplessness—he remembered that in his mother.) Agnes becoming silent, gazing at him, and though she smiled her eyes filling with tears. (He had thought she was remembering Pat.) Agnes wandering alone in her beloved garden, not asking him to come with her as she usually did, and bending to touch a flower or lifting her head to study the evening sky, lost in thoughts he did not know. Agnes not in bed at dawn, but out on the glistening grass watching the sun come up through the gray-blue air of the morning. Agnes sleeping with her rosary twined between her fingers. Agnes suddenly exclaiming, "What a beautiful world! It must be a reflection of heaven." (He had smiled at this, indulgently. There was only this world.)

All these things had begun to happen only over these last three months. Someone had betrayed him, one of those lying doctors—

The soul knows.

"There is no soul!" he exclaimed, full of terror and grief.

He had a shocked thought. Was it possible that Agnes knew but did not wish to burden him by letting him know that she knew? Did she want him to believe she was ignorant of the horror which was killing her? How else to explain things which had puzzled him: Her gaze at him with pity and tenderness? Her mouth shaking with words she held back? Her increasing suggestions of God's mercy and God's will? Her anxiety for him? Her pleas that he attend Mass with her? (He always but gently refused.) Her sudden shy kisses, the way she clung to him? Her hands on his cheeks, pressing, urgent, as if she were trying to communicate with her flesh the words she dared not say?

"Oh, no," he groaned. "I can stand almost anything but that, Agnes knowing."

If she knew then it was possible she was already in pain and did not tell him because again she did not want to burden him. How lonely she must be—if she knew. And then it came to him devastatingly that he was depriving Agnes of her last comfort, a full communication with her husband, a long and loving farewell, a final hope. He had been thinking only of the barren desolation of his own life when she died, the stony places, the lightless hours, weeks, and days, the meaningless years when he would have to walk alone.

You were thinking only of yourself.

Yes, he thought with an old agony, even when Pat died it wasn't Agnes' grief that disturbed me. It was only my own. Yet, she was Pat's mother. He had thought Agnes' fortitude the piteous folly of faith; he had thought her, God forgive him, less sensitive than himself. When, later, she spoke of Pat fondly and tranquilly, he had moments of angry bitterness when he had thought she had loved the girl less than he had loved her, and had resented it. Was it possible that she truly believed Pat was still close to them and safe with God, and that her husband needed her comfort and not her tears? Yes, it was more than possible. It was true. He did not doubt it; he did not question it. It was true.

He had deprived her of comfort after Pat's death. He was depriving her now of the last comfort of her life by his silence. What did she think of him, a man without fortitude, without faith, without courage? He was sure that she did not despise him. She wanted to help him as a mother helps her child. But she was a woman and she needed her husband.

She was walking the last days of her life alone and in silence, because he believed that he was sparing her. But in marriage there should be no sparing; husband and wife were one and they must share everything together, life and death, hope and pain, reunion and parting. He was condemning Agnes to death alone. Whether or not he chose the hour of her death or she died of the disease, she would be alone, going out into the darkness without the last loving reassurance and faith. To a woman like Agnes that was worse than any physical suffering. To be alone.

"I thought," he said aloud in the depths of his new humility and despair, "that it was only I who walked alone, bearing everything myself. And in all these thirty-two years Agnes walked alone, too, because I never asked her to walk with me. I was always 'sparing' her!"

Yet, she had not been spared at all. She had had only the added torment of keeping silent before a man who would not speak to her—out of his stubborn love and pride.

"God forgive me," he said in the white and blue room. Now he knew why Agnes had come here. It had been for his sake because he would not talk to the priest of his parish. She had come here for the courage and the hope her husband refused her. He had refused the necessary part of life, the pain, the struggle, the despair. He had thought himself singled out among men for misfortune. What did he really know of the private agonies of his friends and neighbors, in spite of their smiles and their casual conversation? He had taken them at face value. And now he saw that all men are one and suffer the same in various degrees. Those who suffered very little—what did they know of living, the victories and the exultations, the startling joys and the triumphant overcoming? They were the truly poor.

"I've lived a selfish life," he said to the man behind the curtain. "I've lived bitterly and stonily. I never once left a wound to heal by itself. I've kept it bleeding. I'm a coward."

Once Agnes had said to him, after a cynical outburst on his part about religion:

"I know that my Redeemer lives."

He had laughed and had patted her hand as a father would pat the hand of a child who passionately affirms her faith in a pretty fairy tale. Women's faith! Let the dears have it if it pleased their dreams and fantasies. They knew nothing of reality.

"It is I who knew nothing of reality," he said. "All these years, I really believed. I thought that by—killing—Agnes, and myself, I would be finally revenging myself on God. I would throw our lives in His Face, defying Him. All men are born with faith; it is part of our nature. When we reject it we are really rejecting what we are. We are, with childish petulance, insisting that we aren't men, that we are only animals. We are trying to provoke God—"

All his life ran before him, the hunger, the cold, the fierceness, the struggle, the hopelessness, the winning, the pain, the despair, and he saw it now as a rich life, one for which to be grateful and joyous—for he had been given the strength to overcome misfortune. Those who never knew the battle never knew the victory. What empty lives!

"God forgive me," he prayed. He touched the button near the curtain. "Father, bless me, for I have sinned."

The curtains rolled apart and he saw the man who had listened to him so patiently. He was not surprised and not startled. He only knelt and clasped his hands together and for the first time in all these years he blessed himself and bowed his head.

"Yes, you will give me the courage to go on, as you always did," he said in his mind to the man. "You never once deserted me. I was the one who deserted you, in my childish resentment. You will forgive me everything.

"Now I can go home to Agnes and tell her that I know. I can give her the comfort I never gave her before. She won't be alone any longer. It is going to be terrible for me when she suffers, but I'll be there to help her bear it. I will try to have her own faith and courage. It won't be easy. Men aren't transformed in an instant. But with your help I'll hold on. I can probably even live with some serenity after Agnes goes—to you. With your help.

"But you will have to tell me over and over that parting isn't forever. You will tell me, as my wife tried to tell me, that my Redeemer lives."

When he went out into the autumn sunshine he was amazed. He had not even known that summer was over. Now he saw the brilliant trees, the copper forests of the sun, and

62

life roared into his ears and the men and women on the street down there were no longer lifeless. They were human again, part of himself, and he wondered, with humility, how many of them were brave and how many of them were hiding anguish and defeat and misery under an air of busyness and compact surety, and how many knew that someone beloved was about to die or even themselves.

If they could endure—if man could endure with his awful knowledge of himself—then he, Francis Stoddard, could endure.

The man who had listened to him: He, too, had been a stranger in a strange land, with an accent which had invited ridicule. He had been abused and derided; multitudes had turned from him. He had known loss and grief and what seemed to many the ultimate defeat and humiliation. He had known everything that men ever knew and will know. And out of his defeat had come victory, out of his death—life. Above all things he had been brave and had forgiven.

Pat isn't lost to me, thought Francis Stoddard, walking in the sun once more. And who knows? By dying so soon she was, perhaps, spared what I have been suffering, and what her mother is suffering. If she didn't receive any fulfillment she was never betrayed and never grieved. What did Agnes tell me once? That life is only an overture to living, that its greatest sound and harmony are not in this world. But overture or not, the music is still beautiful if sometimes terrible.

No, I'm not reconciled. How could I be? But at least I'm not hopeless now. I am a complete man as I never was before. For, indeed, my Redeemer lives and because He lives all that I love will live, and I will be with them and this time there won't be any parting.

He had thought of immediately going home. But he turned his car, now, and drove to the rectory of the priest.

SOUL FOUR: The Ostracized

"Am I not a man as you are a man?
Why do you deny to me my manifest humanity?"
SENECA. "Essay on Humanity"

He supposed they had been offended when he had left the lunch so abruptly. He had ended his talk on a note of despair, but they had not heard the despair. Of that he was positive. They never heard anything but their self-congratulation and the applause of their colleagues for their "tolerance" and "liberalism." When he had quoted Seneca and had demanded "Am I not a man as you are a man?" they had only nodded their heads solemnly and had looked at each other with grave eyes of assent. But they did not know what he had meant.

He had meant it for them. They had not known or were too stupid and self-engrossed to know. They had been applauding themselves, as usual. Egotists! Mean little liars! He, Paul Winsor, preferred those who openly despised him rather than those who "loved" him. The despisers were at least honest; he could talk to them and sometimes persuade them. But the fawning liars were a most dreadful danger to him and all that he was. They provoked the violent who could not endure hypocrisy either, as he could not endure it. Let a man hate him, and there was a possibility for conciliation. But there was no reconciling the "loving" who perversely insisted on loving him their own way—which nauseated him and made him so acutely self-conscious. And ashamed, as no man should be made to feel shame. There were times when they put their hands on his shoulder and he was outraged. How dare they touch him as they would touch a dog they did not understand but which they wished to placate, or worse, wished to seduce with a false affection? Would they be so condescending to one of their own, and violate reticence with their kind as they violated it with him?

"Am I not a man as you are a man?" Hah. Was it so much to demand of another human being that one be treated as a

64

man, only, neither with furious hatred and loathing nor with maudlin "love?" Either was an insult to a man's humanity, but the last was the worst of all, the very worst of all.

Paul Winsor. Summa cum laude, Harvard, and Harvard School of Business Administration. Businessman, now worth, at thirty-eight, half a million dollars and every dollar earned with sweat and blood. Fine little factory, employing one hundred people and more during rush seasons. Beautiful wife, Kathleen, an executive in his company. Two wonderful kids, Timothy and Ailsa. Proud of him, proud of themselves. They did not know how much he despised himself sometimes, not that there was anything in him to despise but because of the attitude of others, especially the patronizing. He must stay away from them after this, and remain with his own community where at least he was respected as an intelligent and prosperous businessman and not as a "problem" or a "national cause." He was on the School Board, also, and on the board of his church, and a collector for all charities. A Rotarian, too. (That had taken aback some of the Rotarians on the "panel" at the lunch today. He could see them making somersaults in their minds; they were obviously trying to be pleased. It was just as obvious that they were not exactly pleased.) He was listed in Who's Who in America, because of his business-machine invention which had made his business possible. Last year the company, of which he was president, had grossed nearly two million dollars. Quite an accomplishment for the son of a poor minister.

Only the single Jew on the "panel" had looked at him with wry understanding when he had posed his question, "Am I not a man as you are a man?" Only the Jew had not nodded with solemn, turned-down mouth and sheep's eyes. The Jew had smiled faintly as well as sardonically. Now he, Paul Winsor, wished he had not left so abruptly after the lunch at the hotel; he might have been able to have had an ironic and confidential conversation with the Jew. And probably, best of all, some bitter laughs, with perceptive glances. There had been another one there who might have had something to say privately: an old Irish priest with a brogue. He had given the opening prayer. The members of the Lunch Club were so very tolerant. They had a clergyman of a different faith at every lunch. The priest had not been extraordinarily comfortable either, a rough big old man with a fighter's face and a mystic's eyes. At Paul's question he had frowned, as if the question had been challenging, whereas the priest seemed to believe as if there should be no challenge at all. But there was.

Just before the lunch he had looked down from his window and had seen, in that congested vicinity, several green acres of beautifully tended grass shadowed by trees in all the glorious colors of autumn, gold, brown, russet, fiery red, pale fretted yellow. A lovely park. He had been able to see wandering paths of raked gravel, and grottoes, and marble benches scattered here and there, and a twinkling fountain or two. In the very center, on a rise of land like a small hill, had stood a magnificent white building, low and long, like a Grecian temple. He had asked another guest what it was. "Oh," said the man with contemptuous indulgence, "some people call it the Sanctuary. A sort of chapel or shrine, built by a fanatical old lawyer long before my time; I think my father knew him. Never have seen it close to, myself. It's a kind of disgrace to the city, though it's supposed to be religious. It's a wonder the clergy don't object. You could ask the priest who'll be at the lunch today, what's his name? I don't know; we always have a different clergyman. Maybe he can tell you."

. Paul had asked the priest just before the lunch. The old priest had looked at him with small but brilliant gray eyes. He had hesitated. Then he had said, "It's neither a shrine nor a chapel. We're proud of it in our city. There's an arch of gold over the entrance, *THE MAN WHO LISTENS*. It's been here for many years, even before I came to this city. I think there is—a man—who listens to people in there; their troubles, their problems. Rootless people. Frightened ones, too. People who are outside organized religion, some of them. Lots of them have come to me after they went to the Sanctuary." Again the priest hesitated. "Some of them had been at the point of committing suicide. He—he in there—had helped them. Then they had come to me, or some other clergyman." The priest had then turned away.

The man who listens. Whoever did, in these days, these noisy, self-congratulatory, prosperous, affluent, dynamic days? Everybody made a noise, but no one listened to anybody. Paul Winsor was intrigued; he had continued to look down at the Sanctuary until it was time for lunch. The man who listens. A clergyman, a doctor, a psychiatrist? He must be a rare bird indeed, if he could stop talking long enough to listen to anybody. No one listened now except to himself.

Paul had forgotten all about the Sanctuary when lunch began. He had sat at the right hand of the president, a thin,

66

Noise

skinny specimen with cold and watery blue eyes, a vicious mouth, an impeccable manner, an alert glance, a long gray head, a sharp and penetrating voice, a polite gentleman in all ways. Paul was the speaker for the month. His subject had been: "The Problems of Businessmen in a Controlled Economy." The president had said:

"Yes, that's very important, considering the bureaucracy in Washington. But, and I hope you won't mind when I say we were a little disappointed in your choice of material, we had hoped you'd have given us a talk about Racial Intolerance and Civil Rights. From your point of view, of course."

Paul had frowned. "My point of view? It's a human point of view, that's all, with a wide range of differing opinions. Why should 'my view' be different from anyone else's?"

The president had stared at him with amazement. "You're from Georgia, aren't you?"

"Yes. That's where my factory is, and where I live with my family." Paul felt his forehead grow hot and tense. "I employ both white and colored, of course. I've never had any trouble. Until lately." He had looked into those cold blue eyes and the cold blue eyes had looked back at him, and it was as if wrestlers had locked in mortal combat. He had continued bitterly, "Until professional agitators had tried to ruin it all. People with their own sinister mission."

The president had said with ice in his voice, "I'd hardly call it 'sinister.' Just a word of advice: Don't go into that in your talk. Keep to your script," and the smile that accompanied the words had been purely malevolent.

But Paul, aroused as he had rarely been aroused before, had not kept to his script. He had opened with the words of Seneca—to all these brotherly-lovers!—"Am I not a man as you are a man? Why do you deny to me my manifest humanity?"

It was obvious, halfway through his impassioned and angry talk, that only the Jew, and probably the priest, had really absorbed what he had been saying. The others, as usual, had reinterpreted rapidly as he had been talking, to suit their own prejudices and turn of mind and convictions—their lying, hypocritical, self-loving convictions! Their smug convictions. They had not heard him because they were so busily trying to fit his words into their own stilted frames of reference, to make it palatable to themselves and acceptable in the context of their acquired beliefs which were so popular these days and so lauded in the newspapers and in the more "liberal" periodicals.

What had his father once told him? "There is nothing so hateful to a hypocrite as to have his hypocrisy publicly exposed, or even exposed only to himself. Avoid hypocrites, Paul. They'll have your lights and livers if you don't watch out!"

A number of men at the lunch had finally caught on as to what he meant. They had looked at him with hatred, the hatred of the Pharisee who had tried to conceal his Phariseeism under a gloss of brotherly love and equality. But the others had only solemnly nodded in assent—and damn them! had not understood at all. That was worse than the Pharisees.

There had been no question period. Even the fools had uneasily understood that answers might be devastating. So, he had run away from them, on some vague excuse. They were probably still waiting for him to come back from the men's room.

But he was here, slowly walking up the gravel path to the Sanctuary. The man who listens. Another hypocrite with sweet, lipoid talk, with sweet consolations, and pat answers. "My son, I understand your Problem and regret it. But remember, We are all One with God."

Are we, are we? asked Paul, already hating the man who listened. If so, then there is something terribly wrong. Surely God preferred His saints—if there was a God at all—to monsters in human form, no matter the race or color, or religion if any. Surely God, though Pa had said that God was no Respecter of persons, had a special love for those who served Him in selflessness and hope. Surely He had not regarded a Hitler or a Stalin or a Khrushchev with the same "love" as he had regarded sane and just men!

Surely God had regarded a hypocrite with detestation! Yes, He had said to them, with wrath and disgust, "Liars, hypocrites!" Or, at least Pa had told him that, as he had read from the Bible every evening to his children.

Paul stood now before the bronze doors of the Sanctuary. "Hello, hypocrite," he said. "I know you and your kind of clergymen. You'll give me instant love and sympathy, and wind up, as almost everyone else does, with hatred and animosity. You'll give me the same old disgusting cant, the same old liberal hogwash. You won't regard me as a man but only as a 'problem.' And how you'll pour your scented oil over me—until—"

He pushed open the doors. An elderly man with a cane was the only one present in the waiting room, an old man with sunglasses, sunken in misery. The beautiful waiting room was cool and fresh, after the warm autumn day outside. Paul sat down at a distance from the old man, but the old man looked at him through those dark glasses. Paul braced himself. He knew he was a tall, slender, fine-looking youngish man, with a scholarly face for all he was a businessman. But that did not count. It never counted. The old man said, "I hope he can help me. Do you think he can?" The ancient voice was quivering.

Paul was surprised. He expected a remark—he was always expecting a remark—but not this one. He felt a pang of gratitude. He said, "I hope so." He paused. Then he added, "That's why I'm here, myself," and was astonished at his own words.

The old man nodded sorrowfully. "We all have our problems," he said, a remark surely without originality, Paul thought.

"Now my problem," said the old man, "is that I'm almost blind. I'm going to lose even what little sight I have left; that's what the doctors tell me. How can I stand being blind?"

So, thought Paul, that's the answer. He doesn't even see me. He said, "Blindness can be of the mind, too, as well as the body. Which is worse?"

The old man smiled at him gently. "Yes, I see. I can see you, you know. My sight isn't all gone yet. And I think I know why you're here. Never mind. I don't believe in intruding on anyone. Everybody does these days; no one lets you alone."

Paul was not an emotional man. He had inherited a quiet reticence from his English ancestors, a cool aloofness, a polite distance. (One of his ancestors had fought with George Washington and had later been a Secretary of the Treasury.) But he was deeply moved by the old man's words. That was the very heart of the problem. "No one these day lets you alone." They pried; they stuck their impudent fingers into the very sensitive ulcers of the spirit which every man suffered; they peeked and peered; they demanded, in their vulgar insistence, that you tell them your secret thoughts. They were insulted if you kept yourself to yourself and insisted on your privacy. Everyone should "share" these days. You should indecently expose yourself to the most shameless eyes; you should be "warm" and "outgoing." Especially if you were one like Paul Winsor.

The old man said, "You see, I'm an artist, of sorts. I create, if you can call it that, patterns for rugs and draperies.

Not so much of an artist, would you say? But I've made a lot of money, so I don't have to worry about being indigent and subject to all the busy-loving of the social workers. What bothers me is that I won't be able to see the color of the world any longer, or the shapes and forms. Every morning," said the old man with a beautiful candor, "I see the dawn. And one morning I saw it come up in winter, against a cold dark sky. A crown of crimson fire, a real crown, like the crown of a Titan. It—well, it was the crown of God against complete blackness. And for the first time in my life I said to it, 'Good morning, Father!' I'm not a religious man. I'm an agnostic, honestly; always was. But something happened to me then, when I saw that crimson crown of fire. I think I began to believe. I was happy for the first time in my long life. And now I'm going to be blind and I'll never see anything again."

Paul did not remember the last time he had felt a rush of tears in his eyes. He was glad that perhaps the old man did not see them. What could he say? What was his problem compared to this: a man who loved color and form and who would never see them again? What could he say? He said, "I'm ashamed of myself."

What a ridiculous thing to say! But the old man was nodding seriously. "I suppose we could all say that, if we were honest."

A bell chimed. The old man began to rise, then tottered. Paul went to him at once and helped him, and put the cane into his hand. "Thank you," said the old man. "I don't like it, though. I suppose I never will." He looked at Paul searchingly. "Neither will you. But what does it matter? I'm going in there to ask that man how I am going to live, after I go blind. Don't you think a person like myself should choose a time to die, instead of waiting, helplessly?"

Paul had asked himself that a thousand times, with bitterness and anger. But he said now, "I don't think so. If there is any reason in the universe then we have a reason to be here." Liar, hypocrite, he commented to himself. You are just pouring the same old oil which has been poured on you, too.

The old man laughed a little and shook his head. But he did not object when Paul led him to the door of the other room. "Good luck," he said to Paul, and somehow Paul was reminded of the Jew's ironical smile at the lunch. The door closed after the old man and Paul sat down again. There was a curious agitation in him now, an agitation without a name, a disturbance of the spirit with which he was unfamiliar. As

70

a self-controlled man and a gentleman, he was annoyed. He took up a magazine and began to read. But all he could see imprinted on the page was the old man's words, "No one these days lets you alone." Oh, damn them. Damn them.

After awhile the bell chimed softly and Paul looked up from his brooding contemplation of the floor. He rose and went to the door yonder. He paused, hesitating, with his hand on the knob. What a stupid business this was! He wondered what platitudes had been spewed on that tragic old man's head. Had they been so bad that he had gone home to kill himself, out of sheer disgust, or had he become maudlin? Coming down to it, why was Paul Winsor here, himself? He dropped his hand from the knob and half-turned away. The chime sounded like a voice, so he opened the door and went into the inner room.

There was no sign of the old man. There was nothing here but white marble walls, a white marble chair and a shrouded blue alcove. Theatrical. Paul went to the chair and stood behind it, his hands on its back. He looked at the blue curtains.

"Good evening," he said in his soft, southern drawl.

No one answered. The blue curtains did not move. The white silence of the walls and the ceiling glowed down on him. Had the psychiatrist or minister taken a coffee break, or perhaps a drink to numb the foolishness he had told the old man? Well, that was understandable. And human. No matter how hypocritical the man there were moments when he had a flash of self-revelation and was nauseated. Or he turned his self-hatred on other men. Paul mused on the countless numbers of men who had hated themselves in him.

"Is anyone here?" he asked.

Was that a stir he had heard or only the whisper of the air-conditioning? But all at once he felt that a man was waiting behind the curtains. Paul said, "I'm a stranger in town, and I'm sorry, but I'm not going to tell you my name or very much about me, at that. By the way, can you see me?"

No one really answered him, but a voice appeared to sound within Paul's ear, a man's voice infinitely kind and grave. "Yes, child," it said. Ridiculous. He was using his imagination; Kathleen invariably told him he had too much of it. But he, Paul, though he had anticipated an affirmative answer, in spite of the heaviness of the draperies which hid everything, had really expected a patronizing "Yes, son," or at the worst, "Yes, boy."

But never "child." Only his parents had called him that, in love or admonition or impatience. Child. A child was univer-

71

sal, a young one, an outraged one, a suffering one. Outrage. That was worse than suffering. Any time, that was worse than pain, an affront to what one really was.

"My problem," said Paul, feeling both foolish and formal, "is really nothing compared to the old man's; he was just here. I hope you gave him some consolation?"

Paul felt an affirmation and a tenderness. Oh, that imagination of his! Paul moved from behind the chair to the seat and sat down. He placed his beautifully-formed hands on his knees, as if he were about to address his board of directors and while doing so avoid Kathleen's amused eyes.

"You see," he said pedantically, and he could hear his measured words and see Kathleen's dancing eyes, "no one treats me as a man these days. Once some people did. Not any longer. Now they look at me with hate or with their infernal 'love.' I think I prefer the hate; at least it's honest and sometimes I can overcome it. When I was younger and at school my profs treated me as they treated everyone else. I flunked some tests, and was yelled at; I passed others, at the head of the class, and was congratulated. I was on the high school team, in Georgia, the track, you know, and if I was good—well, I was just good. If I was bad, then I was cursed in no uncertain terms.

"Now, everything's changed. I go North and the most stupid remark I make—and I'm no tyro at stupid remarks, I can assure you—is received as if it were Holy Writ. But that's not what I want to say."

He stopped and looked at the curtain and did not know the leaping despair in his eyes.

"I am a man! It's true I'm a businessman and I'm successful. But I'm a man in my own right! That is what is being denied me these days. I'm not only a businessman. That's my vocation. I'm interested in a thousand things. I'm an amateur musician of sorts; piano. I studied music; among other things. And my wife, Kathleen, has a beautiful voice. She sings when I play. Oh, my God, how can I make it plain to you?"

He clenched his hands into the impotent fists he was always making these days. "I love sculpture. I mess around with it a little. I love architecture; I really designed our house in Georgia, though I'm no architect. I love the classics; I love ancient art. I love the theater, especially the tragedies." He halted. "I come of a tragic people. Tragedy isn't native to us, you see. It is others who have made us tragic.

"It doesn't matter. You see, I travel a great deal. You can't get decent salesmen in this affluent age, so I do a lot of traveling myself. I meet very interesting people." He made a wry mouth. "But, can I talk to them about music, literature, art, science, the theater, the ballet, about human events and history? No! Damn it, no! I try to talk to them as one human being to another. But they won't let me! They either look impatient or they are puzzled. All they want to discuss with me is—Race. And Racial Problems. They deny me my identity as a man, with a man's hopes and love of beauty and concern with humanity and history, and my future as a man. Do you realize how terrible that is—to be denied your identity as a man?"

The faintest sound came to him, as a sigh, as an indrawn breath. My imagination again, he thought. But all at once he felt understood. He moved in agitation on the chair.

"I am a man, with a man's human nature. That human nature is denied me, not by those who ignorantly hate me, but by those who pretend, or believe, they 'love' me. But they don't love me as Paul Winsor, a man, with their own organs and blood and sinews and spirit and hopes and despairs. They 'love' me as a Symbol. A Symbol of their own perverted and inverted hatred!

"That's what it is: hatred. You and I, we know there is little difference between hate and love; the line is very thin. But I don't want to be hated or loved! I don't want to be the scapegoat for those whom James Baldwin called the 'white, liberal bastards.' I don't want to be their pretty sacrifice for the perverse self-hatred they hold in themselves, and through which they would like to purge themselves. They heap their perversities on me, their lies, their hypocrisies; they touch me with their obscene hands, as they wouldn't do their own kind. Pawing me, soothing me! I don't need to be soothed. I want my human nature to be recognized, not with 'love,' but with objectivity. Is that too much to ask?"

"No," said the grave voice in his ear. He started. "But it appears too much for almost all men in these awful days," said the imagined voice.

My God, my imagination, thought Paul Winsor. He looked down at his beautiful hands, his molded black hands, the hands of a sensitive artist, but firm and strong and sinewy.

"What is it that is so frightful in most men these days that they must pretend to 'love' others?" asked Paul. "Never was the world so loveless as it is now, so degraded, so full of hate. Yet, you can't go anywhere but that you hear love, love, love. A steamy bath of it. A miasma. It is particularly smothering for my people. They are choking in it, especially in the

North. But it isn't really love, is it? It is hatred. It is the self-righteousness of the cruel Pharisee."

He turned his head as if choking, his strong and well-marked head with the gleaming black skin, the crisply curling hair, the dimpled chin and the shining cheekbones.

He said, in a gasping voice, "But who are my people? All mankind is my people. I am a man; if others are men, then they are men with me. Those who deny my human nature, which I share with them, deny me my rights as a spirit, as a mind, as an aspiring man."

He got to his feet in his increasing agitation. "But you don't understand! You refuse to me, like your own race, my human nature, my human nature as a person which is precious to me! What does it matter that my skin is darker than yours, that I have a remote African ancestry? Am I not a man, and do I not bleed as you bleed, and do I not love as you love, and suffer as you suffer? I am a man! Until recently I was known as a man. Now I am only a Problem, a Symbol, to those who 'love' me and try to exploit me and relegate me outside of humanity, for their own secret and perverted objectives. As a white man, how can you understand me, and my outrage that I am denied my human nature?"

He ran to the curtain and struck it with his fist. It seemed, in spite of its soft texture, to be made of iron. He did not know he was sobbing dryly. Then he saw the button near it, informing him that if he wished to see the man who had listened to him he had only to press it.

He said, in a bitter voice, "I don't want to see your white face, and to hear you call me 'son,' and to listen to your lies. I don't want your soothing 'love.' You won't talk to me as a man to a man. You aren't interested. You'll talk to me seriously about 'racism,' until I squirm with shame for you, and for myself. You won't say a word about our mutual human interests and our common humanity."

His hand was clenched again. He struck the button with it. The curtains moved aside, heavily, as if pain were concealed behind them. And then, in the glow of soft pale light he saw the man who had listened to him, the agonized, loving man who gazed at him with pain and passionate comprehension.

Paul slowly lifted his hand and covered his mouth with it, his shaking mouth.

"No," he whispered. "I don't believe in you. I don't believe a word you are saying— My father did. He died of starvation, slow starvation. He loved you; he said you were a man as he was a man. Is that how you repaid him?"

74

He turned away and went back to the chair. He stood beside it, with his hand on the back. His eyes met those of the man who had listened to all his agony. For a long time they contemplated each other in silence. Paul averted his head.

"No. No. No."

He felt a presence in the room, enveloping, strong, manly. A father's presence.

He said, "They denied your human nature too, didn't they? You were either a symbol for their maudlin love, or you were not a man at all. You were removed from humanity entirely, or you did not exist. Just as I am, these days, removed from humanity or denied my existence as a legitimate American with a black skin. A symbol, or a nothing. An object of unhealthy love—an insult to my intelligence—or a mark for contempt."

It was the coolness in the room, of course, which was making his eyes wet. He wiped them, simply, with the back of his hand, like a hurt child.

"My wife, Kathleen, and my children. My children, especially. What is going to happen to them? They were never treated in their young lives as I was treated in Georgia, as a human being. They may move North, where they will be glorified as something 'super,' until their blatant human nature asserts itself—when they will be hated for daring to be human! Neither in the South now, nor in the North, will they be simply accepted as human, good and bad, bright or stupid, aspiring or dull. Just accepted. As a human being, punished if they are evil, rewarded if they are worthy. Not coddled, not given special sly privilege, not listened to abjectly, but not rejected when they display that which is human in them, common to all men."

He looked again at the man who heard him and who was regarding him with both agony and mighty love.

"You and I, we have a lot in common, haven't we? We have an immortal spirit, and we have our human nature, bound up in one. Mankind rejects one part of us, forever, doesn't it? Why can't they accept us? Simply, honestly?"

"At some time. Perhaps," said the deep and manly voice.

His ridiculous imagination. The man who had listened had not moved at all, had not really spoken. Had he?

But all at once Paul Winsor felt a rise in him, a gift of brotherhood, a lift of the spirit, a community of being. He got to his feet slowly and went to the man. He himself was tall, and he had to stand on tiptoe to touch the man's cheek.

"Brother," he said. He waited. The great eyes smiled on him. "Brother," he said again.

Then, "Brother!" For the first time in his life Paul felt that the word was significant and not part of the cant which other men used toward him, no humiliating lie, no fawning assertion which rose out of shamed hatred, no condescension from the mouth of a white man who pretended to "equality" and "brotherly love," because he was a liar.

Here was one who accepted him from love, as one man to another, worthy of love as a human being, as a human soul. The man loved him, not as a Cain disguised as an Abel for his own evil purposes. He loved him for what they shared together, body and spirit, with an immortal destiny.

"Dear God," said Paul. "Dear God. With Your help I will endure. We, together, will outlive false love and furious hatred, and lies and hypocrisies. We shall endure together, for eternity. And perhaps, in some far time, our brothers will talk to us as brothers, and will finally know us for what we are."

SOUL FIVE: "Only a Kid"

"Gird up your loins and answer Me."
                                        JOB 38:3

He came smiling rosily into the waiting room, walking with his usual boyish insolence and waiting for every eye to turn on him indulgently and every woman's eye to warm. But no one seemed to know he had entered. His smile faded, and he scowled. Just as he suspected: old bags and crumpled old men—except for that youngish woman over there in the smart summer dress. He sat down near her, his smile ready, moistening his glowing teeth of which he was very proud. The woman did not look at him. It was not that he was deliberately ignored, he saw to his amazement. They had simply not cared to turn their heads in his direction. He stared at the women and thought: Pigs. He glared at the men and thought: Slugs. Several young women and girls had told him he was magnetic, and that he attracted instant attention. If so, his charm wasn't working today. They were all tied in knots, that's what the trouble with them was. Selfish animals. Selfish old animals. The sooner they were dead the better. They'd make room for kids like himself. What was it some famous writer had written about old folks' homes? "I'd like to take a machine gun and clear them all out, for the kids." Right.

He crossed his knees and folded his powerful arms across his chest, seeing himself pleasantly in the mirror of himself. A big kid, with broad shoulders and narrow hips, handsomely dressed in a fine cashmere sports jacket, a deep and lustrous blue, and with slacks of a lighter blue. Blue silk socks, handmade black loafers, blue and white striped sports shirt and no tie. He had a broad pink face with dimples he pretended to deplore, a strong and belligerent nose, a full mouth and eyes the color of his jacket and all crowned by a tousled mop of bright gold hair. His whole body was flushed and tanned by the sun. He loved himself in swim-trunks, and surfing. He

77

loved himself swimming strongly. He loved himself dressing and undressing, eating and drowsing, playing and laughing. In short he loved himself. He knew it. He saw no reason to deny it. After all, he was a handsome kid and the world had been made exclusively for the young. He pursed his lips soundlessly as if whistling. A roaring beat of modern music pounded pleasingly in his head and he tapped his foot on the thick blue rug which covered the white marble floor. Kookie place, he thought with great amusement. A nut farm. He heard a chiming and he saw an elderly man rising and going to another door. The door closed after him. So that was where the headshrinker was, tinkling his stupid bell for the pigs and the slugs who went in there to tell him about their complexes and inferiorities and frustrations. Thank God he didn't have any. But he'd given Sally his word that he'd come here; that was the only way he could get a divorce out of her. He couldn't lie to her either; she'd been here, herself, and she knew exactly what it was like and all about the kook who listened in there, so he couldn't fool her.

It wasn't a hell of a lot to pay for a divorce. After all, he was only a kid and she had almost raped him into marrying her. She was a mature woman, and he was still practically a teen-ager.

The outer door opened and a young girl in a green dress came in, a lovely young girl not more than twenty, if that old, with a mass of fine black hair on her shoulders, a clear fair face and beautiful big black eyes. Johnnie Martin looked at her with intense admiration. A babe. Now, that was more his kind of dish. He watched her openly as she sat down and neatly crossed her ankles and folded her white-gloved hands in her lap. She made Sally look as old as his grandmother, and he felt the freshness of her youth and stared at the full redness of her mouth. Now what in hell had brought that kid here, a kid like himself? Maybe she had an old slob for a husband and wanted to get rid of him, too. The girl lifted the white lids of her eyes and saw him admiring her. She studied him. Then her lip, incredibly, lifted in disdain and she reached to a table and took a magazine.

Johnnie was astounded. Girls never brushed him off like that! He was also angry. Deliberately, then, he stood and went to the girl and sat down beside her. She read the magazine. He bent his head and whispered, "What's a doll like you doing in this menagerie?"

She did not answer for a few seconds and then she said, still not looking at him, "What're you doing here?"

He grinned. "Getting advice on how to get rid of an old bag."

"Your mother?" she asked, looking at him now with intentness. He was pleased. He smiled and his huge white teeth flashed, as he knew they would flash. He had expected that question.

"Believe it or not, my wife," he said, and waited for her expression of disbelief. It did not come. Instead she only studied him thoughtfully.

"She's a lot older than me," he said, a slight petulance in his rich voice.

The girl smiled. He could not dig that smile; it was very odd.

"I was only a kid when I married her," he said. The room was very cool and pleasant and he began to relax and enjoy himself. He did not notice or did not care that the other occupants of the room were giving him glances of dull displeasure.

The girl smiled again. "How long have you been married?"

He hesitated, and she saw it. "To Sally? Three years."

Her black eyes, which had appeared so distant and sad when she had entered, began to sparkle. She made a rounded cherry of her mouth. "Oh? Are you planning to get an annulment? For being under-age?"

He beamed at her, delighted. He scratched his head to make his hair more tousled than before. "Well, you could just about say that! But, not quite."

The girl stopped smiling. "I thought not," she said, and stood up and left him for another section of the room. He watched her go. The delight in his eyes was replaced by rage and hate. Little tramp! Probably made a "mistake" and was looking for the name of an abortionist. She was just the kind, with her dress tight across the rump. Legs too fat, too. He hated girls with heavy legs. Cows. In a few years she'd be a bag, like Sally. Some of the others in the room had noticed all this, in spite of their misery, and they could not help smiling a little, understanding. This made him angrier than ever. His face flushed a deeper pink and his straw-colored brows tightened over his eyes. He'd get the hell out of here.

No. He'd have to see that headshrinker in there. He must be some kind of a nut, to listen for free to every yapper who came in to see him. Didn't charge a cent, either. What did he do? Make sex-reports? On these old pigs and slugs sitting around here, waiting? The idea made him grin nastily. He could imagine the reports these dirty old men could make, if they had the nerve! With bold insolence he watched them stand up one by one at the chiming, and leave the room. He wanted them to glance at him just once; he'd let them know he knew all about them. They did not look at him. The distant girl was reading; he was sure she was not, for she did not turn a page. Her eyes appeared fixed on the print, but did not stir and hardly appeared to blink. A junkie? Probably. She had the color for it, too fair; no healthy tan; no vitality; no hint of sensuality. Then he saw something which freshly delighted him. She wasn't as young as he had thought. There were the slightest hints of crow's-feet at the corners of her eyes. A bag. An old bag. At least twenty-eight; an old bag.

The girl was clutching her composure to her heart. I must be calm, she was thinking. I must hold on to myself. This thing happens to millions of people every year, people much younger than I am. Girls much younger. I've got to keep my head for Tom's sake; I must remember not to tell him until the very, very last. Dear Tom. If only she and Tom could really talk together; but they'd had so much fun these six years of their marriage. There had never been any time for serious conversation; Tom's life had always been too serious, anyway. She hoped she had brought into it all the fun and laughter and joy he deserved. But now—

In her misery she involuntarily lifted her head and turned it and saw Johnnie Martin staring at her with open disgust. She was not disturbed. She could only compare him with Tom, who must be younger. This man must be at least thirty, if not older. But he dressed and acted like a kid, a silly, grinning, worthless kid. There were so many of him around now; she was always seeing them and comparing them with Tom. Aging juveniles, perpetual teen-agers, men who refused to grow up. Didn't he realize how old he was? She wondered, pityingly, about his wife. Whatever "Sally" was she was getting a good deal if she could get rid of him. She hoped that the man who listened in there would tell this idiot to run, not walk, to the nearest divorce court, for "Sally's" sake. Ugh! she thought. How could the poor thing have married him in the first place?

Johnnie Martin could not believe that he was seeing that old bag's black eyes sparkling with disgust and unsheathed contempt at him. Her red lips had parted and he saw how small and white her teeth were. He detested little teeth; he liked huge flaring teeth in a woman, wet and shining. "Horse's teeth," Sally had said once. She had little teeth like this old bag. He wondered why he hadn't noticed that before he had married her; it would have put him off right at the beginning. Everything about Sally was wrong for him; she was not tall, not slender, not fascinating, not sexy, not even pretty. Her hair was only brown, and her eyes also. She had a round sober face, with one deep dimple in her left cheek, and a tilted nose. She had been his mother's friend, and he had known for some time that it was his mother who had engineered his disastrous marriage—his dead mother.

"Sally's such a wonderful girl," his mother had said, his dying mother. "She'll be the very best for the children, and be the mother to them that they've never had."

Throwing up his two previous marriages to him, as if they'd been his fault! He'd been only a kid, and they'd practically forced him to marry them, he, only a youngster, the first marriage when he was only twenty-four, hardly out of his teens and not dry behind the ears yet, and the second at twenty-eight—he had been only a youth, still a kid. Isn't that what the judges called kids his age? Youths. Some of them wanted Youth Courts to handle boys and girls up to the age of thirty-one; they realized they were only kids, after all. Dad had understood that, that little guy. Even when his son had topped him by seven inches and was a sophomore in college, he would stand back on his heels and look up at his son's face and say rebukingly to his wife, "He's just a little kid, Ann, just a little kid. What else can you call him?" Yes, what else? But his mother had been like Sally; they were a pair.

When he was rid of Sally, and got his hands on all that money, he'd really make up for lost time. Two or three years in Hawaii. A year in Rome. Perhaps a season or two in the south of France, and a winter in Paris. He smiled and his heart pounded with the joy of anticipation. The only thing that stood between him and the pleasures necessary to his youth was Sally, and she had promised him a divorce if he would come to this kookie place and talk to the man who listened. Well, he'd listen! And then freedom, like a kid again.

Dimly he heard the bell chime. But he was sunken in his anticipations. Then the girl said to him across the room, in her sweet well-bred voice, "You are next." He started and looked up. They were alone. He winked at her impudently, showing his dimples. She went back to her reading. He yawned, stood up, pulled down his jacket, and sauntered to the door. He had an easy, boyish lope which he knew was very appealing to women. The girl was evidently not impressed for she did not look up. He pulled open the door with unnecessary vigor and entered the white and blue room beyond. He stared.

There was nothing there but marble walls, a marble chair with blue cushions and a blue-shrouded alcove. He grinned, knowingly. Just like those sex-investigations, the Kinsey Report, or something. The interrogator hidden behind a screen so that the one interviewed would have no embarrassment and so would talk freely. He sat down on the arm of the marble chair and felt his quick amusement returning.

"Hello," he said in his insolent and swaggering voice. "I'm here. Me."

No one answered him. There was no sound at all in the room. Was anyone there?

"Anyone here?" he demanded. There was still no answer. He got up and loped to the curtain and took hold of its silk-velvet folds curiously and tried to move them. But they seemed meshed with steel. He saw the button which informed him that he could see the man who listened if he wished. With a flourish and a fresh grin he struck the button. The curtains did not move.

"All right, all right," he said indulgently. "If you want to stay hidden that's your business. Professional ethics? All right. I don't mind; actually, I like it this way. You don't know me; I don't know you. We can't see each other—" He stopped. "Hey, can you see me from behind there? One-way window or something?"

The man was silent. But with a tremor of uneasiness Johnnie felt certain that the man could see him clearly. Suddenly, he went back to the chair, crossed his legs and his arms and gloomily surveyed the curtain. "Let's get this over with," he said. "I'm not here like those old pigs and slugs you've been interviewing. I just want a divorce. Simple? That's right. My wife sent me to talk to you; then she'd talk divorce. That's why I'm here."

When the man did not reply he slapped the arm of the chair with finality. "O.K.," he said, emphatically. "I've talked to you. That's all I promised to do. So why should I stay? I've seen what this room looks like; I can tell Sally all about it. That's all she wants. So, that's it. Ring the bell for that girl who's next. That woman, I mean, with the wrinkles. Goodbye." He stood up. He waited for a murmur of protest. None came. The man was indifferent whether he stayed or not, whether he talked or not. Johnnie Martin was not used to indifference or to being ignored. He hesitated.

"I wouldn't have minded talking to you," he said. It was

his imagination that made him suddenly sure that the man was regarding him intensely from his one-way window. "No, I wouldn't have minded talking to a headshrinker at that, and getting a little sympathy. I'm not disturbed; it's only Sally who is; a frustrated old bag who angled me into marrying her when I was only a kid and didn't know what it was all about." He sat down again, slowly and without volition. "She and my mother. She was even worse than the others who angled me into marrying them—that is, if possible. But though I'm young, I'm fair. Mother didn't have anything to do with the first two of my wives; actually, she tried to stop me from marrying them, and I wish I'd listened. I wouldn't have three kids around my neck now."

He laughed affectionately at himself, and pushed his mop of hair fondly over his forehead. He even pulled one of his ears like a father. "Me, with three kids! Would you believe it at my age? Three kids, and I'm only a kid, myself! A blast, isn't it?"

Then he was no longer smiling lovingly at himself. He had suddenly recalled something. Sally was the only woman he had married in the Church, therefore, according to the natural law she was his only wife, and not the others hastily married before justices of the peace in other cities. Sally was pious. She had an iron will, like his mother, and so to keep her from nagging he sometimes went to Mass with her on Sundays and on holy days of obligation. Last Thursday was Assumption, and she had nagged him to go with her to the late afternoon Mass. The large church had been crowded to its vestibules, but he and Sally had been earlier than others and had managed to find a pew with the two remaining seats. This had irritated him. Sometimes, if he could manage to be a little late with Sally, they had to stand in the vestibules, and then, during a particularly solemn moment when all were kneeling he could silently spring up from his knees—that damned stone floor!—and slip out for a smoke. Sometimes he could return without Sally even knowing he had been absent; she was always praying and rattling her rosary anyway, all her devotion fixed on the mighty events transpiring at the altar, unaware of discomfort.

But last Thursday he had been trapped, and the usher had beckoned them to the last seats. Then the rest of the crowd surged in from the hot August afternoon outside, and he was trapped; people even moved into the aisles along the walls. He scowled. Now he was not only trapped but he would have to trudge behind mobs when Mass was over, to get outside again. He saw that old Father Houlihan was already at the altar; he could see him over the bowed heads of the people. Old Father Houlihan was called Huddling Houlihan by the irreverent, for not only was he almost inaudible and so a bore when it came to the homily, but he was very slow and very ponderous, and Mass went on forever. Johnnie had grunted deep in his throat. It would be forty-five minutes at the very least before he could get out of here. Well, at least he had a leather kneeler to kneel on and not the stone floor of the aisles and the vestibules.

The August sun poured hotly through the tall stained glass of the windows. The doors were all open but the air was heated in here and smelled of old incense and stone and beeswax. Father Houlihan turned and lifted and spread his hands. (Double, white, first-class; his vestments hung on his thin old body.)

"Dominus vobiscum," he droned.

"Et cum spiritu tuo," dutifully responded the people.

Children wailed here and there in the heat. Johnnie flinched. He hated the hard shrill voices of children, and especially the voices of his own. Then he heard a rich and joyous chuckling, and he turned his head to his left. He had the end seat. The aisles were flooded with people. So close he could almost touch him stood a young and very slender boy, not more than twenty-three, dressed in poor dark clothes and with heavy workman's boots. His white shirt was stiffly starched, and his tie was a dark blue. He was not very tall, hardly five foot nine, and his badly made clothing hung on his body as if they had been intended for a man much bigger. He had thick fair hair and a childish profile; he resembled an altar boy. In his arms he held a child much less than two years old, a little rosy boy with dancing blue eyes. It was the child who had chuckled so innocently and so happily. He was pulling his father's ears. He suddenly screamed with delight: "Dada, Dada!" and kissed the very young man who held him.

The boy blushed brightly, tried to look stern, melted, gazed into the face of his offspring, and his eyes softened and glowed with pride and love. Johnnie was caught by that glow; it lit up that snub-nosed profile with a holy and tender light; it gave to that nondescript and undistinguished young man somewhat of the air of joy and exultation. Johnnie had never been pious or reverent even as a child; the saints had bored him; he had never admired the statues or fervently joined in the prayers. His imagination had never been extraordinary. Yet, when he looked at that very young workingman, in his wretched neat clothes, and with the child in his thin arms, Johnnie had thought, struck: Why do all paintings, and all statues I've seen show only women with infants in their arms? Why not a young father like this, with his kid? Why, why— there's something heroic about this, something, well, noble, something basically beautiful! Something movingly poignant, almost unbearable.

He was touched by himself being touched. When tears wetted his eyelids he told himself how actually good he was, how easily moved by beauty. But even then, in the midst of his self-congratulation, he could feel honestly stirred and a little sad and humble. He had forgotten the young man and his child at once when the priest had announced the end of the Mass, and had not thought of him since. Until today, in this cool white room with the blue curtains confronting him.

As clearly as though it was his first sight he saw the young father again with his infant. And again he was deeply moved and again he felt that nameless sadness, that sadness mixed with compassion and inexplicable yearning. "What the hell?" he muttered and rubbed his cheek. "I suppose it's because it was pitiful, a kid like that married and with a kid of his own. Only a child, himself. A little kid." A poor young bastard, already tied down to some woman who had burdened him with a baby, and he hardly out of his teens; he worked hard; it had been evident in his worn young hands; he had all a boy's shining innocence. And why not? If he hadn't let some woman blind him and drag him into marriage, and if his parents had had the money, he'd be doing graduate work in some university and having himself a ball, playing around with the gals and driving a sports job all over the country. Poor kid. Only a child.

Is he?

Johnnie started quite violently. "What?" he stammered. "What did you say? Why sure he was only a child, that boy! There ought to be a law—"

He stopped abruptly. Had he really heard a voice full of sternness and deep wondering quiet? No. It was all his imagination. The man behind the curtain could not possibly have heard his thoughts, and he had not spoken aloud. It was all the fault of his deep imaginings; Sally said he lacked imagination, but she was a liar! He had just proved it, not only by seeing that boy again in his mind's eye so vividly but in having the hallucination that the man had answered his thoughts.

"I was talking about my three kids," he said to the man. "A blast! It's ridiculous. Sometimes I can't believe it; I don't

85

want to believe it. After all, I'm only a youth, and my youth shouldn't be spoiled like this. You can't live your life over again, and your youth is all you have. I'm only thirty—" He paused. He winced at the dreadful word. He was past thirty-two, but he did not find it contemptible to insist that he was younger. He felt like a child, like a very young man. And so did everyone his age think so, and they were right. Adolescence went on, these days, to thirty-five at least. Even the doctors hinted that, and basically they ought to know. A man wasn't even mature, now, until he was in his late forties. The forties were far away to Johnnie Martin, eons away in time.

"Sally, my wife, says everything is really my father's fault. That's another lie. Oh, the old guy wasn't bright except when it came to money, but he did understand that your childhood and your youth are the most important parts of your life. He'd never had any, himself. He was twenty-three when he married my mother—and she was seventeen."

Only children?

"It was different in those days," said Johnnie in a loud and emphatic voice. "People were born old and responsible. My mother said so, herself. She was still only seventeen when I was born. Dad had a hardware store; he had had it since he was eighteen. When I was about a year old he invented some kind of a stupid small tool, and when the war came along—the second one, I mean, you know?—he sold the patent to some company making war material, and overnight he was rich, on the royalties. And royalties aren't counted as earned income for tax purposes; they're sort of capital gains. So Dad made it big, all at once.

"He saved half of it and spent half of it. Right from the beginning, before everything got so expensive, we had it made, wonderful house, maids, cars—everything. I went to a rich nursery school. Dad filled my room full of marvelous toys; I had everything I wanted; I only had to howl a little and it was there as fast as he could get it for me. He'd say to Mom, 'You and I had it tough, but the little kid is going to have anything he wants, anything, to make up for what we didn't have.' And I did, too."

Johnnie frowned bitterly at the curtain. "Mom never stopped interfering. She'd nag and complain when Dad would bring armloads of toys home for me, and new clothing, and candies. I can remember that just as if it was only yesterday— and it was at that. Mom would say, 'You are spoiling him now, and he'll be ruined for the rest of his life.' Stupid, wasn't it?

I had a hell of a good time. Dad worshiped me, poor old little guy. He was an old man when he was born, and Mom was an old woman. But at least Dad understood."

He rubbed his warm pink forehead. "Yes, he understood. I went to a private Catholic boarding-school; that was Mom's idea, not Dad's. I couldn't stand it there, all those grim old priests and solemn brothers. When I was kicked out the first year Dad only laughed, but Mom cried. I can't ever remember her laughing and having fun like us. I can see now that she should have been sent to a psychiatrist like you; she was mentally ill. She was always talking about responsibility and self-respect and maturity, but anyone who knows anything about these things knows she was totally irresponsible and lacked maturity in her outlook on life. She didn't understand that things are different these days, for everybody. What right did she have to talk about maturity, for instance, to a little kid only sixteen? Why, she'd actually tell me that I was a man—at that age! Isn't that a drag? Just because, at sixteen, I was only a freshman in this private high school, she thought it scandalous or something. At sixteen, she said, she had been graduated. But look at the schools in those days, before the war! They had the idea that schools were just places of learning, and not happiness-centers. You were supposed to crouch over books for hours, just studying, instead of having fun and fun-courses, and enjoying yourself. You were supposed to fill your mind with learning and waste all your childhood in libraries and at your desk.

"Yes, Mom was mentally ill. She'd say, 'There's no royal road to learning.' As if learning from books was all there was! She said nothing of playing and being happy and carefree. She thought that sinful. That's because she had been raised by nuns. We know better in these days. We young guys know that this life is all you have and if you miss enjoying it you've missed it forever."

Have you?

Johnnie started again. "What?" he exclaimed. But only the soft whispering of the air-conditioning answered him. Talking to myself, he said ruefully. And no wonder, with all those damned women!

"Well," he said, smiling affectionately at himself, "I was kicked out of that preparatory school after the first year. Mom cried like she was sick, and she probably was. So, I had a tutor. He was an old man, too, though I think he was only a kid in years, about twenty-two. He really twisted my arm. This time Dad didn't interfere much. He was afraid I wouldn't make a good university, and that was his goal. I didn't make it," said Johnnie Martin, flatly. "But what the hell does that matter? You're only a kid once. I did get into a college, a small private one, that emphasized sports, and had no real grading system. They didn't care much about that. Most of the kids were kids like me, who had Dads like mine. Living it up. We had good cars, nice apartments off campus, all the girls we wanted, the best of clothes, all the money we could spend."

Johnnie sighed, remembering those joyful years of heedless life. "It was a shock to me when I was graduated. Mom didn't come to the exercises. She said, later, that my diploma didn't mean a thing. 'It hasn't any verity,' she said, and isn't that a stupid remark? I got it, didn't I? What did it matter that the college had no accreditation? A diploma's a diploma, isn't it? Dad thought it was wonderful. He bought me a fine foreign car to celebrate. I was twenty-three years old, just a kid."

He smiled deeply. "Dad gave me another present—a trip around the world. A whole year! I didn't miss a thing." He stopped smiling. "Two days after I got back Dad died."

He leaned earnestly toward the curtain. "And that's what I mean! Dad had been earning his own living since he was only a child, about fifteen. No wonder his heart was worn out; he died of a heart attack, you know? Well, he was old; he was forty-nine."

A small cold finger laid itself on the base of his neck and he shivered. "Too much air-conditioning," he muttered. Forty-nine. His father had been only forty-nine when he had died, and forty-nine was only, these days— His mother had been forty-two at the death of his father, only ten years older than himself, now. The cold finger pressed itself heavier on his neck. She had been an old woman! When he was forty-two, ages from now, he'd still be young, still almost a youth.

Will you?

He raised his voice over the terrible question. "I think Mom really went round the bend when Dad died. She accused me of causing it! She said that Dad hadn't really been fooled by me, at the last! He'd realized, she said. And what had I done? Nothing but what Dad had wanted for me: Enjoying my childhood.

"Is that a crime? No. Isn't that what childhood's for?

"I really think, looking back, that Mom had been mentally ill all her life, with her peculiar distorted outlook on reality.

She proved it, later. And what happened to me next was her fault, not mine. My first marriage. You see, Dad had left me half his money, and the other half to Mom. That was a bad mistake, considering her mental illness, and her extreme conservative ideas which she tried to force on me. Though I was still only a kid when Dad died I should have known more about her symptoms. I should have insisted that she undergo therapy; I once mentioned it to her. She actually hit me across the face!

"Then and there I should have consulted with Dad's lawyers about having her committed and treated by psychiatrists. Menopause and all that, you know? She was out of her mind, frankly. Screaming at me all the time, saying poor old Dad had been a criminal to leave me half his money outright. I couldn't take it. I'm a patient sort of guy, good-natured. That's my fault, actually. So, I left home, not long after the funeral. I went around the world again. When I came back I took an apartment in New York and looked up old friends from my college days. Fun! Except some of them had elected to settle down—at their age! Only kids. What a waste.

"I don't know just how it happened. There were these girls, you know? Models. Debra was the prettiest we knew. I should have known she was a tramp, but I was only a kid, after all. She thought I was a multimillionaire; she played up to me. Then one day she told me she was pregnant. Well, what was I supposed to do about that? She also said that she wasn't yet eighteen, so that, under the law in New York State I was guilty of statutory rape! Isn't that a blast? I went to lawyers, and they tried to buy her off. But no, she wanted to marry me. She brought her parents and all the rest of her stupid family from New Jersey. Grocers. Me, marrying the daughter of a grocer! Then I thought, 'Hell, I can always divorce her, later.' So, I married her. To give the kid a name, you know? Not that I cared much."

Again, and with blazing suddenness and vitality, he saw the youthful father in the church, with his child in his thin young arms and the glowing look of melting love and joy on his boy's face.

A father and his child.

"That's the poor kid's fault," said Johnnie in answer. But the curious sadness, which had in it a sense of unbearable loss, moved like a dark wing over him. "We were married in City Hall. I thought, in all justice, that Mom ought to know, and we came back here on our honeymoon, though by this time I was sick of Debra. Mom had a shock. She's the old-

89

fashioned, down-on-the-farm type, you know? I could see what she thought of Debra, and in a way I know she was right; she came from behind her clouds of mental illness for a little while, though she had a relapse when she insisted we be married before a priest. Debra refused, and so did I. I couldn't tell Mom outright that I intended to divorce Debra as soon as I could. She thought it scandalous enough that we weren't 'validly married.' She said I was excommunicated, and she called for the priests and they told me the same thing. It was a drag. Who cared?

"Well, Debra wanted two hundred thousand dollars to give me my freedom. I sent her to Reno after the baby was born. He lived with Mom. Then Mom asked me how much money I had left. I couldn't believe it! I had only two hundred thousand left—after all that money! Worst of all, there was a provision in Dad's will that after his death all royalties from his small tool invention were to be put into trusts for his grandchildren. Mom and I couldn't touch it. He'd thought that what he'd left us outright was enough for us—me. He was wrong. How far does six hundred thousand dollars go these days? Nowhere. My share was six hundred thousand, and so was Mom's.

"She didn't realize how fast money can go in this generation. She flipped. How could I have gotten rid of half a million dollars so fast? Easy, I told her. Living it up, like Dad taught me. I didn't live like a schoolteacher on a Sabbatical in Europe, you can bet! And women cost money, and so do cars and apartments and good clothing, and belonging to decent clubs. What did she want me to do?

"She wanted me to 'settle down' and do something! Here I was, only twenty-six years old, only a kid, and she wanted me to be an old man, like my father. I'd given Debra two hundred thousand, I reminded her, and I had two hundred thousand left, and I'd spent the rest of it. Wasn't it mine? Mom said for the sake of the kid I had to 'become a man.' At my age! With all my youth in front of me! She wanted me to go back to a good university and get a 'real' degree, and then study law or something. I thought of Dad, and I could see him laughing at her. Poor old guy."

His father. His father had been about the age of that kid in church when he, Johnnie, had been born. Had he ever stood with his son in his arms, or on his knee, and had he ever beamed with such pride and tenderness at his child?

Yes, thought Johnnie. That was the kind of man— kid—my father was, too. I can remember him looking at me when I was in nursery school—with that same expression. And he was still under thirty then, years younger than me.

The impulsive thought shocked him, struck at him. He had always thought of his father as old. Would his own children, at his age, think he, too, had been old? No. No! They'd remember him as a kid like themselves, full of fun. But, thought Johnnie, I never spend the time with them that my Dad did with me. I've never sat with them or talked with them or sung to them, as Dad did to me. Not once. Why? I guess it was their mothers. And I'm always having too much fun to look at them. That was my mother's department, and now it's Sally's. Kids these days—their fathers are too busy. Are you?

"I'm still young," said Johnnie, in answer, and he spoke desperately. "I don't want to be old before my time, damn it! Broken down, like my father. Dying of a heart attack before I'm fifty! What for?" Then he remembered that his grandfather had been a farmer and had married late in life. He had lived to be nearly eighty though to the day he had died he had worked his land from sunrise to sundown, and had died of an accident. He pushed the thought from him almost physically, as if he had hit it.

He began to speak hurriedly. "Mom said she was sick, as if I didn't know it! Didn't I pay her to take care of my boy, and didn't I hire a nurse for him? Yes. It's true that I went to Europe again; after all, I had been shook up by my early marriage. And in Paris I met Justine with her 'father.' He'd been yachting around and having himself a ball. How could I have known he was a con man and no more Justine's father than I am? Anyway, we all fooled each other, and it was a kind of a laugh at that. I married Justine in Paris, and then the whole story blew, but by this time Justine had managed to get pregnant and I was stuck with her, and the con man disappeared with his yacht. I tried to get a divorce in Paris, but they're sticky about things like that over there, and so we came back home, and Justine was fun for a while. Then she took fifty thousand of what I had left to give me a divorce, after the twins were born, and I took them to Mom. Girls."

He glowered at the unresponsive curtain. The guy behind it ought to make some noise like sympathy, shouldn't he? But he said nothing.

"Well," said Johnnie, angry again, "Mom went out of her mind entirely after that. What did she expect me to do? She was hoarding her money, wasn't she, and living like an old woman on Social Security, counting every penny, and I was almost broke. Who else did she have in the world? Didn't she realize that she'd practically driven me into all that hard luck? Did she care? No, she didn't! All she could do was stare at me and cry, but she did take the kids and I helped out when I could with their support. Not much. Did I drink and make a mess of my life like a lot of kids I know? No, I didn't. I just wanted to be happy, like Dad had wanted for me, but everybody had set out to deprive me of my youth and my happiness. Damn it, I'm not going to let them!"

He was sweating with fear of the future and with indignation at his predicament. "Hey!" he shouted at the curtain. "Don't you think I ought to have some happiness in my life and not be forced into old age before my time?"

There was no sound from the man behind the curtain but Johnnie felt that he had moved.

"Nobody," said the young man, "should be expected to 'face life,' as my mother called it, at my early age. It isn't fair. It's ridiculous! It's anachronistic in this day and age. I suppose it always was. To tell the truth, only adults refused to acknowledge it. All the trouble in the world is caused by adults not understanding us young people. Don't you agree? Lots of educationists do. They believe in kids enjoying their childhood, and not being pushed out into life when they're not mature enough. That's what happened to me; my mother really was the cause of those two disastrous marriages of mine, when I was only a kid and didn't know what I was doing, actually. How could marriage mean anything to me at my age? Or now, even? I'm too young!"

So am I.

Hell, he was losing his mind! He had heard, yet he had not heard. He strained forward. "Did you say you were young, too? My age? Then you do understand! I won't be thirty-three for a whole month yet—" He stopped, and almost cringed. He spoke again with hard defiance, "What's thirty-three these days? Nothing at all! It never was—at least not for a man. For a woman it may be old—but not for a man. I bet you have a ball, yourself, when you're not hiding behind that curtain!" He grinned at the lustrous blue hanging so motionless before him, and winked.

Then he was gloomy again. "What's the use of my going on and on? I was broke, after Justine. I asked Mom for an allowance; I wanted my own apartment. But she refused. Imagine that, she refused, my own mother! I could live at home with her and the kids—a screaming household—or I could go to work. In fact, she tried to get me to go to 'a real university,' as she called it. Never once in my life did she want me to enjoy myself and be carefree like Dad intended. Oh, she gave me money for clothes. I told her to let me go and give me some money, and then in a few years I'd settle down. But she was like a stone wall, sunk in her mental illness. I went to her lawyers to talk about committing her, and giving me power of attorney to manage her affairs, but they actually laughed in my face! So, I was stuck. It isn't fair; life was never fair to me."

Nor to me.

"Hey, I heard you then, didn't I?" He was quite excited. "You understand how I'm stuck?"

Yes. The world is "stuck" with you.

"Wait a minute, wait a minute!" said Johnnie, hurt and indignant. "You don't even know me!"

But the man was silent. I didn't hear him, did I? Johnnie asked himself. It's this damned silent place with nothing to look at and nothing to hear but your own voice and your own thoughts. Shut in with yourself. It's giving me claustrophobia; it's making me see and hear things— His heart began to beat loudly, as if he were about to witness a terrible revelation which he could not endure even in anticipation. To delay it—for he had such fear—he hurried on.

"Mom had an old friend; she'd known her all her life. And that friend had a daughter, Sally, older than I. Well, a year older, but thirty-four is old for a woman. When the friend died Sally was invited by Mom to move in with her to help with the children—my children. My God, were we crowded in that little house, the little house Mom had bought after Dad died. She sold our old wonderful house; too expensive, she said. Hah. Mom began to go downhill not long after Sally moved in. She called me into her bedroom one night and told me she was dying. I suggested a mental sanitarium for her; if I could once get her in there I'd have it made. I could get power of attorney and my hands on that money which was really mine. But she gave me the sickest smile; man, she was really sick. And she told me that she was leaving me exactly twenty thousand dollars and all the rest to Sally!"

He waited for the hidden man's gasp of incredulity. But there was only the cool quiet of marble wall and floor.

"I went to other lawyers then, and told them the whole story, and they said I could fight the will if I wanted to but Sally's lawyers would, and could, put up a good fight. After all, they said, I had 'wasted' the money Dad had left me, and that would be held against me. Oh, hell. They'd also say I didn't contribute anything to my—the kids' support. All this was after Mom died, you know? She died a month after she'd told me the outrageous provisions in her will. And the kids had their trust funds, and I had nothing but that lousy little legacy. It didn't last me a year."

He tousled his bright hair pathetically, and blinked his eyes.

"Before Mom died she suggested I marry Sally, that old bag. I couldn't stand her. I guess that isn't quite true; she was kind of attractive in a sober way, with what I thought was a great sense of humor. She seemed like a warm human being—before I married her. Sweet and kind, too. Warm. Good to the kids. She kept them out of the way, most of the time. But sometimes—before and after we were married—she tried to push them at me, as if at my age I had any paternal affection!"

Again, like a blinding vision, he saw the young father with his child in his arms, and he moved restlessly. "Oh, they're attractive enough, the boy especially. They all look like me. Sometimes I play with them, when they aren't screaming or wanting something. But I'll be damned if I will act like a father to them, at my age. You know how it is? Married too young, too much responsibility before I was an adult. Sally keeps telling me that the boy has made his first Communion, and that I have duties to him. She, like Mom, wants me to take a job or go back to school and 'learn something.' Well, she has the money. I don't. But I'm not going to let her spoil my youth, as my mother tried!"

Now tears of anger and despair rushed into his eyes. He pulled out his fine linen handkerchief and blew his nose. He said in a choked and vindictive voice, "I've been giving Sally hell. We've been married three years now. I was determined to make her sorry for what she had done to me, using undue influence on my mother and robbing me of my own money. For the last few months I haven't talked to her very much, and I refuse to do anything for the kids, just to spite her. I stay out of that lousy little house as much as I can, and that isn't very much. I don't have any money but the hundred a month Sally gives me for spending cash. Is that fair? My own money!"

He blew his nose again. "Anyway, that's about all. A few nights ago Sally said to me, 'You are unhappy because you refuse to grow up, and you're almost middle-aged.' Middle-aged, me! Then she said, 'And you are making me desperately unhappy, too. I married you because I loved you and your children, and not because your mother wanted it that way. I thought I could make you face life before it's too late for you. I thought I could make you into the right kind of a father to your children, who need you. After all, if I'd wanted to, I could just have quietly inherited your mother's money and gone away, leaving you with your children to care for any way you could. As their guardian you'd have been given an allowance and money from the trust funds to support them, until they reached the age of twenty-one when they'd come into their own money. Perhaps I should have done that; in a way it hasn't been fair to you for me to assume the responsibility for your children, and not demand that you be responsible, too. Of course, you wouldn't have received a penny when your children inherited. I think,' she said, 'that it was more of a sense of responsibility to you that I've stayed this long.'

"Did you ever hear anything so insane? I said to her, 'Give me at least half of my own money, and I'll be satisfied. How about it?'

"She really thought about the whole thing. Then she said, 'Yes. But only if you'll go up to that Sanctuary and talk about it all to the man who listens there. I did, once, after my mother died. I thought I couldn't stand it; we'd been so close. But he made me understand. Well, I'll do what you want; I'll even let you divorce me, if you'll talk to him.'

"And that's why I'm here," said Johnnie Martin. "So I've talked to you. I can go back to Sally and describe everything, and then I'll be free again."

He smiled with the sudden volatile happiness of a child looking forward to Christmas.

And your children, your little ones?

"I'll send them to some boarding-school. The boy can go to a military academy. And a convent will take the girls. I know just the place. Then I'll be free."

For what?

"To enjoy my youth, as my father wanted."

He turned his head and though there was no window in the room the marble wall appeared to shine, and in that shining he saw the young father again with his child, the proud and responsible young father with hands scored by hard work. Poor young bastard. What did he do after his day's labor, and he only a kid? Help that woman of his with the diapers and the dishes, or run the washing machine, or give the kid his baths, and maybe mow the lawn—if he could afford the

95

lawn? What did he and the woman who had married him—for surely he hadn't been the aggressor!—do in their free time, if they had any free time? Talk about formulas, and the future of their kid? What future?

A man's future, for the child has a man for a father.

"You think I'm not a man?" exclaimed Johnnie. He got to his feet. "Of course I'm not; I'm only a kid! I've got years to grow up, many years. In the meantime I'm going to enjoy my youth!"

Thirty-three years old.

"Only a kid!" protested Johnnie. "Only a youth!"

He stared challengingly at the curtain, but it did not move. He sat down again. His hands came to rest on the arms of the chair. Thirty-three years old soon, and broke. Not even a job. A father who was not really a father. A strange weighty feeling came to him, like the dark premonition of a desolate and lonely future. Where would he be in ten, in fifteen years? Would his money be gone by then? Would it go as all the rest had gone? Women, cars, rich apartments, travel, fine restaurants, wonderful clothing. Money had no real quality in these days; it literally melted away. And what would he have, after it was gone? His children? They would not know him, he who had abandoned them. They would not want him. They would not say "my father," as that poor young bastard's kid would probably say of his father. He would be old— old!—and there would be nothing. Only memories—of what?

He jumped to his feet, feeling imprisoned and choking.

"It isn't fair!" he cried. "Why do I have to grow old? I'm young, young!"

He ran to the curtain, overcome with a despair he had never known before, and he struck the button only half-knowing he had done so, and while it was rolling aside he repeated, "I'm young, I tell you, I'm young! I'm not really a full adult yet!"

And then he saw the man who had listened to him. He stared, stupefied, blinking helplessly, and swallowing very hard. He began to fall back, slow step by slow step. He reached the chair and felt behind him and clutched it. The awful fear was on him again, and another emotion which he did not as yet recognize as profound and shattering shame, for never once before in his life had he felt that shame.

He could not take his eyes from those somber eyes which gazed at him so sternly—he was certain that admonition and sternness gleamed from them at him, and that if the man was not actually despising him he understood him fully.

I was only thirty-three when I completed my work, the man seemed to be saying to him. I was in years only your own age. I was not a child, a youth, even in my human flesh. I had not been a child since I had been twelve years old, though I was subject to my family as you were never subject. I was a man, and never have you been a man.

"God help me," Johnnie muttered. "It was not only my fault. It was my father's, too. I'm not judging him, not condemning him. I am only speaking the truth, as I never spoke it before. He was wrong. He should have helped me to be a man, and not have encouraged me to be an everlasting child. But he is not more wrong than millions of fathers in this country. They are making perpetual children of their sons. They are denying them their manhood and their responsibilities as men."

He looked at the man pleadingly, but the stern eyes did not appear to soften or show sympathy.

"All right," said Johnnie with a humility totally once unknown to him. "I'm not a complete moron. I think I knew all the time, and that it was my fault, even more than my father's. I wanted it that way! I wanted to be a kid all my life, having fun. Yes, I think I knew. The priests tried to talk to me, and my mother, and Sally. But—I was afraid. I was afraid," he repeated, marveling in disgust at himself. "I was afraid to be a man!"

He saw himself completely, big, bluff, overgrown, a little too heavy, revoltingly boyish, tousled like a two-year-old!, manicured, bathed, healthy—and useless. A stupid, middle-aged juvenile, big-footed and relentlessly young and grinning, denying his adulthood, denying that he had been an adult for eighteen years! Thinking of himself as a teen-ager, and who had invented that actually cruel and repulsive term, anyway? After puberty a child was a man, with a man's powers of body, and a man's maturity. After Confirmation he had been responsible for his own sins and his own life—hadn't the priests told him that? He alone was responsible, and he had refused the manifest responsibility. Why? Because he had been afraid to be a man. His father must have guessed his terror and in his love had tried to soothe and reassure him. He was wrong, said John Martin. It was his duty as a father to lead me into adulthood and to have set me free. He was not kind to me at all. He and I—we made me, together, what I am.

But he died of seeing what I really was. Yes, I know that now. Just as my mother died.

He thought of his own children, the boy, Michael, with his strong young face, and the little twin girls, merry and blue-eyed and humorous. He had never seen them before as he saw them now in the full light of the awful revelation of himself. Why, they were fine kids! They needed a father, not the sort of father he had had, but a man who could guide them and teach them and not romp with them like a child, himself, playing with toys which quickly bored him. Why, now he could remember the cool speculation in his son's eyes, the reserve. Of what had the boy been thinking? John Martin winced. I know, he thought. He thinks I'm a stupid big bastard, and that's what I am. That's all I am. What a terrible thing it is when a boy thinks that of his father!

And Sally. Patient, kind, loving Sally, his wife. Why in hell had she wanted to marry him, anyway? Beautiful Sally. He had never realized she was so beautiful, with her shining brown eyes and her tenderness to him and his children, and her goodness. I don't deserve her, he thought. Does she despise me? Not half as much as I despise myself. Is it too late, now? Perhaps not. She did send me here. I wonder if she saw him—too?

He looked at the silent man who was gazing at him. Now the tears of an adult came to his eyes. He went slowly to the man and slowly dropped to his knees, and he bent his head and kissed the man's feet.

He said, "Lord have mercy, Christ have mercy—"

He stayed on his knees for a long time, praying as he had never prayed before in his life. Slowly the self-disgust and the new self-hatred left him as he knew he had been heard, and forgiven and that he had put his childhood and his youth forever from him. When he stood up, he was clothed in manhood.

"Please don't ever leave me," he whispered. "It isn't over. I have such a long way to go."

When he was out in the hot August sun again it came to him that he was looking at a world he had never known, a world of men and duty and stern responsibility and struggle. He was not sure he liked it yet. But he would have to like it! It was his world. It was the world of himself and his children. My God, Michael! he thought. My son. I can't begin soon enough.

Then he saw Sally coming up the long graveled walk toward him, Sally with her pale and anxious face and mute, questioning eyes. He started to run toward her as a child runs to his mother, and then he stopped himself. He walked firmly

98

down the path to her with quick but controlled steps. She halted while she waited for him. He took her hand.

"Hello, Sally," he said, and smiled. "Let's go home, to the kids."

Her whole face began to shine radiantly. He saw her wet eyes, her trembling mouth. Not caring for the people sitting in the shade on the marble benches, he bent down and kissed her.

"Let's go home," he repeated.

SOUL SIX: The Senior Citizen

"The righteous shall flourish like the palm tree—
they shall bring forth fruit in old age."

PSALM 92:12-14

The mauve-blue twilight lay over the snowy city and the street lamps began to bloom like faint golden balls. A cold and ruthless wind lifted the snow and threw it into the air in powdery "ground blizzards." It was the dinner hour for the majority of the city's working people, but in the great apartment houses men were just arriving from offices and preparing for a relaxing cocktail. Now, one by one, the floors of office buildings glowed as cleaners moved about and one by one the apartments lit up and draperies were drawn against the winter night. Weather like this was unusual for the city; the inhabitants enjoyed it, if young. The old shivered.

Except Bernard Carstairs, who was sixty-five and abroad in the twilight and walking from the Senior Citizens Center to his home in one of the apartment buildings nearby. He strode like a young man, though he was somewhat too heavy for his height, which was only average. He had put on these extra pounds since his forced retirement six months ago, and neither he nor his doctor liked them. "Better than getting shriveled, though, like a lot of you retired men," the doctor had said to him. "Bernie, biologically you are less than fifty. A damned shame, a damned shame." On this they were both agreed. "Better look around for something to do," the doctor had added, looking pityingly at his friend, who had hardly a gray thread in his fine crop of dark-brown hair. Bernard's blue eyes were strenuous and young and alive, and he needed glasses only to read fine print. His features were blunt, his cheeks taut and well-colored, his lips firm and strong, his chin defiant though now there was a roll below it due to his increased weight, a roll which had not been there a year ago. All his actions were vigorous and definite, and he had never had an ache or pain in his life before, until now. Sometimes

100

he was so weary that he could scarcely move, and for this weariness his doctor had prescribed a tonic. "It won't do any good, I'm afraid," said the doctor. "You've got an active mind and it's going to seed, and it doesn't like it, and so it reflects itself in your body and complains."

"Well, what shall I do?" asked Bernard. "I was only a minor executive in the company. If I'd been major maybe they'd have kept me on. But I didn't have much ambition, I suppose. I was the contented kind; I didn't like the rat race of competition; never did. I did my work more than adequately, but Kitty and I, not having children, jobbed along nicely, saving, seeing friends, having social affairs, joining a few do-good clubs, sleeping well, eating well, having a nice apartment, some good clothes, a car every three years, taking vacations in the summer. It was enough for us—me. I didn't particularly like my job, but it was all I knew. I married young and took the first fairly good job I could find, book-keeping, and I figured—hell—it was a living, and then I went slowly up the ladder to my last position, where I was paid twelve thousand a year, with a pension plan, and Social Security, and fringe benefits, and I thought—hell—the other guys in the big jobs were dropping dead all the time or getting ulcers and having no fun, and here I was, contented and safe, with a secure future after retirement, and why should I worry? Or want more pay, which would only go to taxes anyway? No, I didn't like the job, much, but I did it well; treadmill like they say, but a comfortable one. I guess I'm just an ordinary guy."

"Who isn't?" said the doctor.

Bernard looked at him shrewdly, and his blue eyes were not the eyes of "an ordinary guy." "Some aren't, Doc," he said. "And a hell of a lot of us settle just for contentment—like me. It isn't enough."

" 'Though our outward man perish, yet the inward man is renewed day by day,' " said the doctor. "St. Paul."

"What's that supposed to mean?"

"Better find out, Bernie. No one can find it for you; just you."

Bernard's wife was fifty-five, busy with many pleasant things. She loved her husband. But after the first two months of euphoria over his retirement at sixty-five, and a first trip abroad, she found her husband's constant presence wearisome. He was not the kind to grow old over the TV set, nor the sort to bury himself in "community activities" or in busy-work, or tinkering. He had no hobbies; he did not even

101

play golf. He had never cared much for alcohol, but now he was drinking too much beer, and he walked some, and yawned. He had not, during his busy, active days at the office, and his social affairs at night, become much of a reader. He had declared that when he retired he would "read all the good books I've missed." But he was essentially an "outward" man; reading constantly, for weeks, had wearied him. His education had not gone beyond high school; he found many of the allusions in the better books bewildering and unknown to him. He began to haunt the library. But his muscular body rebelled at so much quietude and inactivity. Unfortunately, too, he did not find the classics relevant to modern life; they had been written for a contemplative people and Bernard was not contemplative in the least. They had been written for those who had many long twilight hours, and Bernard disliked twilight hours intensely. They had been written for those who calmly accepted life and lived serenely, but Bernard had not been trained to a fatalistic attitude nor was he basically serene.

No, he had not liked his position as assistant traffic manager in his company; but he had not really disliked it, either. It was a living. For the major part of his life he had considered that quite enough; he was "only an ordinary guy." Now that he was retired he could not claim that he missed "the old gang at the office." He didn't miss them at all. He had never gone back for a visit even once.

Financially, he was comfortable. He and Kitty had always saved a fixed sum of his income, and he had three nice annuities due on his sixty-fifth birthday. He also had his Social Security check, and his pension, which amounted to fifty percent of his salary. Sometimes he and Kitty vaguely considered "a house in the country, or in the suburbs, anyway, where we can potter around in the garden and raise prize roses or something." But both he and Kitty were city people, and Kitty had all her friends in the city and so did he. Moreover, the very thought of moving, of disorder, of decisions to make regarding old furniture and buying new, repelled both of them. They owned the nice and pleasant apartment where they lived and which they had occupied for twenty-five years. They knew every corner, every door. They felt homesick when they merely considered leaving it all for a strange raw place in the suburbs.

The thing was that the apartment had become, lately, less a home to Bernard than a comfortable, warm prison. While Kitty was off at her luncheons he sat in the living room and tried to read, and he would become conscious of the total silence about him, the lack of movement, the hiatus. Then he would go out and walk restlessly, staring at shop windows, visiting the zoo in nice weather, wandering in the library, buying groceries, going to afternoon movies.

For the first time he began to think of the years ahead. How long would he live? Then another thought would intrude itself: "Not long. One of these days I am going to die, maybe in a couple of years, maybe ten years, maybe fifteen. Is that all there is, just sitting around like this, waiting to die? What has become of my life? And what will I do with the rest of it?"

"Why don't you see what you can do at the Senior Citizens Center?" Kitty had asked a week ago. She had infused enthusiasm in her voice, and Bernard understood at once. He was getting on Kitty's nerves, and he didn't blame her. He was getting on his own nerves. His strong and youthful body seemed to be straining at its seams; he had never been very conscious of his mind, in the busy years. Yet somehow it had come alive with all sorts of uneasy and disquieting questions and restlessnesses these days. To please Kitty he had gone to the Senior Citizens Center this morning, and he had stayed the day.

It was a terrible mistake. Bernard was not a man for violent emotions, but today, contemplating and talking to the men and women of his own age at the Center, or older, had given him his first taste of active and overpowering despair. What had merely been a vague uneasiness in his mind these past months became panic and terror. It was not that the sight of the aging appalled him so; it was their complacent acceptance of uselessness and their empty waiting for the death that lurked in all the shadows of the various comfortable rooms of the Center. Some rocked and talked together before a nice fireplace, their hands folded. They talked of their children and their grandchildren and the trips they had taken the last summer. (They did not talk of any future for themselves; they had placidly accepted the fact that they had no future.) Some of them droned on endlessly about the important positions they had once held and how their superiors had regretted their retirement. Some of them were engaged in the "hobby shops," creating mediocre and clumsy objects which no one would ever buy, like, or use. Some of them played pinochle, or bridge. There was a small library, and tables covered with magazines. Every day earnest youngish women came in to give "talks" about gardening and other hobbies, about health and exercise, about "great books," and Bernard heard that clergymen came here also once or twice a week to hearten "our wonderful Senior Citizens" and to tell them how really important they still were to the world. ("How?" asked Bernard of one of the older men he had met. The other had had no answer.) There was, tactfully on the part of the clergymen, no talk of death and the everlasting life.

Some of the younger Senior Citizens ladies engaged in volunteer hospital work, but they found it tiring at their age. They preferred their plastic photographic folds of featureless grandchildren and boasting of their sons and their daughters or growing gently spiteful at the spouses of those sons and daughters. No one listened to them, of course; the other ladies also had their plastic folds of photographs and wanted to talk of them. Some of the men were sometimes occupied in charity drives, and house-to-house calls. They met "such interesting people." Social workers, ardent young women with intense faces, came every morning, with solicitous "help" for those whose Social Security checks were all they had, and with psychiatric jabber about "adjustment," or with urgings to the indolent to engage in the half-dozen hobby shops, or take more exercise. "After all," said the ardent young ladies, "you must Continue to Take an Interest in Life."

The majority nodded contentedly and went back to their dozes or their cards and their conversation about their grandchildren. A few, a very few, looked at the girls cynically, and sighed.

"I think," said the vigorous Bernard to one of the social workers, "that what most of us need is a job."

He received applause from the few, and an affronted stare from the majority, and a look of bafflement from the girls.

"Come now, Mr. Carstairs," said one of the girls, "you know very well that no employer these days will hire a man of your age, or older. There are the pension plans to be considered, and the Social Security, and the natural infirmities of the old which make them a hazard in some employment, and employees' benefits which no employer wants to pay for in the case of the—well, the older folks. And there are the government forms, which demand—"

"Too much goddamned government!" Bernard had exclaimed, and was astonished at himself, for he had always thought it very comforting to people to know that the government was looking after their interests these days. "Maybe if we didn't have Social Security and all the pension plans and fringe benefits most of us here would have jobs and be of use to the world, and not thrown-away garbage. That's all we are: thrown-away garbage. Even worse, we're a burden to the young husbands and fathers who have to pay out those Social Security checks to us in the form of taxes."

"You paid for Social Security yourselves," the girl patiently informed him.

"No, we didn't. I figured it all up, one day. I figure I'll have outrun what I paid in in about six years. Who pays for the rest? The young people, and I think it's a damned injustice!"

His firm full face became quite florid in his new indignation. The girl gently smiled. "Well, their own children will pay for them that way, too."

"Why should they? Why should the generations be supported by someone else? So long as we can move and have breath in our bodies we ought to support ourselves, and not expect younger people to carry us on their backs."

An outraged clamor from most of the old people had drowned him out. One old man said, "I had my quarters and I retired, and I get my good checks and trot right down to the bank and cash them! Why shouldn't I? Don't I deserve it?"

"No," said Bernard, "you don't. We don't deserve anything we haven't earned."

"I raised a family," said another old man. "Isn't that doing something for my country?"

"Yes, and so your children should be supporting you, themselves, instead of letting other folks' children support you. Haven't they ever heard of the Commandment, 'Honor thy father and thy mother'?"

The social worker had smoothly interrupted, for so many of the old were becoming too flushed and too vexed. "In these days," she said, "we all Care for each other. Isn't that the better way?"

"That isn't what I was taught when I was young," said Bernard. "I was taught that every tub should stand on its own bottom. Never be a burden to anyone else. You know what I'm going to do tomorrow? I'm going right down to the Social Security office and tell them what they can do with their damned checks and not send any to me! Outside of what I actually paid for."

"But you're fortunate, Mr. Carstairs, very fortunate," said the young lady with sadness. There seemed to be a rebuke in her voice that he was "fortunate," as if he had committed some crime against Society and should therefore be overcome by guilt. "Others here have nothing but their Social Security checks—"

"Why don't they?" he asked, bluntly. "Why didn't they save a little? I saved a dollar a week sometimes, and that's all I could afford when I was young, but by God! I did save! Sure, we had our illnesses, at least Kitty did. But I managed to pay for them, and save some money. It was very little at first; then it was more. I never made a lot of money, but I put what I could into annuities, and now I've got them, and I paid out more than twenty percent on my pension fund, and maybe I'll stop that, too, when I've gotten back the amount I paid in. After all, a man has to have self-respect, and he doesn't have that if he lets someone else support him in his old age! You should provide for that, yourself. When you're young you shouldn't have more children than you can support, so that you can't save any of your money during your working-days. My own parents never asked a cent from me! They didn't need to; they saved their money."

The young lady was now definitely not liking Bernard, nor were most of the old people.

"Mr. Carstairs," said the young lady with reproof, "your parents lived in a Simple Day when people didn't have all these Wants and Demands, legitimate felt needs, and there were no taxes."

"Damned right!" said Bernard. "There weren't any taxes! That's the whole trouble. Taxes. And people demanding more than they're worth and what they paid for."

He was now utterly beyond the pale to the young lady. She cast down her eyes as if he had uttered blasphemy against nature and Society. And government. She peeked at him with bright malice.

"Who are you, Mr. Carstairs, to say what is the 'worth' of a person?"

"All I know is what I was taught. Ever hear of the ant and the grasshopper? The ant worked all summer, laying up food for itself, but the grasshopper played and danced the summer away, and when the winter came it had nothing. And it complained, sure it complained. And what was the answer God gave it? 'Go to the ant, thou sluggard, and consider her ways.' There wasn't any sympathy for those who didn't plan for themselves for the future."

The young lady coughed. "I hope this discussion won't descend into a religious controversy."

Bernard was pleasantly conscious of the life now stirring in his body. "Why not? Why does everybody here avoid discussing religion? Are they afraid it might make them think of what's waiting for them around the corner? Death, that's what."

This was the worst obscenity of them all. The old people shuddered. The girl became mute. Bernard's eyes were all sparkling blue. He looked slowly around the warm room and saw the fallen faces. "Death," he said. "That's all you're waiting for; that's all you're afraid of. Why do you want to live, anyway? You're useless; you're hopeless. You'd rather have this Center and your ridiculous hobby shops than face life, wouldn't you? Maybe that's the trouble with you; you never faced life at all, even when you were younger."

Because he was a dogged and resolute man he stayed the full day, observing and commenting to himself. Very few spoke to him after his "anachronistic" outburst. (The young lady had called him an "anachronism," which in her vocabulary meant anyone with self-respect. "Yes, it's certainly an old-fashioned virtue," he had agreed, but his agreement had not pleased the young lady. She had said, "In these days, we are interdependent, Mr. Carstairs." She had no answer but silent umbrage when he had replied, "Why should we be? I'm not against charity. Those who are too old to work and are penniless, and the broken and the blind and the diseased, should be taken care of by private charity, as they always were, and not be a burden to the present generation. I've been reading, lately, of young delinquents attacking old men on the streets and calling them useless, and perhaps they have a legitimate gripe, at that."

(This had further diminished him in her regard. Finally she said, "You think juvenile delinquency a proper protest, Mr. Carstairs?"

(He had grinned at her. "Maybe," he said. "Maybe we should read those placards they're carrying around and try to find out what they are really trying to say!")

By the end of the day he felt a total hopelessness for himself and the others. Now he was on the way home. What was there? Dear Kitty, of course, with her account books, for she was chairman of so many clubs. The TV. The late news. Perhaps the late, late show. (He wasn't sleeping so well these days.) And then bed. And then tomorrow. With what? I am no longer engaged in mankind, he said, as the cold fierce ground blizzard cut his face. I am a real anachronism, and not the kind that girl spoke about. I'm of no use to anybody. If I died tomorrow Kitty wouldn't have to worry, financially. She has a lot of friends, and activities, even if I think those activities are only busy-work. She would cry for me, and then would forget me. Isn't that all I deserve? She doesn't need me. No one needs me. And that's the awful answer to all this security. Not to be needed. Not to be depended upon for anything.

This storm was really something. He had always had "good wind." Now he was gasping. He stopped a moment on the empty street to catch his breath. He looked about him, huddled in his good Montenac coat. He saw the neatly-shoveled gravel paths leading up to what people cynically, or piously, called the "Sanctuary." He knew all about it, and was indifferent to it. A clergyman up there, or a silly social worker, or a grave psychiatrist, all handing out cheap advice to the troubled or the despairing or the inadequate. It was a pretty place in the summer. After his retirement he had often gone into the small park about the building and had fed the squirrels and had enjoyed the lawns, the fresh sweet air, the trees, the fountains. He had never thought of consulting the man who listens. He had no troubles.

He had troubles today. His mind roared with them, and with its hot uneasiness. He was also full of a nameless and restless anger. What did I ever live for? he asked himself. I didn't like my job; I didn't dislike it, either. What do I have to show for my life? All those traffic records, and files. Were they important to me, as a person? No. Now they are gathering dust in the company's attics. Who remembers Bernie Carstairs? My life—a pack of dusty records in dark files. I never did one damned useful thing in my life! I never contributed any real labor, just paper.

Something stirred in his mind. Labor. Only labor was significant, adding to the treasure of the world, something done with one's hands, something that would live after you. He thought of the antique shops to which Kitty had dragged him. Beautiful furniture, not just hobby-shop stuff which was worth nothing. Chippendale. Sheraton. Duncan Phyfe. Something authentic, something with authority. Something that lived after a man with beauty and soundness. Something that was admirable. He remembered a hutch cabinet made by sturdy hands of Amish farmers: good fine stuff, plain, humble—but with authority.

If a man left nothing behind him of authority he left nothing. He had only, as Samuel Butler had written, left a platter licked clean and a pile of offal. That was all his generation of white-collar workers was leaving: a licked platter and a pile of offal. And, he thought with grim humor, they don't even use our offal these days. They use chemical fertilizers. Sanitary. That was the trouble with the world now: It was so damned sanitary, and sterile.

Everything in plastic. He had often gone with Kitty in these past months to the supermarkets. There was no fragrance in them. The vegetables and the meat and the fruit and the butter and the potatoes were all wrapped in cellophane—very sanitary—and they all smelled of—paper. Just paper. Glaring lights, piped-in music, glass. But no scent of celery and tomatoes; no pungent odor of carved meat; no earthy smell of potatoes; no sweet fragrance of warm melons and apples and pears; no heady spice of ground coffee and open tea. No cedary wood floors. The wares on sale looked artificial, too. The chickens were bloated and enormous, and had no taste at all when cooked, and no exhilarating perfume while they were roasting or frying. Everything deodorized. Everything bland and tasteless. Everything neat and orderly—and without life. That was the trouble with living now: there was no life to it. The old people he had just left: They had no life. They had no fruits after a lifetime of working. Dead Sea fruit, full of dust. God help them, Bernard thought. God help me.

Who had done this violence to hot human nature? The government? But a government was only the people. What generations have we spawned? Sterile young people with no bowels, no real vitality, no honest lust, no sweat, no labor. They had only shrill voices that were demanding— What?

What we have deprived them of, thought Bernard Carstairs. The right to have honest authority. We have sanitized all the food they ate; we gave them paper instead of the bread of life. We gave them government forms which guaranteed that they would survive in the sterile world we made for them. No wonder they were protesting, without knowing what they were protesting against. They wanted to live and to have adventure. We removed adventure from them—with a guaranteed income. They had no uncertainties, no struggle, no hope and no victories. Just as I never had. Oh, we live longer because we killed all the germs! But is life only length of days?

He found himself walking up the gravel path to that low white building whose red roof was drifting with cold snow. He began to hurry. The man who listened in there ought to hear, for once, what a Senior Citizen had to say! And be damned to him. The Senior Citizens had been betrayed, too, as well as the young.

There was no one in the waiting room, for it was night now and the city was eating its tasteless dinner, and hurrying to watch television, which had no verity either. Bernard had no sooner closed the door behind him than he heard a chiming. They were very efficient here, just like the world outside. They chimed a bell when the outer door opened. He took off his snowy overcoat and shook his hat. The bell chimed again. "All right, I'm coming," he said impatiently. "Though God knows why."

The man who listened in there was probably anxious to go home too in this windy white wilderness of winter, and to eat his flavorless dinner and to watch TV, listen to the late news, and then go to bed—to confront another day as meaningless. Another day without authentic authority. Just like me, thought Bernard, pushing open the other door and entering the quiet room within, with its blue curtains over a hidden alcove and its lonely marble chair with the blue cushions. He sat down in the chair and was conscious of his new heavy weariness. He faced the alcove.

"I've been thinking," he said abruptly, not greeting the man who waited to hear him. "I've been at a Senior Citizens Center. A living cemetery. All clean and warm and peaceful, like a nice grave. The living corpses just sit around and talk about the past, as if there is no future for them. Damned if there is, anyway. But me. I want a future! I don't want to wait for death, like a sheep before the knife. Even a sheep is more important. It's eaten. I don't have any food for anybody, least of all for myself."

The man did not answer. It was very still and remote in here, and very peaceful. There was no hurrying, no sound of footsteps rushing to go nowhere. It was said that the man who listened had all the time in the world.

"I don't," said Bernard. "I have no time, and yet I have too much time. I'm not old, and I'm not young. I'm useless. I'm a retired man. I've been active all my life, and I can't be satisfied with toys now. I don't want made-work, and pretend-activities. I'm not a child! I'm a grown man! But now everyone has decreed that I must retire—to what?"

The man did not answer. "When I was young and went to church," said Bernard, "the minister used to talk of the 'harvest of old age.' Golden fields heavy with wheat; trees heavy with fruit. Work well done. But in these days there is no wheat, no fruit, no work well done. There is no personal satisfaction for there is no life worth the living. Only files, and paper. There isn't even any satisfaction to a worker in a fac-

110

tory; he never sees the finished product for he had part in only one piece of it. That's necessary, they say, in an industrial civilization. I don't have any quarrel with an industrial civilization, I suppose. But where is there any meaning in it? Any joy of accomplishment? Now, you tell me."

The man said not a word. Bernard shifted in the chair. "Perhaps we have no real harvest because we never plowed and laid the seed. Is that it?"

There was no reply. "But everything is compartmentalized," said Bernard. "You do this one little job and hundreds of other men do their own little job. There's never any sight of what is finally done. There's so many of us! Perhaps it's necessary that we do just a part and never see the over-all design, if an industrial civilization is to flourish. But we are men, too! We aren't satisfied with being part of a machine. We aren't 'units,' though some government officials call us 'units.' It isn't so bad when we are young; we have families to raise and to talk to, and to pretend with that life has some meaning. But when we grow old and are thrown out on the garbage heap we have nothing to look back on that we've accomplished, nothing substantial, nothing marked with our own hands. Then we become Senior Citizens, taking up useless hobbies and trying to believe that we are important or were ever important to the world, and talking to others like ourselves, who were, and are, just as useless."

Bernard suddenly struck the arm of the chair with unusual emotion. He leaned forward toward the hidden alcove. "If a man can't say, 'I have lived, and this is what I did,' then he never lived at all! And all the security and the government checks are only narcotics to quiet his desperate mind and make him willing to die and leave a place for some other 'unit' to fill!"

The warm fresh air of the room flowed about him, and in spite of himself he relaxed. He said to the man behind the curtain with the utmost earnestness, "Look at me. Modern medicine and natural good health have kept me alive and young for my age. I'm sixty-five. I'm not decrepit. But I've been thrown on the garbage heap, rejected, and sent out to pasture. What pasture? A procession of useless days? Some are satisfied with that; some want nothing more. But there are more of us who don't want to sit and wait to die in a warm cozy place. Some of us look for jobs; there aren't any. They all want youth, youth, youth. It isn't the employers' fault. They're all wound up in government tape, and fringe benefits and pension funds, and that keeps them from hiring men like me, who still want to be useful and have some hope, and who want to believe that what we do is important.

"Why don't they simply kill us when we get old?" cried Bernard. "That's not as bad as letting us live on the sidelines waiting for death! We get so sick of our lives that we fall into nursing homes, and then wither away, and then we're buried. We men in the most vital part of our lives—condemned to a slow death. I hear that in Russia they just murder us; maybe that's not so. Maybe they just let us work. That's better than what we have. Anything's better than what we have."

The man did not speak, but Bernard did not care. He leaned back against the blue velvet cushions. His eyes became far-away. He began to smile.

"My father was a carpenter," he said. "He had his own shop. He made furniture and built houses. Sometimes we'd go for walks together and he'd show me houses he'd built. They weren't notable houses, but they were houses, and they were sound and strong. He was proud of them. Sometimes people would let us in their houses and let me see the furniture my father had made. Nothing fancy or elaborate. Just plain polished tables and good chairs and cabinets. You could touch them and they weren't flimsy. Hand-polished by my father. He used to build barns, too, old barns I still see when I take my wife out driving in the country.

"My father went to school for only four years. But he left something behind him. He lived to be eighty-six, and he was still working in his shop, making furniture. He sold it, too. He had more work than he could handle. I remember his shop. It smelled of unfinished wood and varnish and paint, and the floor was covered with sawdust. There were saws on the walls and hammers; and barrels of nails, and lathes, and wheels. I used to watch a rough piece of furniture grow smooth and mellow and shiny, and it was like a miracle! My father's furniture will last almost forever. It had verity.

"I liked it so much that I was hungry for it. My father used to let me help him after school. Everything must be just so; turned just right; polished like this. No nails must show, just satiny wood. I wanted to be a carpenter, myself.

"But my mother said no. I must be a white-collar worker. I must have some education, and not be almost illiterate like my father. She'd come into the shop and take the hammers away from me, and the saws, and scream at Dad. I was going to be a gentleman, and not work with my hands. And my father would say, 'What's wrong with honest labor? It shows.' But my mother would sniff and make me go back into the house and study. I didn't want to study. I was never a brain. I went to business school after high school, and learned to be a bookkeeper. I hated it. God, I never knew until now how much I hated it!

"You know? I think women have too much to say these days, and in my days, too, about the future of their children. They all want things to be 'nice' for their children, and never soil their hands. They don't think about the world's work. They think of paper.

"And too many of the old men I saw today had mothers like mine, silly pretentious women who think they know 'what is best' for their sons. That's why the goods we buy these days, even in the best stores, are mechanical and don't have any personality. No one is proud of labor any longer. So we were condemned to desks and offices and files, and air-conditioned cubicles, and were never let out into the air. Yes, even in the days when I was young—people began to think that labor was somehow disgraceful.

"But even the factories now and the big shops are depersonalized. Maybe it has to be. I don't know. Everybody thinks only of 'gross national product,' and not the terrible product of men's minds when they are deprived of personality. They never think of the old-young men sent off to Senior Citizens Centers. To wait for death."

Bernard felt the weariness in him which was of the mind and not his healthy body.

"Why isn't some decent provision made for us who want to work? Why can't the government forget its forms and pension plans and fringe benefits? Why don't they let us work until we fall at our jobs? Welfare, they call it! A decent old, protected old age, they call it! Well, there are millions of us who don't want that! We want to work at something we can be proud of, if it's only handiwork or being a carpenter on your own, or a bricklayer or a plumber! We need to be useful, and not parasites."

He wanted to weep. "I want to be a carpenter, like my father," he said. "What's so shameful about that? Wasn't Christ a carpenter, working with His adoptive father, Joseph? Was He ashamed of honest work? No. He chose fishermen and carpenters to be His disciples. And they went out into the world, without the benefit of Social Security and paid pensions, and preached to the world, and worked with their hands, and they lived to be very old men, full of years, as the preachers used to say, and full of honors. They worked until the day they died, and went everywhere on foot—old men,

113

and not garbage. No one ever consigned them to Senior Citizens Centers and said, 'You've earned the right to loaf the rest of your life and draw checks.' No one has ever earned the right to leave the harvest."

Again he struck the arm of the chair with his fist. "I'm not ready to die! I want to be in on the harvest, too! I want to be useful; I need to be wanted; I want people to say, 'This is what Bernie Carstairs made for me, or did for me.' I want to walk home from an honest day's work done among honest people and not clerks. I want to wash my hands and look at the dirt rolling from them. I want to—sweat. I want to be useful.

"But I'm denied that. They treat us like children, senile children, when we're full of health and life! They pamper and coddle us and take away from us the little self-respect we have left. They coo at us. It makes me sick right down to the bottom of my feet. Why do they retire us when our life isn't over? Answer me that!"

He stared at the curtain. "I know. They want us to die quick. They want the space for the young, who will be just like us in a few years. Useless."

He waited, but there was no answer. However, he felt a loosening in himself as though someone had been listening who understood and sympathized.

"Do you know something?" he said. "Life has become meaningless to everybody now. Who's responsible? The government, the unions? I don't know. But we're all washed and urbanized. Everything is mechanical, and fitted and adjusted. Even amusement. Is that what we really wanted? I don't think so. Every man has the right to be an individual and to have some meaning in his life. We've been deprived of that. No wonder people are losing their minds.

"I don't want to lose mine. But where shall I go? Tell me, where shall I go?"

He stood up. He had had enough of listening silence. He went to the curtain rapidly and stared at it. He saw the button which informed him that he could see the man behind the curtain if he wished. He touched the button quickly.

The curtains soundlessly parted and a warm glow of light rushed out. He saw the man who had listened to him. He stood and looked and could not have enough of the looking.

He began to smile. "Why. Greetings," he said. "I'd forgotten all about you, and what you did. You were a carpenter, weren't you? An honest, hard-working carpenter, like my father. The kind I wanted to be, myself. Your father worked to

114

the day he died, didn't he? I bet you both built good sound houses and made good sound furniture. I bet you were proud of them, too. I bet your father wasn't retired on Social Security, and he didn't end his days in a Senior Citizens Center, either. He was useful until the end of his life. And the men who worked with you—no one ever sent them to a nursing home. They didn't need it. They were too busy working to be sick or. helpless."

Bernard returned to his chair and sat down, still smiling. His heart rose in his chest and he felt renewed life and vitality. "You know, my doctor said more illnesses are caused by people not having enough to do, or anything to do, than anything else. They rust out; they don't wear out. That's supposed to be secular charity. It isn't. It's cruel. It's barbarous. We old guys have a lot to give the world yet, if they'd only let us. But everything's bound around with rules and regulations and pension plans and fringe benefits. That's nice to think about, I guess. Nice to think that if you get very sick and old you won't be thrown into a poorhouse. But only nice to think about if you're still strong and willing to work. A sort of money-in-the-bank, the kind you don't use until you are forced to. But why should we be forced to spend the money-in-the-bank when we don't need it yet?"

He leaned eagerly forward in the chair. "I've got it! I'm going to find an independent carpenter who can use me, and teach me to be a real workman! If I can't find him I'll set up shop for myself. I'll hire men my age, who know something about carpentry. No artsy-craftsy stuff. Good honest furniture, made to order, handmade, hand-tooled. If unions try to interfere I'll say to them, 'Look, I'm a Senior Citizen, boy, so stand out of my way and let me earn an honest living.' I'll turn out work no mechanized factory can turn out. It'll be lovingly made, as it used to be. Why, I'll even hire retired upholsterers. There's no limit—"

His mind, revitalized, raced. He said, "I'll go back to that Senior Citizens Center place and look around for men like me who really want to work, and forget the paper work they did, or anything else. I'll pull them up from the graves they're falling into. I'll say, 'There's real honest work, real work, for you if you want it. Don't sit and snooze here until you die and they carry you out. Use your hands and your pride and live again.' "

He stood up, joyous and refreshed. "Thanks, Brother," he said to the smiling man in the alcove. "You didn't live long enough to be old in this world. But I bet you know about

115

men like me. I bet you wish we'd spit on our hands and get to work again, and not lie around whining and thinking of the past.

"I bet you wish everyone would work for the harvest, and bring in the fruits again. God knows, there's plenty of work to be done, and what's that I remember? The laborers are few. Yes, I know that was meant in a more religious sense, but I also remember that my father used to say that to work was to pray, and giving older people a chance at living again and being needed, and proud of themselves, and adding to the treasure of the world, is surely religious in concept, and who knows what harvest and fruits they'll bring in to everybody?

"Somebody has to start somewhere, and I'm going to start—tomorrow. I'll get in touch with Senior Citizens Clubs and Centers in other cities, too, and perhaps we can put pressure on our representatives in Congress to do something about the situation, such as getting unions to waive restrictions for men after sixty-five, or even sixty, and let us waive all the fringes, too, while we're at it so that employers can afford to employ us.

"Let the old who want to vegetate and die, do it. But for those of us who want to live—we shouldn't be condemned to death. We, too, have a right to pray and to work."

He smiled at the man who had listened to him so patiently and in that patience had given him life again. "I'm going back to church, too," he said, "and get acquainted with you all over again. You've always been waiting, haven't you, but you won't have to wait any longer for me. I'm coming!"

SOUL SEVEN: The Shepherd

"Feed My Sheep."

The month of May, the flowering month, the month of the Queen of Heaven. Isn't that what his friend, Father Moran, called it? Yes. A beautiful month, full of light and promise, gold and green and blossoming, with the heady scent of jubilation and rejoicing. But when did I feel that last? asked the Reverend Mr. Henry Blackstone of himself. I am as old as death, honestly, in these days, though by modern calculation I am only sixty. I'm not with it, as my younger parishioners would say. No, I'm not "with it." It's strange; I was always such an optimistic man until the last few years. Now I feel totally despondent; I walk despondently; I think despondently. Who is wrong, the world or I? Am I of the past, hopelessly? I'm so damned confused, so helpless. Once I could "talk" to God but now there is only the darkest and most reproving silence, as if I had committed some terrible sin. But what that sin is I don't know. Does God think I'm "not with it," too? I wish, sometimes, that we had a Confessional so I could—but what should I confess? That I've fallen behind some place, and am mired behind all the generations, or that something is wrong with modern man, something too terrible to contemplate? When I think that, am I guilty of the sin of pride, that I'm convinced that Harry Blackstone has all the answers? What am I going to do?

He did not wear his clerical collar, not because the younger people smirked at it these days but because he felt unworthy of it. The May day was warm and fair and full of radiance and the scent of the holy earth. So he wore an old sports jacket; it had always felt awkward on his shoulders as did all secular garb. He walked slowly up the gravel path toward what the community laughingly, or reverently, called the Sanctuary. A scandal to some; a pride to others. Old John Godfrey; he wished he had known him. But Godfrey had been dead many years, long before he, the Reverend Blackstone, had come to this city from the lovely small town where he had been born, where he had been ordained, and where he had had his first parish. He paused on the path. Midville. He hadn't visited Midville for over fifteen years, since his parents had died. He was taken with a sense of nostalgia so intense that his eyes ached and his heart felt sick. Perhaps he should go back, to the peace and harmony and stillness of Midville. Then another thought came to him: Perhaps Midville had changed, too. Perhaps he would feel an anachronism if he returned, just as he felt an anachronism here in this great city. Anachronism. That is what the younger people said of him, and even the middle-aged and his own generation. Something hovered in his mind, but it seemed blasphemous to him and he hastily turned his attention to the beautiful white building he was approaching, and all the innocent colors in the flower beds, the tulips, the daffodils, the lilies-of-the-valley, and, in quiet spots, the bursting lilacs, white and blue and purple. A fountain sparkled and spoke laughingly, and the marble young man within it lifted up his eager face to the sky and was bathed in falling and rainbowed fire. "So lovely, so beautiful," said the minister, and stopped to watch the eager birds skimming from tree to tree in the sheer excitement of sinless being, in the passionate and simple celebration of life.

Somewhere, he thought, there is the answer. I wish this dim confusion in my mind would lift, that I could be sure again as once I was sure: That there was an answer, not to God who needs no answers, but what is pleasing to Him, and what, in particular, I should do.

He had reached the bronze doors. The brilliant sun shone on the golden letters above them: *THE MAN WHO LISTENS*. Do you? asked the minister in himself. And what do you say then? Will you have an answer to what is crushing me? Will you tell me why I've come to you today? My own despair, my own doubt of myself and of others, my own lostness and uncertainty: Will you explain them? Can you explain them? You see, I have a profound decision to make. I hope you can help me; no one else, not even God, appears to be able to do that. Must we always be alone, but most especially when we are in the deepest need?

He hesitated, then opened the bronze doors. Two elderly women were sitting in silence in the pleasant waiting room, which was filled with lamps but had no windows. Mr. Blackstone looked carefully at the women and was relieved that they were unknown to him. They were leafing through some magazines lifelessly; the glasses of one glinted, and the glint was like the sharpness of pain to the minister and he did not know why. He looked at the women more closely. Did they suffer also? What had brought these undistinguished and ordinary women here, plump and gloved and sedate? Both seemed fairly prosperous if one was to judge by their clothing and their casual attitudes. Yet, some problem had drawn them to this spot, some overwhelming misery. He was suddenly struck with pain again. Had they no ministers in whom to confide, no help from any man? Were there women like these in his congregation, who saw nothing in him, heard nothing in his voice, that they must go to an anonymous psychiatrist? Doctor? Clergyman, like himself? He was ashamed and stricken. Yet he, the shepherd, had come here also. Was he as lost as these?

One of the women glanced up mildly as if she had heard some sound from him, some sound of despair or muffled suffering, or a question. She saw a tall and robust man in his middle-age, with thick gray-brown hair, a full kind face both strong and thoughtful, and brown eyes that drooped at the corners as if he were unbearably tired. She noted that his clothing was ill-fitting and that he did not seem at ease in them, as if they were not his customary garments. But she was so wretched that her silent comments on him wearied her and she returned to thinking of her own problems and to the wonder if the man who waited and listened in the other room could help her at all.

The minister listlessly picked up a current news magazine and looked through it. Was it only his imagination which made the contents seem hectic, flaring too vividly, and screaming so excitedly? Crisis, crisis, crisis! Was it all false, or was it really so avid, so demanding, so scorching, so vehement? Did man need his daily news all in black, capital letters because there was no verve any longer in his soul, or were black, capital letters really an expression of some rushing horror in the world which must be shrieked, as crows shrieked at the sight of an appalling danger? Was it all only a banal scarecrow in a really indifferent landscape, or was it a specter of horror visible even to the dullest eye? Was it only his imagination that today all children appeared to shout incoherently and never spoke calmly? Were all men frequently too breathless, and did they honestly move too fast in such a hurry—to what? Did even older women give the illusion of galloping, of talking too rapidly, of being fevered in spite of their vivacious laughter, their glowing and too-dominant teeth, and their air of being young, young, young, when it was obvious that they were becoming older, older, and older?

Or was the Reverend Mr. Henry Blackstone feeling his own age and shying like an elderly horse at things which did not exist except in his jostled existence? Was the world always like this? Did merely time and care make a man feel rudely buffeted when in reality all was as it had been and only his own eye had changed? How had it been in his youth, when he had been a very young child before all those wars? He could recall only a sunlit autumn garden heavy with the scent of warm apples and slumbering grass, the tinkle of a distant bicycle bell, the slapping of a screen door, the eager cry of a child, the serene laughter of women, and the striking of the church bell on a languid and unhurried hour. He could remember the swing on which he idled, and the back of the old white house where he had been born and the shine of the sun on the polished kitchen windows. It came back to him so clearly that again he could see the young face of his mother smiling at him as she busied herself at the sink, and her wave across the shadows and the grass. He felt contentment, forgetting, and he smiled tenderly. Forever, now, his mother would be young to him, and sweet and ardent, and forever she would laugh her soft mirth and wait with his father for him.

It had been peaceful, then. But had it been so peaceful for his parents? Was his only the illusion of childhood, or had it been so in verity? He pursued the quiet days of his early years, and the sound of Saturday afternoon with the lawn mowers and the whistling of boys and the rattling of the skates of the little girls, and the women busily preparing picnic baskets, and the hiss of hoses as men watered their small lawns and the busy barking of happy dogs. Was it possible that children today felt such a deep placidity and contentment, and that children were always children?

Had his parents' lives been filled with crises as were the lives of almost everyone in this modern world? He sank deeper into thought. His father had been a railroad clerk with a small salary; he had been so proud of his green celluloid eyeshade and the garters on his arms, holding back the striped cleanliness of his shirt. His hours were long and tiring. His wife had had no modern equipment in her big old kitchen. (How he, Harry, could remember, now, the *rub-dub-dub* of the Monday washboard in the basement as his mother sang and drubbed soiled clothing and splashed water! Was there ever a more consoling sound to remember?) There had been no automobile in the family until his father had been middle-aged, though many neighbors possessed automobiles which they used only on the weekends. There had been the movies, of course, furious wild things which everyone was always condemning, especially the old ministers who thought them "sinful." But all in all there had been peace. Hadn't there?

His father had never mentioned taxes. Washington was so far away it was almost a myth. The Fourth of July was an occasion to gather in the park to hear the German band, and then to eat from the fat picnic baskets and listen to the orators and to stand and sing patriotic songs and wave small flags. And then the home-going, happily weary and surfeited with ice cream and fried chicken, in the warm dusk with the birds sleepily cheeping in the trees, and windows lighting up along the street, and hot cocoa and cookies in prospect and then his bed, tucked away safely for the night. Of what did his parents speak?

Of the Depot. Of neighbors. Of the minister's sermon last Sunday. Of the need to cut the grass; of the new baby down the street, of fellow-workers and their wives and children, of the worry over their own parents, of hopes of their own. Above all, of their innocent faith in God and the acceptance of everything He was pleased to send them, whether good or distressing. He could hear his young parents' voices so clearly far over the arch of the decades. His mother was annoyed that the sponge cake had fallen today, and that the milk had soured too early. He heard his father laugh at her lovingly, and kiss her. They talked then of the raise he expected after Christmas, and what they would do with the money, besides saving some of it. But there was no talk of taxes, of deductions, of juvenile delinquents a mile away, of "misunderstood" girls who had "made a mistake." (One didn't mention such girls; he had never known such a one in his youth; they were not only unmentionable, they were unspeakable.) There was no frantic conversation concerning a new gadget which a contemptuous neighbor was loftily showing to her envious friends, no insistence that his mother should have the same. There was no fast and jerky talk from his father, full of greed that others had more than he or any resentment against fellow-workers or derision for "the boss." The planning for the future was certain and contented. Harry would have the best education his parents could afford. Harry would marry and give them grandchildren. Harry would walk humbly with his God, and in safety and in peace. In the meantime the roof was sound above them all, and the old walls sheltering.

There was no war. There was no clangor, no shrilling, no beat of undisciplined feet, no slogans, no hot wearinesses of the uncontrolled, no anarchy, neither of the body nor the mind, no lawlessness of spirit. No rootlessness, no running to-and-fro to nowhere.

Am I sure? the minister asked himself, and for the first time in many days the answer returned to him: You are sure. It was so.

If so, then what had happened to the world? Why had it become—what was the graphic word?—sleazy, in the old meaning of the word: raveled, cheap, second-rate, flimsy, gaudy, without strength.

Suddenly the minister heard his young mother singing her favorite hymn to him as sweetly and as confidently as he had heard it in his childhood:

"Long have I loved Thee, Lord!
Long through my days.
Long have I loved Thee, Lord!
In all my ways.
Dark though the nights at times,
And sad and forlorn,
But long have I loved Thee, Lord!
And bided the morn."

Long have I loved Thee, Lord, thought the minister. But somewhere we parted, didn't we? Was it my fault, as they say it is? Is that why I don't hear You any longer?

He heard a soft chime, insistent, as if questioning, and he started and looked about him. He was alone. So the chime had sounded for him, and he stood and hesitated again, sadly wondering if the man who waited there had any answer for him. What if he were a clergyman also, but of another kind than himself? Then there would be only renewed confusion, more distress, more uncertainty, and more despair.

He went into the other room. He was not surprised by its gleaming yet gentle austerity, for someone—who?—had told him what was there, white marble walls indirectly lighted, a white marble chair with a blue cushion, and a great blue alcove behind the draperies of which waited the good man who listened so patiently and gave good advice. A little confidence returned to the tired minister.

"Good evening," he said in his great voice, which needed no amplification in his large wooden church.

No one replied to his greeting, but the minister was sure he could sense a presence behind the curtains. He felt no hurt that no one had replied to him. He sat down in the chair and gazed at the intense blueness that shielded the alcove.

"I've heard that you are a fellow-clergyman," he said. "I hope so. Only one of us can help the other now, isn't that so? We should have a union of sorts, shouldn't we?" His laugh was deep and sincere. "Oh, my name. The Reverend Mr. Henry Blackstone. Or, as my younger parishioners call me, 'Hell-fire Harry.' That should reveal a lot to you!"

He laughed again, but there was more sadness in his laughter than amusement. "Perhaps you'll call me that, yourself. And maybe I'll deserve it. I don't know, and that's the trouble. Is the world out of joint—or is it I alone? I—I have some friends in the clergy. Smart and keen and aware. They don't have the highest opinion in the world of me. If they were much younger, or very young, I'd understand. Youth is always intolerant. Or at least that is what people are always telling me, with indulgence, as if intolerance were a kind of heroic virtue in itself instead of a boredom to men my age. Well, anyway, most of the clergy who have a low opinion of me are my age, or just a little younger, and some are even older. That's what bothers me. Some are older, and yet they are 'with it,' as they say now. Silly phrase, isn't it, and yet it's pithy.

"You see, my problem is simple. Betty, my wife, is disgusted and heartsick. She's fifty-three, and not smart and young and modern like other clergymen's wives these days, eternally young, God help them, poor things! We've known each other almost all our lives. We're from Midville, five hundred miles from here, almost in New England. We had the same kind of lives, and we have the same point of view. For a long time we were reasonably happy in this city. In spite of the fact that we don't have any children, and all those damnable wars which seemed to get in the way of honest, sound living. After they're over no one seems to know what they were really about, after all, and worse, no one seems to care.

"But, my problem. I'm no use to my congregation any longer, not to the old, the middle-aged, and not, especially, to the young. I had five hundred souls, once. Now I have only about two hundred. My congregation dwindles year by year. My people go to the smart ministers who can satisfy them and give them what they want. I don't try to dissuade them—"

He paused. There it came again, the vast uneasiness, the

sense of reproof, the feeling of being reproached—but for what?

"After all," he said, "we are to be free in religion, aren't we? Sometimes, you know, I envy the authority of Catholic priests. But maybe they don't have much authority any longer. I don't know. I've seen some of the older ones, friends of mine, suddenly becoming very still and very silent, sometimes, when we've been talking of our people, and sometimes they look lost, too, as I probably look lost. I gather the impression that many of them have their doubts about all that 'updating' you hear about—as if God isn't the Eternal, and never changes. Yes, we have our worries, the old guys and I. But, somehow, that seems to be a subject we can't talk about freely. I don't know why. It's as if something is too powerful—too powerful— Oh, I don't know. As if we were beset, to use an old-fashioned phrase. I'm an old-fashioned man, you see.

"In any event, Betty wants me to resign and go back to Midville or anywhere else provided it's a small town. It was Socrates, wasn't it? who said that men should not live in large cities, but in hamlets, that men's souls wither in the cry of the streets and the leaflessness of their lives, and that tranquillity and contemplation and the knowledge of God can only be found on the land, in the sight of great forests and noble mountains and flowing rivers. And the peaceful long lawns at sunset in the shadow of high trees after the day's work is over.

"They haven't yet said so, my Board, but I know no one will regret my resignation. Betty and I—we'll have our life again, in contentment and in quietness, among a few friends and in the company of those who know us and understand us. Something we can't have in this stony wilderness, this noisy wilderness, this feverish, frantic, and heated wilderness, where there is no rock in a weary land."

The feeling of reproach struck his heart so heavily that it was actually physical, and he caught his breath.

"The wilderness," he muttered, and stared at the closed curtains. He was positive that the man was gazing at him through some aperture and that he was affronted.

"You don't understand, I see," said the minister. "You agree with the Board. But don't condemn me, please, until I've finished. As a minister, yourself, you should wait to hear my side of the story. Again, as they tell me, I'm not 'with it.' No, I'm not with it, I can't be with it, because I'm not part of it! I never was. I never will be. No, no, don't speak yet. Let me tell you, and then we'll talk it over together reasonably, and perhaps you can give me some advice. God knows, I need it.

"Why don't I talk to my superiors? I have. They're displeased with me; I can tell. After all, a minister isn't much of a success if his congregation keeps dwindling. One or two suggested that a small congregation, in a town like Midville, would be best for me. I think it would; Betty is sure it would. In time, anyway, I'd be mandatorily retired and sent out to pasture. Probably in ten years, though there are old ministers who are still in their pulpits at eighty. If I stay here, until I am retired, then my congregation will wither away more and more, until there is nothing. At the rate it is withering I won't need to wait! They'll all be gone in a couple of years.

"And yet, and yet. You see, God and I walked together until about fifteen years ago or so. I was so certain I had His ear, and that we understood each other. But now, He is far removed from me. Perhaps it's because I didn't conciliate my congregation as I ought to have done, and updated myself to be one with them, as some of my clergy friends have advised. They don't worry and torment themselves as I do. They live very snugly and very neatly, and speak of this best possible of worlds—when," and the minister raised his voice in a shaking cry, "when it is obvious this is the most terrible of all worlds and the most lost!"

He got to his feet. "You don't agree with me! Hardly anyone does, except old Father Moran and one or two other clergymen. You think I should have brought myself up-to-date, and been one of the boys with every man in my congregation, and an indulgent confidant to the girls and the women and the children, and talked of every damn thing in the world except about what it is: The terror of everything innocent that lives.

"Listen to me, before you pass judgment on me as an outdated old body who can't, and won't, understand this modern world! I beg of you, listen. Do you know what Christianity has become, in the main, in these days? Secularism. Not one with the people, as Christ was, but worldly, busy with many things except simple faith and the Fatherhood of God. Oh, they talk a lot, professing Christians do, about the brotherhood of man, but suggest, just try, that there is no brotherhood of man without the acknowledged Fatherhood of God, and there is an embarrassed silence or a few superior smiles.

"I'm not sophisticated, I confess it. I'm not urbane; I don't 'understand this changing world.' That's what they say. But when was not the world changing from the very moment it came from the hand of God? It is always in flux; they don't understand that, my people. They think there is something unique in this instant moment, something that has never been before, something so far superior to the past that the past should be totally forgotten, and all the heroic things that lie in the past. Including, most of the time, God. Oh, they are willing to profess faith, but there is no faith in them. In more ways than one they are a faithless and adulterous generation. As one clergyman to another, I must be honest. A faithless and adulterous generation. Is that lack of charity to confess the truth? There is so much talk these days of 'charity,' and 'the spirit of the modern aspiring man,' but there is no charity any longer, and the aspirations of modern men are the frivolous aspirations of an eternal child.

"Whose fault is it? The clergy's? But what can we do when they turn restlessly away from us, with covert smiles? We can't forbid them; we don't have the authority, either secular or spiritual, as once we did. This is the Day of the Layman, some clergymen say, smilingly abdicating their position as shepherds and contented, even proud, to be one of the herd. Brotherhood! No authority, though authority was given us when we were ordained. Is the shepherd less than the sheep? If so, who will guard them from the wolves?"

Sweat stood in large drops on his forehead. He shook his head heavily over and over. He held the back of the chair in his right hand.

"Don't condemn me yet. Please let me finish. I look at the world. It's crowded with things; just things. And not one of them of any verity or soundness. It's crowded with gadgets, with machinery, with automated houses and factories and offices; it's clangorous with hideous noise. The worst noise of all is people-noise, heedless, quarreling, discontented, rootless, demanding, petulant, dissatisfied, asking, wanting, or just making clamor.

"I've lived sixty years," said the minister, "and I've never known a world like this. I knew the Great Depression, and it was better than this, believe me. At least people were face to face with sharp reality, and not the ugly 'realism' they talk of now. They knew stern privation and hunger and the frightful face of despair and a profound fear. But these were real things, and could be surmounted, for always there was hope.

"But now everyone has everything. Wasn't it Ibsen who said that when every man has everything no one has anything of value? And nothing is real when man has no longer any

126

need to struggle. I've known awful poverty. I tell you, I prefer that to coziness and luxuries and all the affluence I see about me. For at least in poverty I had certitude, and so did all the poor people with me. But the luxurious about me now, from machinist to businessman, from doctor to plumber, from secretary to housewife, have absolutely no certitude, no roots, no calm stature, and so no hope.

"They don't want what I have to give them. They reproach me that I don't talk to them about 'social justice' and 'social problems,' or whatever is the frenzied fad of the moment. Once I quoted the great English statesman and philosopher, Edmund Burke, of nearly two hundred years ago:

" 'No sound ought to be heard in the Church but the healing voice of Christian charity. The cause of civil liberty and civil government gains as little as that of religion by this confusion of duties. Those who quit their proper character to assume what does not belong to them are, for the greater part, ignorant both of the character they leave and the character they assume. Wholly unacquainted with the world in which they are fond of meddling, and inexperienced in all of its affairs, upon which they pronounce with such confidence, they have nothing of politics but the passion they excite. Surely the Church is a place where one day's truce ought to be allowed the dimensions and animosities of mankind! We need no political theologians nor theological politicians.'

"But they know nothing of that great man, Edmund Burke, though most of the young people know all about Marx!

"Well, they accused me of being 'outdated,' as if truth is ever an anachronism! I talk to them of the eternal verities of God and read to them from the Gospels, and tell them that when men walk with God and His truth and His justice, and practice them humbly in their daily lives, social justice will inevitably come about and social problems will solve themselves.

"Then there is the silly talk these days of 'the search for identity,' but they do not know what they mean any more than I do! I told them once that they had 'identity' from the moment they were conceived, and that their sole duty in life is to save their individual, immortal souls.

"Do you know what they did? They gave me their sickening, indulgent smiles. And there was the Sunday that I talked of the solid reality of Satan, and his great triumph when he had persuaded men he did not exist. I talked of sin—imagine that, sin! The Board told me later that it was unrealistic to talk so, and insulting to the intelligence of my congregation, and that 'sin' was only a matter of bad 'mental health' and not the fault of the 'sinner' at all! They gently suggested that I 'try to understand these modern days' in which everyone is now so science-minded and so psychologically aware.

"I blew up. I admit it, and I'm sorry, but I felt besieged.

"I told the Board that I knew all about 'mental illness,' as they call it, and all about the blather you read in the press concerning it, and the solemn mouthings over it by people who have ignorantly learned a new vocabulary of pseudo-science and wish to impress others with it. Forgive me, but I've never known more truly ignorant and more pretentious men and women than I do now, God help them. They know nothing of God, the human soul and the mind of man, and what they don't know they speak of loudly, and never stop. The more ignorant, the more noisy and insistent, until you feel embarrassed for them just before you feel alarmed about them. They seem a new kind of people, and all of them vulgar.

"Yes, I told the Board, when I was a young man every small town had its harmless eccentrics and the senile, but they were accepted as part of the community and didn't need 'therapy.' But why are so many others now 'disturbed'? 'I'll tell you,' I said, 'it's because they have lost God and religion. Whose fault is that? The clergy who are so modern and up-to-date? I won't join their ranks! I may not be the best of shepherds or the wisest, but I won't betray my people to passing 'intellectual' fashions, and the silly, feverish preoccupations which will be laughed at or forgotten tomorrow.' "

Now he had the strange impression that the man was listening to him not with reproach or reproof but with sadness, and with understanding. He was so grateful that he sat down again, leaned forward with his hands tightly clasped between his knees, his tired face very earnest.

"They think I know nothing, that I live in some sort of simple past. But I know all that they know, and more. I'm an educated man; I read—which is more than some of the more glib and knowledgeable of my congregation do! I know about the desperate illness of the world, and the depravity, and the lack of peace and the turmoil and hate and the threat of the holocaust. I know about homosexualism and all vice. I know of the terror in which the majority of mankind now lives. And I know something most of them don't know: They have left God; they have no frame of reference; they accept the world of their feeble senses and reject the world of their immortal souls, which is the only reality.

"They are avid materialists, smugly rejoicing in their 'sense of what is *relatively* true.' You see, they believe in relativism; truth has no eternal verity to them. It is protean, to them. It changes hour by hour and never has the same face. They love it. They find in 'new truths' excuses for their excesses, for their lack of fortitude and courage and strength. They are dishonorable, for they owe no allegiance to anything, not to God and country, not to each other as true men and true brothers, not to law and order. They are the cruelest generation ever to have cursed this world, for they do not love each other as once Christians loved each other, verily, in the Name of Almighty God. Now they pretend to love each other in the name of 'social justice,' or their fake brotherhood. Liars! Liars! They would, without the slightest qualm, cut a 'brother's' throat for any damned reason at all!

"They have no tender concern, one with another. A neighbor could die on their doorstep and they would not answer his call, while listening all the time to some television story about 'involvement with all mankind.' A woman is attacked before their very windows, and they draw their blinds, and read all about their community obligations and how well they are engaging in them. They talk about 'responsibility' and they are abjectly irresponsible. No, not abjectly. Monstrously, sinfully irresponsible! Once a man was proud of his work and his competence at it, no matter how humble or how important. Now, everyone wants his children to háve a college education, and as most men are very ordinary—something they didn't mind once or admitted happily—only a very small percentage of our young people are college material. But most would make excellent workers in the service occupations, something which they despise and think 'beneath them.' I tell them that Christ, Himself, The Wonderful, with the Government on His Shoulder, was a carpenter, sinewy and strong, and proud of His work. They think I am a fool. Christ is a shadow to them. He lived so long ago, you see, in the past, and what have they to do with the past?

"If it were the young people only who were so sadly stupid, so heartbreakingly stupid and irrational, one could have patience, and wait, and patiently teach, until they saw the mighty face of the only Reality for themselves. But it isn't just the young people who babble so endlessly and so foolishly and so mindlessly. It is their parents, also, their up-to-date, 'these days' parents. The parents who tell them that it isn't what you know that is important, but who you know, and get with it and become fat and rich and successful and well-adjusted and a leader. Be a scoundrel; be a liar; be exigent and merciless. Everything goes, so long as it leads to material success.

"In the meantime, of course, you must keep up the chatter of loving your brother, and pretend that you care about him. It makes you seem such a civilized, nice person. Such an admirable nice person. And admirable nice people are liked, and when you are liked others will promote your welfare and your happy future.

"As if, my God, this world is all there is! But the trouble, you know, is that they believe it is all there is, even my most regular parishioners who come comfortably to hear me every Sunday—and never really hear a word I say."

His tiredness took all his body until it seemed to him that he could never move again. "No wonder," he muttered, "that so many young people are strange these days, and disordered. No wonder the girls love to dress and behave like hard, bold young men, and the young men love to dress disreputably and behave like weak women. What have their parents and their teachers given them but falsities, false values and slogans? They are 'rebellious,' they say. Against what are they rebelling? They don't know it, but they are truly rebelling against the lack of values in their lives, against the lack of authority and discipline, and the lack of decency and honor in their elders. I've seen them picketing or mouthing noisily and incoherently, and I see their parents as only a minister can see them: Silly fools who never possessed authority in their lives nor had any values in their lives, nor any faith or pride.

"Sometimes we clergy are blamed for all that. We didn't give the people what they wanted. Shall the sheep tell the shepherd where he is to take them, and what they shall eat? Shall the sheep lead the shepherd, and he indulgently permit them, until they wander into the valley of the shadow of death?"

He stopped, struck. He blinked at the blue curtains. He bit his lip.

"But what of us who try, and who are laughed at, and ignored and derided? What are our struggles worth? If we lift our voices they tumble out and leave us hastily. If we admonish, they pretend to hide their smiles. The sheep have left their shepherds, and they no longer hear our voices or respond to them. My own sheep call me 'Hell-fire Harry,' because I tell them the truth and the awful danger in which their souls now stand. The older people smooth their furs or their gloves and make large eyes at us and talk of 'young people these days, who are more sophisticated and more educated.' We are supposed to applaud that callowness, that stupidity. We are supposed to smile approvingly.

"I can't do it!" He sprang to his feet again. "I'm not going to update myself and talk of secular matters in my pulpit! I'm no worldly Sadducee, like so many of my kind! I'm getting out; they don't want me any longer. I have no sheep. I must go where I'll have some, and where they will listen to the shepherd!"

He was breathing loudly. He was desperate, and desperate with impatience, for the man behind the curtain said not a word at all. He only waited. But there was no more to say. The minister recalled that someone had said that you had only to touch the button near the curtains to see the man who had listened to you.

"Oh, my God!" he said. "I don't want to see you. I don't want to hear you tell me that I must 'update' and 'modernize' Christ for a blind and silly and weak and degenerate and immoral and wicked generation—the worst this world has ever seen! How can I help them if they refuse to be helped—"

He halted. What had he seen in the wall in the waiting room, and which he had read but had not felt? "I can do all things in Him Who strengthens me." Once that would have struck on his heart and his soul would have answered. But now he was too broken, too besieged by despair. He stretched out his hand and touched the button, preparing to brace himself for the smooth and urbane words of the clergyman who had sat there, hidden, and had smugly listened to an "oldtimer."

The curtains moved aside and a light burst out from behind its silent folds, and in that light he saw the man who listens.

They looked at each other, and the minister turned ashen white and he staggered back step by step until he was pressing against the wall and the door through which he had entered.

The man did not turn away his eyes. He gazed at the minister long and sternly, and the Reverend Mr. Henry Blackstone was sure he heard, in his inner ear, a mighty voice say to him: "Feed My Sheep!"

The minister held out his hands straight before him, as if in self-protection. "No, no," he said, "you don't understand. They don't want me to feed them. They don't even see me. They left me; I didn't leave them."

131

Again he heard the voice, more penetrating now and more inflexible, in the corridors of his mind: "Feed My Sheep!"

"With bread they won't eat?" The minister implored the man. "With bread they reject? With bread they despise? Let me go! Let me end my life in some quiet place, with no turmoil and no heat and no derision—"

Feed My Sheep.

The barren places where the sheep lay and sweltered and were blind with dust and the fierce light of a sun from which they could find no shelter. A weary land. A land of rocks and rivers of fire, and no living waters. The sheep lay there and died, far from a life of certitude and true security. And where was the shepherd?

He was turning and leaving them. They had wandered from him and he had not stayed with them and had not led them—because they had despised him in their sheeplike folly. If the world had been too much for him, how much more terribly had the world been too much for them!

The minister felt that he dared not approach nearer the man. He knelt where he had stood, and he put his hands over his face.

"I see," he said, "why I felt so separated from God in these past years. What had mockery and scorn meant to Our Lord? Nothing. He had fed the hungry sheep, though they had bared their teeth in derision at Him. They had laughed at Him from the thresholds; they had jeered at Him in the temples. They had shouted their contempt for Him in the market-place and in the streets. They had tried to seize and destroy Him, and He had slipped gently from their ravenous hands.

"But always He taught His sheep. Despised and rejected—He still taught. And eventually, because He was so steadfast a few listened.

"Only a few. But they saved the world. And only a few now, even now, can save the world."

The worldly Sadducees who had believed in mortality and not immortality; who had sponsored ethics and right behavior in man, but had denied their Source; who had politely talked of enlightenment and had lived in darkness! And the Pharisees who detested the people and honored only the letter of the law and not the Lawgiver! Which was the worst? Was he, Henry Blackstone, to be numbered among them? Or was he worse than they, a shepherd preparing to desert his sheep for his own peace and his own contentment of mind?

"Forgive me," he prayed. "Lord, forgive me. Does it matter what they call me, or how they laugh at me? I shall struggle with them more passionately, and with less meekness and less self-consciousness. I shall not be afraid of their fear, nor shall their monstrous world ever intrude on me again. Not again.

"They may drive me out, as they drove you out. They may shatter what is left of my life, and trample it. They may exile me because they can't 'update' me.

"But never again—if you abide with me—shall I dream of deserting them and leaving them hungry.

"And we shall walk together again—and, who knows? —the sheep may follow."

He smiled timidly at the man who appeared, now, to be tenderly smiling at him. He said, "My mother used to sing a hymn, and now I truly know what it means:

> " 'Dark though the nights at times,
> And sad and forlorn,
> But long have I loved Thee, Lord!
> And bided the morn.' "

SOUL EIGHT: The Husbandman

> "—when that it remembreth me
> Upon my youth and on my jolitee
> It tikleth me about min herte roote—
> *That I have had my world as in my time!*"
> "WIFE OF BATH."

"Well, hello, Parson," said the old man with gravity as he faced the calm blue curtain of the alcove. "You are a parson, ain't you? That's what everybody says, anyhow. You listen to folks' troubles and then you tell them what to do. That's real kind of you. Didn't know there was that kind left in the world, no sir. Everybody loving each other and nobody loving anybody: that's what goes on now. Like the patriotism you read about in the newspapers and nobody's patriotic, seems like. Why, there was a time, I remember, if folks had trouble, even in the city, everybody'd come with baked goods and fruit and maybe a roast chicken, and there'd be real sympathy. Now it's all fake, newspapers full of brotherly love and the rights of everybody, and people talkin' and the pastors telling you, in their pulpits, to do good to everybody, 'specially people you don't know in foreign parts, and nobody gives a damn about their next-door neighbor. Easy to be sympathetic about people a thousand miles away or more; costs you nothin' to roll your eyes and make your voice all deep and soft. But gettin' off your butt and doin' something about the people next door, with your own money and your own work: Oh, no. That doesn't mean anythin' now. It isn't havin' a sense—what do they call it with their mealy-mouths?—of world-wide responsibility. Hell."

He settled back comfortably in his chair and felt for his pipe. He'd prepared it outside, and he had that lighter Al, his son, had given him, and so it didn't make no difference smoking in here, and that air-conditioning took the smoke away anyway. He hadn't felt this comfortable since Beth had died: relaxed and at peace, talking to somebody who understood.

"There's that young fellow I just saw outside, in his fancy city clothes, big city. He tells me he don't have any troubles. Well, if that young feller don't have troubles I'll eat my hat.

134

Just smells all over with 'em. Like all the city folks, and some of the country ones do, these days. All the 'love' and the rushin' and bein' alert and mindin' your neighbors' business—'specially if the neighbor is clear around the other side of the world—is sure not makin' people happy. Downright miserable. Never saw such miserable people in my life, like you see nowadays, and people so full of hate they're mean as sin. Somethin's wrong."

He smoked a little, reflectively. "When Jesus talked about lovin' your neighbor, I reckon He didn't mean runnin' off from your own country as fast as you could and lookin' for a 'neighbor' in Greece or Rome or whatever to do good to. He meant the feller livin' right next door to you, with his troubles. Why, there's Missuz Campbell, next farm to mine, a big farm, collective like the Chinese and the Rooskis, from what I hear: She's in the Fairmont papers all the time collectin' for this and that for people she'll never see, what we used to call the heathen Chinee and Darkest Africa, and workin' for the United Nations, and all that, and on the other side of me, little farm, there's that young widow with three kids strugglin' alone and not makin' ends meet with the poor land and all, and only her oldest to help her, and I says to Missuz Campbell, 'There's Susy Trendall, and she ain't got money this year for fertilizer, and how about ante-ing up and helping her out, she don't get much in the way of subsidies,' and Missuz Campbell, she says, 'All our money that we're collectin' is goin' to the Association for the United Nations and the Emerging Nations, and Mrs. Trendall should go on Relief if she's so poverty-stricken.'

"Now, I tell you. Is that Christian charity and helpin' your neighbor? No sir. It's fake. Fake and cruel like the jaws of charity. So, I go over there to Susy's and help with the tractor and fix it up, and I tell Missuz Campbell to go love her neighbor and not look for Causes to make her feel important and good. Goooood! What a hypocrite. Seems like the whole damn country is a-seethin' with liars and hypocrites now, and not fine sound people like I'd always known since I was a kid on the farm that belonged to my granddad and my father and now to me. All the goodie-goodies I see around these days got hearts of solid iron and eyes like wildcats. It makes me feel sick at my stomach."

The pipe was puffing agitatedly now. "One time, we had mean folks that used to hide under what we call the 'religious cloak,' that helped hide their meanness and greediness and hate for their neighbor, while they quoted Scripture and

135

watched their bank accounts grow. But those same folks don't go in for religious cloaks to hide their sinfulness of heart any longer. They go for somethin' some parsons call 'the social gospel.' It works just the same: Keep your money, talk big about 'love,' try to fool your neighbors about what a soft heart you got, and get a wonderful reputation for bein' a fine feller. Funny thing. When folks hid under the lyin' religious cloak we all caught on and made fun of them. We don't do that with the 'social gospel' folks. Some of us believe 'em, and that's part of the general foolishness that gives me a pain in the—well, you know."

He nodded his head bitterly. He had the strangest feeling that the man behind the curtain was agreeing with him.

"And there's the government always interferin' with your life. Once we'd have gotten out our guns and chased the government men right off our land, and we had the Constitution to back us up. Well, I can say, and I got pride, that never once did I take one of their damned checks, though they offered it over and over. Take a check from government and you put a chain around your neck. No sir, not for me. I got to pay that social security or whatever they call it, but that's all, and so long as I got one shake in my legs to help me walk I don't go on any social security, no sir. And maybe not even then. I got my pride.

"And that brings me to what I'm doin' here, takin' up your time.

"One time, when I was a kid, and even up to twenty years ago, there was eighteen farms around me. Now just one family owns them, the Campbells! Think of that. The other folks sold up their land to those damn greedy Campbells, with their 'modern' industrial farm, and went off to live in town in one of them boxes they call housin' developments. The towns always did stink. They stink worse now. And the stink isn't just in the dirty air and the soot; it's in their souls. Babylons. Not real hearty sin that a person can understand, sins of the body. No, they got sins of the soul, real black sickenin' sins that scare the hell out of you. Babylons."

He shook his head. "Damned if I'm not glad I'm seventy-five years old and lived when the world was solid and sound as a good winesap apple, even if everybody, town and country, worked ten–twelve hours a day. Everybody talks about 'this wonderful era' and it's just like a play-act you see on the stage; everybody pretendin' and runnin' around and gaspin' and makin' a big show with their teeth and their eyes, and babblin' like fools. They're all so busy. They work eight–nine hours, even on the farm, and they don't have no time! No time! No time to visit neighborly, to sit on the porch and talk and watch the fireflies on the bank and listen to the wind. No, they roar into town and they roar back, and they're all exhausted, and they got yapping TV and radios, and they never read a thing in their lives after school, but damn! they all act like they're educated when they're just plain fools who don't know anythin' at all, either about themselves or the world. If they do read anythin' it's just dirty books, and they wink and feel up-to-date. Hell, all them words was written on the backs of barns when I was a kid, and you got the —— whaled out of you if your dad caught you. What's so all-fired modern about dirty words, anyways? I tell you what: The world's full of grown-up kids now, with their fancy clothes, and I got a feelin' they'll never grow up.

"Wonderful era. Space age. And everythin' about as solid and real as the clown-faces we used to make ourselves when we was kids and it was Hollow'E'en. Everybody's got clown-faces, maybe to hide the fact they don't have real faces of their own. Makin' little faces, as Beth used to call it, and not showin' the sunburned flesh at all. Maybe they don't have sunburn now; all I know is they don't have real eyes and real souls.

"Well, anyway. The Campbells, the big Dad, with his sport coat imported from New York, he keeps comin' over to me and askin' me to sell my farm to him, him with his big industrial farm like a factory. I say no, I won't. And the taxes keep goin' up on my farm all the time, and you know what? I think it's that Campbell feller, he who had an honest dad with honest dirt on his hands, and not farm-experts as they call 'em now, with TV in their 'units,' and runnin' hot and cold water, and big shiny cars. Maybe that's progress. I call it gettin' away from God and the earth, and knowin' what you had to do. If it made 'em happy I wouldn't mind. But, like I said, it's makin' them miserable and mean with hearts like old withered apples you'd find at the bottom of the barrels in the spring. No sap. No taste. Just old dried skin and dead seeds. Not even fit for hogs.

"Sometimes I look at my cows and my horses and my dogs, and I go out walkin' over my fields and see the polecats and possums and chipmunks and birds, and I say to 'em: 'You're real. You're what you are. You are all cow or horse or dog or whatever. You ain't tryin' to be what you're not. You got your nature, and no fake.' And it kind of raises my heart and I come back to the house and feel that here, anyway, things are what they are and not just pretend. They're as God intended: honest and sturdy and good.

"Well. Beth and me, we had just the one boy, Al. We sent him to agricultural school. But he didn't want that. He wanted to be a lawyer-feller, in the city. No more farm, no more drudgery for him, he says. He wants to make a lot of money, and even the money's fake these days. Well, he was the only one we had and we wanted to make him happy, if he wanted to live in the city. So, now he's a lawyer in a big city six hundred miles away, and doing well, and he's got ulcers and three yappy kids who're as miserable as could be, with all their advantages. I can tell. They sometimes come to the farm in summer. The girls just sit around and whine and do their hair and race into town and paint their faces; little girls, too, one thirteen and one sixteen. But there's Roger. He kind of likes the farm— He quiets down here. He gets that restless look off his face, and walks slow, not runnin' the way he does when he first comes. And last summer he runs the harvester for me, and didn't mind gettin' all sweat and dust.

"Well, I had to borrow money from Al last year to pay the big taxes the Campbell's got for me, to force me off the land. And Al—he's a good boy and got a nice city wife—he says, 'Dad, sell the farm at a good price and come to live with us. We love you, and we'll make you happy.' Happy! And he says, 'Dad, I'm all you have since Ma died, and why'd you want to live there all alone when you have a family in this city who want you?' The worst of it is, I know they're tellin' the truth. They do want me, and I like to see 'em when they come, and it's almost like old times. But I don't want their damn city and the cars racin' around and not a piece of earth to set your foot down on."

He paused. "I forgot. Adam Faith's the name. My mother was fanciful. But I kind of like the name now, though people used to laugh at it. It don't matter. The thing is, the pressure of taxes is maybe goin' to get worse, and maybe I'll lose my farm. Al says he'll send me the money to make up what I can't pay, but I don't like to take it, though Al remembers about honorin' your father and mother, and he sure does that. Always did. What do you think? Think I should sell up and move to the city?"

He'd always had a big imagination, Beth used to say, so it was only imagination—but a warming one—that assured him that the man behind the curtain was saying an emphatic "No!"

"Comin' down to it," he said in a suddenly dreary voice, "I guess I'm just not important at all, just a nobody. Like Al

138

says, all I ever knew was work. Hard work. Like Al says. I
didn't get to school much, that school five miles away, and
hell and all in winter to get there, and it was only for six—
seven years. Got up at sunup and fell into bed, upstairs in
that room that burned all summer and froze all winter, when
the sun went down and the cows were safe in the barn and
the hogs and chickens fed. Fell right asleep, like I was dead.
And up again, and the chores, and then runnin' off to school,
and then runnin' home for more chores. Maybe Al's right
after all. I didn't have a chance to be anythin' but a fool
farmer on a farm that don't pay no more, what with the
taxes and the acreage restrictions, from the government. I
don't take their checks, but they come a-threatenin', and tell
what I can raise and what I can't, and is that a free country
any more? No, it ain't. But lots of farmers like it. They get
'security,' they say. Security from years of bad crops, and
pullin' in your belt. Security, they say, from the 'whims' of
weather and good and bad years. Security to buy cars and
run into town to them saloons and movie places, and buy TV
sets and wear fancy clothes.

"Maybe Al's right. I'm seventy-five. Can't afford to hire
a hand no more, like I sometimes used to. Got to do it all
myself. And it gets awful lonesome at nights and on Sundays.
No neighbors to talk to like I used to do. Why, I remember
the time I met Beth—"

The Zimmers had the farm next to his father's, good, industrious German folk, and they had made their farm rich
and their farm buildings as solid as stone. Mrs. Zimmer, like
his own mother, seemed to have lots of time to do everything. She was up before the sun, feeding the chickens and
the hogs, and then milking the cows and attending to breakfast
for her eight children, then working in her vegetable garden
most of the day, and putting up preserves and sewing quilts
and making clothes, then feeding the stock again, then having
a Bible reading in the parlor, and prayers, then going to bed
to prepare to start all over again. And she had time to work
at the Ladies Aid at church, and church suppers and picnics,
and go to quilting bees and help neighbors with their babies
and young ones, and to knit and scrub her big house and take
care of all her children, and make butter and collect her
eggs and milk for the market, and to act as midwife, snow or
no snow in the winter, and to read every book she could get
her hands on which her husband would bring to her from
town every week. All the time in the world. Placid, calm, unhurried Erna Zimmer, with her big rosy face and big jolly

laugh. All the time in the world, unlike the frenzied Mrs. Campbell with her high blood pressure, and empty Causes.

And the Zimmer kids, as big and rosy as their parents. His own mother used to envy that large brood, for he, Adam Faith, was the only child. Well, they had their young cousin, Beth Steigel, visit them one summer, from far off in the West, a girl looking to be a schoolteacher right here. Graduate of teachers college, a big strapping girl with a glowing face and bundles of bright auburn hair and a deep breast and strong brown hands, and a mouth like a red apple. Great big blue eyes, too, lake-blue. All the young fellows around fell in love with her at once and wanted to marry her right off.

The Zimmers gave a huge picnic for her, for dozens of people miles around, and Mrs. Zimmer and her girls cooked ten hams, sides of beef, countless pies, cakes, huge bowls of potatoes and summer squash and sauerkraut and cole slaw, and boats of gravy, and hot bread and gallons of coffee. It was all set out under the giant elms on the rough lawns, on the grass and on wooden tables, with real linen napkins and not paper as they had these days, and a big barrel of cold beer for the men, and all those sweet, sour, and dill pickles and all those cherry pies smelling like heaven, and the hams glazed with honey and cloves, and the children screaming and running and somebody playing a guitar and singing soft, and the sun coming through the trees in rays of quick bright light, and the soft summer wind laughing in the leaves, and the blue hills beyond, curving like velvet against the hot sky, and the river shining in the distance. Even the birds seemed excited and sang like crazy and flew everywhere, and the cows stood in the green fields and watched. And there was no sound but the laughter and talk of the people and the wind in the trees, and the shouting of the children and the clatter of plates. It was like heaven. It was a peace that was not really stillness. It was a living peace.

"I took a shine to Beth the minute I saw her," said Adam Faith, smiling all over his lean brown face which had been plowed by the years and by work and sun. "And she took a shine to me. We were married in time for the harvest."

The little country church, as white and brilliant as the moon, in the hot noonday of early autumn. Everybody came from miles around, hundreds of them, dressed in their best store clothes, the men with ties about their warm sun-reddened necks, the women in flounces and lawn and voile, printed all over in bright colors, and the children with shiny shoes on their feet and their hair slicked down. All farm folk,

140

smelling of sweet hay and clover. The horses standing in the shade of trees about the church, their heads hanging, their tails switching, and the bells in the steeple ringing, and the choir singing:

"Holy, Holy, Holy,
   Lord God Almighty!
   Early in the morning our song shall rise to Thee!
   Holy, Holy, Holy,
   Merciful and Mighty,
   God in Three Persons, Blessed Trinity!"

The sun on the roofs of the little village and glittering on the glass and making the stained glass of the church windows blaze like rainbows. And the people standing and singing their hearts out, while he and his father waited in the vestry and the parson stopped for a moment, pulling on his black robe, and some of the men helping to tie and button him up, and the cool purple shade in the church and the scent of grass outside and sweet dust. He, Adam, was sweating in his thick black suit and his feet were hurting in his new boots and his neck scratched from his new haircut, and his heart was beating like the rain on a summer roof. He could hear the singing of the people and the labored groaning of the old organ, and he did not know if he was frightened or not, and he wondered how Beth was feeling.

The parson went into the church and when he opened the door the sound of the singing became the sound of rejoicing, the sound of faith and glory and gladness. Then Adam heard a different note in the church. A silence, a ringing silence. Suddenly the choir sang out, and it was the wedding march, tentative, and his father laughed in his face, caught his arm and hurried him out to the altar which was all-over mums and ferns, and the other men poured out after him and hurried to their wooden pews, which were sticky and newly varnished, and there was a storm of palm-leaf fans among the congregation and joyous faces looking up at him, all burnished by the sun, and children staring. And as the wedding march soared exultantly there came Beth up the aisle with her Uncle Zimmer—for she was an orphan—and she was dressed all in flowing white, a lovely dress she had made herself, and wearing her mother's white lace veil over her face. Beautiful Beth, as strong and noble as the earth. When he had looked at her it seemed that he expanded, became great and tall, with a heart that was too big for him, and he wanted to weep.

Then she was standing beside him, her large warm hand in his and her eyes shining at him through the meshes of her veil and the dimmed glow of her auburn hair framing her pink face. He had the impression that the women were crying and smiling and that the men were grinning, but he was only really aware of Beth and the blue twinkle of her eyes.

"Dearly beloved," said the parson, "we are gathered here today—"

Gathered here with hearts truly full of love and earnest wishes for happiness, and neighborly rejoicing and simple pleasure! Neighbors on whom a man could depend for comfort, help, work, a strong hand, a good word, kindness, fortitude, hope, and honest prayer. The knowledge was a fortified city, a walled city, a sense of true security, of safety against storms and grief and terrors in the night, a familiar strength compounded of faith in God and faith in the good earth, and affection and promise, of manly and womanly acceptance.

He kissed Beth through the veil, as her bridesmaid was a little slow in lifting it, and he recalled now the taste of starched lace and sun-warm lips as sweet as a pear, and Beth's hand on his shoulder and the sight of blueness through the veil, and her silent promise to him that she would never leave him and that he was hers and she was his, as a tree belongs to the land through winter and summer and all the thunders and all the lightnings and the snows.

"Weddings ain't like that any longer," said Adam Faith to the man behind the curtain. "I know. I've seen twenty or more over the last years. What do they promise each other now? Work and courage and strength, labor side by side? No, they don't. The man promises to hurry to an office and make money; the woman promises to stay pretty and keep her figger. They promise new cars and a new washing machine and lots of gadgets and vacations. They don't promise each other faith in God and themselves and help in pain. No, they don't. It was wonderful, then."

He smiled at the curtain and it trembled through the mist in his eyes.

"It was good. I remember."

Then young Albert was born, when the snow was as high as the windows, worst snow he could ever recall. He went through the blizzard for Mrs. Zimmer, and she came sturdily behind him with her oldest married daughter, and two sons with big baskets of hot food, and fresh warm linens. Within an hour Beth gave birth to her son, and she sat up in bed and laughed with everybody, and there was much bustle in the kitchen and the fragrance of new apple logs on the fire and the blizzard screaming against the windows and rattling them, and he, Adam, "breaking out" the barrel of beer which he had saved for this occasion and men suddenly knocking loudly at the farmhouse door bearing more gifts and their wives shaking off their snow-covered hats and coats. It was an Occasion, a new man born of and for the earth. The very frost on the windowpanes sparkled and shone as if it, too, was happy. Beth sat in the big poster-bed with her son in her arms and her first kiss was for her husband, the second for her child, and she shouted to the women in the kitchen that they'd find the new bread she had baked today under that counter where the pump stood, and the apple pies in the "safe."

"It was good. I remember," said old Adam Faith now, rubbing the thick white hair on his head and smiling tenderly.

It was an occasion, too, for the whole community when little Albert Faith was christened, for all respected the father as a good farmer, cherishing his land, and everyone loved Beth who stood so tall and whose voice was so gentle and kind. There was a prize heifer for the newborn, and a prize young bull—both established a very profitable line—and other proud gifts, joyfully given, joyfully received. "That was before the war, long before we got in, the first one, I mean," said Adam to the blue curtain over the alcove. "A wonderful, peaceful time. There wasn't no dictatorships and fightings and murderers in government, then. Why, there was freedom all over the world for everybody, except in Russia where they had that Czar, and in some places in the bush in Africa! Real freedom, where nobody bothered an honest, God-fearing man with government forms, and everybody minded his own business and worked at an honest day's work and raised his family to be decent men and women who loved their country and their God and went to church of a Sunday and took care of neighbors when they were sick or couldn't work or had babies or were hungry. There wasn't any juvenile gangs and girls gettin' into mischief and social workers running around minding everybody's business except their miserable own, and fighting in the streets. The woman who worked the hardest in the garden and in the house was the one who had this 'status' you hear about these days, and the man who took care of his land the best and raised the best stock—he was the one the community looked up to. You never heard, very often, of a man takin' to drink or a woman to whorin', in those days. We was too damn busy living and enjoying life! And workin' as God intended men and women to work, in His clean sunshine and in His rain. Yes, it was a free world then, a really free world, and not a society hedged all 'round with a lot of nosy bureaucrats and free-loaders at the public trough. A man could walk tall and proud on his acres, and even on his streets, and feel safe, and that's somethin' no one feels these days—safe."

He sighed. "Guess the world's now full of cryin' men, seems like. Everybody's afraid of everythin' and they with their big pay and their cars and their mortgaged ranch houses and their kitchens full of shiny junk and their garages full of shiny cars. Scared to death of everythin', jumpin' at funny sounds and readin' their newspapers, scared. What're they afraid of? Dyin'? Hasn't anyone ever told them that death is just as natural as life, and that all their vitamins and health foods, as they call it, won't keep them alive any longer than their dads lived, or their granddads? And if it does keep them alive, why, anyway? What good are they to the world, scaredy-cats as kids used to call cowards? Why, they aren't even free men any more! Not free like we knew it."

There was no use denying it, life was hard on the farm, but it was a wonderful, real hardness, for it was engaged with wind and snow and tempest and floods, with droughts and storms.

"I remember when the river flooded," he said to the listening man. "Lots of us got washed out; washed out the winter wheat and killed lots of the stock and filled our barns and houses with mud. But we all got together and built everything up; you could hear hammers and saws for miles around, and men workin' in the sun and women bringing lunch baskets and pails of fresh milk and even the toddlers workin' as hard as anyone else, sorting out and bringing nails and water. Everythin' so bright after the storm and flood; the river had poured good fertile soil on the land and we never had such crops like we had that year. It was like a renewal. I remember. It was good."

Then he laughed wryly. "You don't see folks like mine any longer. Just fake people. Last summer, my grandson, Roger, the one I told you about, came to stay two months with me and we had a heck of a time. Roger set up one of them roadside stands, and we sold watermelons and squash and corn and cucumbers and fresh cold milk and some of young Missuz Trendall's pies she made to sell—good pies like Beth made. And some of her real bread. We put a big price on 'em and sold every one, and she needs the money.

"Well, sir, up comes one of them big shiny station wagons they call 'em, with a woman in high heels and a big puffy lot of hair standing on end on her head and a tight short skirt that was a scandal, and two big fat boys older'n Roger, and a scaredy-cat of a husband. Out for a ride in the country, she says, in that hard impudent voice the women have these days, and the bad, greedy look in her eyes, all painted up—the eyes I mean. And she points to the milk and says, 'Is that dairy?'

"Well, that kind of puzzles me. Where in hell would you get milk except out of a cow in a dairy? But that's city folk now. Roger says as smooth as silk, 'Why, ma'am, it's pasteurized, of course.' And she says, throwing her hand around at the wrist, 'That's not what I mean. Is it dairy?' I scratched my head, but Roger was sober as a parson and he shakes his head and says, 'No, ma'am, it was made in a factory.' And she nods real fierce and knowin' and says, 'That's what I thought. You can't have it, boys.'

"Before I could say anythin' she pounds on the watermellons and says are they clean, and Roger says, still sober as a parson, 'Why, no, ma'am, they didn't have a bowel movement today.' And that's the first time the scaredy-cat of a husband makes a sound. He busts out laughin', cacklin' like a hen, and his woman gets mad at Roger, and they all pile in that wagon of theirs and roar off with a stink.

"Fake people. They don't even know how or where their food grows; maybe they think it grows in factories or on top of skyscrapers. They don't even care where their water comes from, that precious water which keeps their worthless bodies alive and washed. They think it just comes out of faucets instead of hill streams and rivers and lakes, and it's all polluted now with people-dirt and factory-dirt and it's dangerous to drink it, not like my well that's just like diamond water.

"When I was a boy half the people, or more, lived on the land, and even the city folk were near fields and forests and rivers and lakes and could walk out in the greenness and smell the good earth. But now I hear hardly anyone lives on the land; it's farmin'-combines now, like factories, and as much real life on them as there is in cans. Farmin'-combines, like the Campbells have. Maybe that's 'efficient,' as they call it. Maybe it's true we couldn't feed the country on family farms any longer. But I don't believe that! We could.

"Anyway, what do city folk these days know about the country, the land? Nothin'. Most of them never saw a cow. One city woman, buying some of our stuff near the road, jumps real scared when she sees old Betsy, our queen cow, and asks me if Betsy's tame, and I says, followin' Roger, that no, she was a man-eater, and the fool screamed like a factory

145

whistle and got in her car like a squirrel, and she a three-hundred pounder if I ever saw one. I tell you, Parson, a people that don't know the land is a dangerous, bad people, a fake people, always ready to scream and panic and run like them lemmings you hear about—I read it in *Reader's Digest*—every year a generation of 'em leaves Europe and they swim right out into the sea and drown.

"I heard once, a story, that a scientist asked a lemming why lemmings do that, and the lemming said, 'Why, sir, we often wonder why the human race don't do that.' He sure was right!

"Well, I'm glad for one thing: I lived my life in a world of real people and not fake people with rubber hearts and paper heads and loud noises in their mouths instead of common sense. I lived my life in a time of peace and good neighbors, and love and kindness, and hard work and thrift and firelight and lamplight, and the smell of apple butter cookin' in big copper kettles under the oak trees, and the sound of church bells rollin' over the hills and the sound of the river in the summer, singin' to itself, and the sound of the wind when the winter snows were high. I lived my life with a good wife beside me, and the smell of her good bread bakin' in the woodstove, and her hymns in the mornin' and the way she laughed at the colts when they was playin' in the fields. I lived my life with God and the earth, with livin' roots in my hands and the winter wheat green as the snow melted, and the orchards full of pink flowers and bees. I lived my life with life and death, and it was all real and round and as full as a cup of milk. And just as sweet and just as life-givin'.

"You know somethin', Parson? Jesus knew all about the land. Remember His stories about the sower and the seeds, and the lilies of the field, and the vineyards and olive groves, and the fig trees, and the hills and the waters? He was a Countryman, like me. He talked our language to us. We loved Him, in the country. It took the City to kill Him. What do they know about life or He Who was the Life? Nothin'. How could they understand Him and His ways? They couldn't. They always kill the Life. That's why they're so damned dangerous, with their silky sluts they call modern women, and their stupid kids full of sin, and their frightened men. Maybe the government really does need to keep an eye on 'em. Any farmer can tell you that a scared cow is a mighty dangerous beast, worse than any bull or a poison snake. She gets to be a killer, once she's scared. Just like most people; they're mostly scared out of their feeble wits more often than not. So maybe the government has to watch them all the time, the way you'd watch crazy people escaped from the asylum."

He shook his head over and over. "But it wasn't like that, fifty years ago. It was good. I remember. A man was brave in his mind and his body. He was always, even in the cities, in the sight of grass and trees.

"Why, even death wasn't so terrible when I was young. Now they call it passing-away, all their silly talk, their scared talk, not bein' able to face the truth and callin' truth by prancy words and mealy-mouthed words. We laid our dead next to their fathers and grandfathers, under the trees behind the church, and we knew in our hearts that they wasn't lost to us. We knew it surely. Their love was all around us, for-ever, and one day we'd see their faces again and there'd be rejoicin' in the Golden City. We knew that for sure. And we'd go to their graves with the flowers we grew in our own gardens, big red roses hot with sun, and bunches of daisies and heliotrope, and lilies-of-the-valley, and branches of apple blossoms. We'd sit by the graves and we'd talk to our dead, and the peaceful sun was all around us and the Eternal Love. The graves were our homes, just as our sound houses were; both sheltered us from storms. Oh, we cried all right. It was a parting, and the parting'd last for life. But it wouldn't last forever. All things are born and bloom and give fruit, and then they die. A countryman knows that. It's natural, even if it's sad. We'd cry. But there were the strong arms of our neighbors around us, and the neighbors cryin', too, and you'd feel comforted for you knew for sure that you were loved and that the dead were loved, too, and always remembered.

"It was that way with me when Beth died, sudden, ten years ago, between one breath and another. But she smiled at me when I held her, and she kissed me, and then she slept just like a baby in its dad's arms, at peace. It wasn't 'til Beth died that things came apart in my mind, and I sort of looked around me and saw this new world for what it was, and I almost died, myself, sick in my heart and soul."

He drew a deep breath, and wiped his eyes with the back of his hand. "Funny. I never saw what a terrible place the world'd become, until Beth died. She was like a tall tree trunk that shuts out the sight of a wild animal. And then I saw it. Yes, sir, it made me sick in my heart and soul. I couldn't tell Al that; he wouldn't understand. Now, he's a good boy, a man, fifty-two years old now, and what they call successful, and he loved his parents, he still loves me, but he wouldn't understand. Sometimes he calls livin' a 'rat race,' and I guess he sometimes remembers the farm, but he never really had a feelin' for it and that's why we didn't try to keep him on the land. He looks older, at fifty-two, than my father looked at eighty, and the look in his eyes is older than death.

"It's that way with his wife, too, a good fine woman as city women go. She tells me they're 'trapped.' Well, why don't they get untrapped? Just give up their second house on the shore, and the three cars they have, and the big house in town and the maid, and their country clubs, and make less and live on less. And Clare, that's her name, says, 'It wouldn't be fair to The Children. The Children need and deserve every advantage we can give 'em.'

"What I'd like to know," said Adam Faith, his brown face flushing with exasperation and pain, "is what children need besides the love of their parents and learnin' how to do a good day's work, and havin' self-respect, and the fear of God in 'em. And learnin' to hate sin and debt. What do they need with country clubs and private schools, if they have good schools with the kind of teachers Beth was, who knew how to discipline kids and teach them and keep them in order? Why do they need cars, any of them? What's the matter with their legs? Oh, I could talk about that all day—the kids they have now, the tired-looking, mean-looking, greedy-looking, kids they have. Little girls dressed up like street-sluts; little boys in long pants. Old before they're even young. But then, they're not young at all, any of them. And the mothers say, puttin' their heads on one side and givin' sweet smiles, 'Well, the children these days.' And who the hell made 'these days'? That's what I'd like to know. It was the parents! And it's a black sin on their souls, this ugly, empty, stony, lifeless world, full of noises and fear.

"Now me, I remember how it was when I was young. It was wonderful." He laughed a little. "Swimmin' in the cold water, in the spring, when the river was as green as grass and frothin' along the banks. Seein' the sun come up, all afire at the edge of the east meadow, like that army with banners the Bible talks about. Hearin' the silence. And seein' the sun set over the western hills, so that it looked like bonfires on them, they all black below and the land quiet and shadowy. Gatherin' the nuts in the fall, with the air all golden and smoky and full of spice near the house, where my mother would be makin' ketchup. Ridin' the hills on sleds in the winter, with everything black and white and steel-colored."

He looked at the blue curtain with startled wonder. "Yes. I

remember. It was wonderful. You made me think of all that, Parson, just listenin' to me. You made me remember a poem Beth read to me, just the night before she died; she was always reading poetry. I don't remember much of it rightly, just the end:

" 'I have had my world as in my time!'

"I didn't know what it meant until right now, thanks to you, Parson! It means that I really lived—had a real world, and enjoyed it and loved it, every minute of it, every smell of it, every sound of it, even the grief and the droughts and the bitter work and the pain. 'I have had my world as in my time.' I did, a wonderful world, all peace and work and satisfaction. The world don't owe me a thing. It gave me everything. God gave me everything, a strong body and love and neighbors and a good wife and a fine son—even if Al don't like the land, he's a fine boy, God help him.

"Maybe Beth knew she was goin' to die, had a premonition. She was tryin' to tell me that she, too, had had her world in her time, and it was complete, and nothin' owed to her or from her. It was finished, like a careful quilt, patiently sewed, patiently patterned, with pieces gathered over a whole lifetime, red and yellow and green and white and blue, some flowered, some kind of shadowed, some with patterns you couldn't tell, some from spring, summer, fall, and winter goods —a whole lifetime, put together and always useful, new or old. And every piece of that quilt had a story to tell, and a place to remember, whether it was joyful or full of pain or sadness.

"I tell you, Parson, you've made me ashamed! Comin' here to you, whimperin' and kind of lost, not knowin' what to do. Why, I had a wonderful life, a free life! What is any life today compared with what I had? Nothin' but dust and ashes, as the Good Book says. I tell you, I'm ashamed. Whinin' about the hard work I did, as if man isn't made for hard work, the muscles in the right places, the bones just right, the shoulders set and strong. You ought to kick me out, yes, sir.

"But you know what I'm goin' to do?" He leaned toward the silent curtain eagerly. "I'm goin' to keep my farm, where my grandfather lived and died and my father after him, and Beth. That's what I'm goin' to do, come hell or high water. Somehow I'll get along. I'll hire a hand; seems like I haven't had the heart to work real hard lately, and it ain't my age. My granddad's father lived to be ninety-six, and every day in the field to the day he died. It's just I got discouraged, and got to thinkin' Al was right, and I should sell up and go to live with him and his family.

149

"But I'll do a lot more for his family than that. I'll keep the farm for my grandson, Roger. He loves it. He's a countryman at heart, just like me. And it'll be a place to run to, my farm, when the world gets black and red with death and terror, and I know as sure as God that that's what's goin' to happen, and maybe sooner than most of us think. It'll be a safe place to come, to hide, to be sheltered from the storm. No matter what man does, the earth remains. It can be burned and broken—but it lives, and then it is green again and full of life.

"No one's goin' to have my farm but me and my blood kin. It's all the world for us. It always was, it always will be. I'll get along, with the help of God. I remember what it said on that marble tablet in the other room: 'I can do all things in Him Who strengthens me.' "

Adam Faith stood up, half-smiling, half-weeping, and nodding his head. "Yes, sir, that's true. I'll find a way. I'll keep the land for the day of the abomination of desolation, as that prophet said long ago.

"Somewhere, a man in those days must have a real place to run to, and it won't be any city or any housin' development or big glassy government building. It'll be farmhouses in the country, under the trees. It has to be an honest-to-God place, where men can learn to live again as God and nature intended, and not like those synthetic vegetables they cultivate in laboratories in artificially fertilized water. When that day comes, it won't be a retreat. It'll be a return. To where men should live."

He picked up his hat from the floor near the white marble chair and hesitantly held it in his hands, and he smiled at the blue curtain.

"I wish, Parson, I could do somethin' special for you, you bein' so patient and listenin' to me so long, and showin' me just what I've got to do, and makin' me remember all the wonderful things I'd forgotten. But I reckon you've got all you want. What I could give you wouldn't be anythin', would it?

"But you've given me back my real world and the sun and the fields again, and all the hope I ever had. Parson, all I can say is, God bless you."

He did not touch the button which would have revealed the man to him, for he had not read the inscription above it, nor had he approached the curtain. Shyly, he bent his head in farewell, then stood up as straight as a youth and went out of the room.

SOUL NINE: *The Richest Man in Town*

"Thou sayest, I am rich and increased
with goods, and have need of nothing;
but knowest not that thou art wretched,
and miserable, and poor, and blind, and naked?"
                                    REVELATION 3:17

It was ridiculous, of course, for him to be here at all. He could not understand what had brought him to this absurd—what was it the proletariat called it?—Sanctuary. That was the name which had become very popular these last few years. Sanctuary! A man got enough "sanctuaries" all through his life, nice and cosy and at the last like a down-lined grave. A lovely, soothing cradle; the transition from cradle to comfortable grave—on a spring mattress, courtesy of expensive undertakers—was hardly perceptible, and hardly differed. From nothingness into nothingness, with "life's fitful fever" in between, if life these days had any fitful fever at any time, or ever had, except in a few rare instances in history, or in the more frenetic novels. From sleep to sleep, with a few pleasant dreams and a little pleasant activity in between, but nothing disturbing to a well-bred man whose parents and grandparents had had the kindness to lay up a fortune for him.

Even if one were comparatively poor, especially now in days of affluence, the pleasantness differed only in degree. All was secured, all was provided, all was contentment and gaiety—except for death, of course, which was not undesirable after all, for it was only another comfortable sleep.

It was enough to make a man kill himself.

He, John Service, had been seriously considering this for over six months. Or was it longer? He could not remember. He was bored to death, bored by pleasantness, smoothness, affluence, laughter, cocktail parties, wood-paneled offices, amiable employees, serene wife, well-established children, rosy fat grandchildren, summer homes, winters in Florida or the Caribbean, or in those exotic out-of-the-way places in Mexico and Central America, or in Paris, or London or Madrid or Mallorca. The world was really small; one finally ran out of places to visit and explore. Besides, everything had become Americanized and sterile and cellophaned and sanitary, with excellent bathrooms, fast jets, gourmet meals, and tender stewardesses. Sweet and Lovely. As he waited in the quiet room John Service hummed that old popular song from his boyhood. It rang in his brain now, not liltingly, but with a kind of horror and terror, mocking, a refrain of demons, a refrain from the very black pits of hell. Sweet and Lovely. An excellent epitaph for a world—and especially for a human life.

The trouble was that he could not lay a finger on what the trouble was. This century was surely, in spite of wars and the rampageous voices in the United Nations, and skirmishes here and there, the dream of men long dead who had struggled for an existence and had fought the frightful wilderness and had set sail on dark seas. They had dreamed of all this—the Sweet and Lovely. Paradise. A cradle that was a grave, really, and a grave that was a cradle, all scented and pink. Especially in America. As he waited among the silent men and women in the calm and quiet waiting room, John Service wondered about Russia, where all was still comparatively grim and the color of iron. But Russia looked enviously at the rosy and perfumed dream of America, and struggled to attain it for her own people. Other European countries had already attained it. What was it he had read recently? Suicide was rising rapidly in the "happy" nations. It was the leading cause of death, outside of drunkenness, in Scandinavia, just as, if all were known, it was truly the leading cause of death in America. There was more than one way to cut your throat. You could induce fatal illness, or at least that is what the head-shrinkers said.

He had come to this ridiculous place for no reason that he could remember. But it was autumn, gold and crimson and russet, and there had been a tranquil wood fire in the library at home, and a tea table and a beautiful, placid wife presiding, and a few relatives present, murmuring gently and with tinkling laughter or peaceful masculine chuckles. A typical autumn Sunday afternoon, with yellow light at the tall windows, and yellow streaks of sunshine on the carved walls, and last sun on the old slate of this house where he had been born. Contentment. It had glowed everywhere. Peace. It lay in every great room of the gracious house. Pleasantness. It

152

reflected off the ancient silver, satiny with thousands of minute scratches. Wood smoke and the smell of tea and brandy and pastries and the women's discreet perfume. Soft classical music from the hi-fi. Clink of china. Rustle of a woman's expensive dress. A murmur: "It hardly seems possible that Sally will make her debut this year. Why, she's hardly out of her crib, my dear!" Fond laughter. "More tea, dear? Do have one of these napoleons. Really excellent. More soda, Bob? John, why are you sitting there so quiet? Is something wrong, dear?"

He had been more aghast than the others, and more horrified and appalled, when he had heard his voice saying, abrupt and harsh, "I am just wondering why the hell we are living, anyway, any of us, anywhere!"

And then, partly because he was appalled at himself, and partly because he had thought of death with an overpowering and desperate desire, he had gotten to his feet and had left all that pleasant tranquillity and the wood smoke and the silver and brandy and china and had literally fled from the room and the house—fled like someone under desperate threat. His feet had pounded on the raked gravel of the turntable outside, and along the paths, bordered by lawns still brilliantly green and filled with flower beds burning with salvia and calla and shaded by trees in the carnival colors of autumn, and he had not thought of one of his expensive cars. He had simply run like a flying youth, and he a man in his fifties. He had run until he reached the road beyond the house, after bursting open the grilled gates. And then, sweating like one who had just escaped death, he had stood there and had panted, bareheaded in the still warm sun, and saying over and over to himself, "God, God, God!" A bus—he never rode buses—came along stinking and grinding, and he had flung himself into it and had fallen on a seat, still panting. His hands were wet and his forehead.

He had ridden a long time. Blue twilight had fallen by the time he finally lifted his head and looked through a grimy window. The bus had stopped at one of the walks leading to that foolish "Sanctuary," and several people had gotten off, young and old, male and female, and on an impulse—he never knew why except that he had excited interest in the bus and he was suddenly aware of embarrassment—he left the vehicle too and trailed the silly little gathering up the red-gravel path to the gleaming whiteness of the building at the top of the low hill.

The group opened the bronze doors—beautiful doors

really; he was surprised at their expensive artistry and their evident age. The door closed behind the group with no sound at all, and he was left alone on the wide marble step, staring at the doors. Italian. Probably from some very old church. Expertly polished; they glimmered like old gold in the last light of the day. Here and there, along the many winding paths that led to the Sanctuary, soft gaslamps were burning. Not electricity, bleak and constant. What an affectation! And coming down to it, how had he gotten here, and why?

He turned his back to the doors and surveyed the immense and silent lawns all about the magnificent low building which was windowless, flat-roofed, smooth as silk and as white as milk. He had often driven past this area, these four acres of park filled with flowers and blossoming trees and little grottoes. An Italian fountain had been added several years ago, a tall marble youth, chastely naked, with head thrown back and lifted to the sky, and an expression of joy on the noble young face, the arms tautly held back as if preparing for flight. Pagan. But really a fine example of neo-classical art. The gemmed water sparkled to the very top of the large head so that always the statue shone and twinkled as if in a mist. He, John Service, had brought visitors to the city to look at the lawns of the parklike land, a green carpet in the very midst of towering apartment and office buildings, holding off progress with the hands of leafy trees and the frail bright arrogance of flowers. He would point out the Sanctuary to his visitors, and they would laugh at his humorous retelling of the tale of its origin. He had laughed, also. Once he had been on a committee which had made a resolution to the effect that it was "depriving our people" to let such a charming place remain in the hands of a "private group." "We could," said the resolution, "establish a small zoo for the benefit of The Children on this land, or make it a picnic ground, or build a music hall on it, or assign it for Community Activities. Even a school." "By all means, a school!" cried some members of the PTA who were on the committee and who never would have been satisfied even if there had been classrooms of only five students each in every school in the city. It had been the members of the PTA—and the memory of rising school taxes—which had induced John Service, to the surprise of everyone, to vote against the resolution.

But he had always been conscious of the fact that the Sanctuary was an embarrassment to him personally, and to his friends. It was offensive, really. People came from all over the country to visit the Sanctuary, and even from foreign countries. Once, it was rumored, an Indian group from the United Nations had called here, jeweled and exotic. John Service was always apologizing to visitors. "Maudlin, of course. Tasteless, of course. Some old man, years ago—sentimental nonsense! Catering to the popular taste— Extremely mortifying, actually. You mustn't judge our robust and expanding city and our realistic and modern point of view by this anachronism, this absurdity. No, we can't do anything about it, unfortunately. A private group runs it, on the income from a tremendous amount of capital. We don't even know their names. Yes, I've tried to find out— No one will talk."

He had never come as far as the doors until this evening. What would people think if the prominent John Service were seen here, at any time, even on exploration? He could imagine the laughter of his friends, and the affectionate ridicule. He began to whistle soundlessly as he stood on the wide marble step, surveying the grounds, his hands in the pockets of his Saville Row suit, his lean shoulders back, his tanned face expressionless, his light blue eyes quiet, but knowing and frank as in his youth, his lightly grayed hair just stirring in the evening breeze.

Then he was conscious of something terrible. His mind was signaling nothing to him, nothing at all, that active, alert mind which was his pride, which was always commenting on something vigorously. His skull felt as empty as if all its contents had been poured out. And in the place of emotion and conjecture there was a dark and awful silence, a numbness, a nothingness. It was too massive to be despair, too quiet.

He tried to think about it, to comment on it, to wonder about it. But every feeble thought was like a dying blade of grass, crushed down by a heavy heel and killed at once. He struggled, mentally. But it was the struggle of a man in paralysis. Only one thought came and stayed, a bright flicker in that ghastly blackness: Death. All sound left him; he did not hear the dry rustle of the flamelike trees and the music of the fountain. He did not hear the clangor and roar of the great city beyond these silent lawns and the soft lamplight. He was like one in a vacuum. He was alone.

He found his hand on the bronze knob of the door; he found himself opening the door and glancing within. A pleasant enough room, he thought vaguely. Quite nicely furnished. Books and magazines on glass tables. And about six people waiting. Waiting for what? Yes, he remembered. They went into the room beyond, it had been told him with easy laughter, and a psychiatrist or a clergyman or a social worker was there, behind some theatrical curtain or perhaps a carved screen, and the unfortunate person listened to the illiterate wailings and whimperings of unimportant, inconsequential housewives and laborers and teen-agers, and then gave some sound advice, suited to the infantile personality which had approached him. How humiliating, how disgraceful. How, really, unsophisticated. He wondered why the city fathers and the clergy had not done something about it long ago, had not put an end to such a medieval situation.

The people waiting did not look up at him as he stood in the doorway, his hand holding the door open. (He had heard that once it closed it could not be opened from within.) They sat there, the ridiculous dolts, the superstitious peasants, sunken in their own petty and obscene little problems which they would pour out to the long-suffering sentimentalist who awaited them. He looked at their clothing, their shoes, their faces. He wanted to laugh at the cheapness of it all, the mawkish comicality. He tried for derisiveness. But nothing came. The solid and stony blackness in his mind did not move.

He found himself, to his utmost surprise, sitting on one of the chairs, a really comfortable chair in blue velvet. Then his face flushed hotly. In a moment these peasants would recognize John Service, the Leader of the City, the art connoisseur, the adviser of mayors and governors, the elegant counselor of politicans, the familiar of Presidents, the Richest Man in Town, the lawyer, the chairman of the board of directors of several banks, the man whose face was constantly in the newspapers. Then they would stare like owls and whisper to each other and furtively point. He began to rise, his temples throbbing with mortified blood.

But no one looked at him. No one was even conscious of his presence. They were armored in their own pain.

It might be interesting, he thought. It really might be interesting, once and for all, to know what the devil is beyond that door in that other room. If he found out, he desperately assured himself, then he would be in a position to put an end to this blot on the city. Once and for all. He would call in all the newspapers, and they would bring TV cameras, and in a stately and judicious fashion he would explain why he had decided to help rid the city of something which was a constant embarrassment to the inhabitants and an insult to the intelligence of the community. Why, the President, only a few months ago, had mocked at him about the Sanctuary.

The President would be running for re-election next year, and he had said to John Service, "I hear you have a fortune-telling establishment, or shrine, in your city, John. I'm thinking of going down for a palm-reading, myself!" He must remember to quote the President. But he would not quote the Archbishop who had said to him very rudely, "Why the hell don't you mind your own business, Jack, or visit the place, yourself?" John had never liked clergymen. He liked them less now.

This damnable black stone in his skull which had replaced his brain! A chime sounded and a stout old woman rose, fumbling with her knitting, and went to the farther door, opened it, closed it behind her. Fat old frump. No doubt she was seeking advice on how to reduce her enormous grease. The psychiatrist in there would probably tell her to stop eating. Detestable people, the working class. Now he, John Service, was a liberal, of course, but one drew the line somewhere. Draw the line, draw the line, draw the line, said the suddenly awakened demon in his skull, which immediately began to sing again, "Sweet and Lovely!" There was a sound of thinly tapping soles in his brain, tap, tap, tap. "Sweet and Lovely!" screeched the demon's voice, and then there was a howl of mirth. John Service put his hands against his temples; he was certain that the screaming mirth was pounding at his fingers. I am losing my mind, he thought. I must go somewhere— But where? Death. "Sweet and Lovely!" shrieked the hellish voice in the chamber of his skull. Then the voice dropped to a dulcet murmur. "Everything always so pleasant, so peaceful, so regulated, so serene, so satisfying. It is nice, isn't it? That's the way life should be, shouldn't it?"

Someone nudged him. It was the gentlest of nudges, but John Service felt it as a blow and he recoiled in his chair. A young girl with a piteous white face was trying to smile at him. "You're next," she whispered, a look of surprise in her weary eyes at his extravagant recoil from her. "Pardon me," he answered with automatic politeness. He did not stir. She pointed, after a moment, to the farther door. "In there," she said. He stared at the door. "I?" he said. "You," she said, more surprised than ever.

It was to escape her imminent recognition that he got to his feet and went to the door, past others who had come and whom he had not seen enter after himself. He opened the door, hesitating, partly because his legs were trembling violently. He paused on the threshold. He had not known what to expect, for no one had ever told him. He had thought to find a large desk there on a carpeted floor, and an easy chair facing it for the "client." He had thought to find a business-like person behind the desk, with a kind and harried face, probably a psychiatrist. But there was no one there, not even the previous visitor. Tall white walls of marble, softly and mysteriously lit. One carved white chair covered with blue velvet. And an alcove, entirely hidden by a blue velvet curtain. He thought, irrelevantly, of the marble tablet in the wall of the other room with its flowing inscription: "I can do all things in Him Who strengthens me."

So, that was it. A clergyman with psychiatric training. He wanted to burst out laughing. He leaned against the door he had closed behind him and his laughter came, terrible, raucous, horrifying even to himself. But he could not stop it. It burst from him like a poisoned spout, like vomit. Like vomit, acrid, burning, tearing, hideous, roaring from some secret place in himself, some desperate and dreadful place. He heard the hoarse echoes of it. He put his hands over his mouth. But behind his fingers his mouth was open and convulsed. Finally, after an awful struggle, it died away.

What, in God's name, would the man behind the theatrical curtain think of him from that perverted noise? That indecent noise? And from where had it come? He had never made such a display of himself before, no, not even in his childhood.

He swung about, aghast with his shame, and tried to open the door through which he had entered. But there was no knob. He had an impulse to scream like a child and batter the door. Only lifelong training prevented him, and he dropped his clenched hands. At least, there was no sound in the room, no murmur of consternation or of mortifying pity. Nothing stirred behind that curtain. The man who listened merely waited. But he must know his "client" or at least whether he was male or female, and his approximate age. There must be a one-way mirror, or something, or a peephole. John smoothed his hair automatically and straightened himself. My God, he thought, he will recognize me! Of course, ethics will prevent him from gossiping. But, who is he? Someone I know personally? If so, then I'll see a smirk on a hundred faces in town.

"I should like," he said with dignity, "to find a way out of this room. I came on a personal investigation, for the sake of the community. You know what a scandal this place is to thoughtful people. I'm surprised that a man of your status should be an accomplice to this rot. Oh, that door in the rear.

Thank you, very much. Goodnight. I've seen all I wanted to see, and believe me, it is quite enough!"

He went to the door near the curtain, and opened it. A wave of fresh evening air, scented with wood smoke, came to him, peaceful and fresh and autumnal. He drew it into his lungs. Then he thought of his house and the tea party, and the stunning numbness hit his mind again and again he heard the insidious whisper: "Death." Sweet and Lovely!

The door slipped from his hand. He turned about. His wild eyes saw the tall marble chair facing the curtain. Slowly, step by step, he approached it. Weariness fell over him, and he sat down. "I probably know you," he said to the curtain. "I can trust in your discretion, can't I? After all, if anyone heard —I'd never hear the end of it! Mary, my wife. She's tried for years to get rid of this place, and you. Humiliating. I can trust you, can't I?"

He waited. And then he started. Had he really heard a deep masculine voice say, "If you cannot trust me, then you can trust no man." Crazy. He had really heard nothing. But the voice was echoing in the stony corridors of his mind.

As he was courteous by nature John said, "Thank you. Of course you as a psychiatrist, or a clergyman, are bound by the ethics of your profession. I'm very fond of psychiatrists, actually. I've even thought of consulting one lately—" He was freshly humiliated that he had revealed something he had thought of only in the recesses of his mind and then had laughed it off. John Service going to a psychiatrist! It was laughable, he the well-adjusted, the serene and tranquil Leader of the City, who had never known a moment's disquiet in his rich, well-ordered life!

The curtain did not move. But all at once John was conscious of a presence, of someone who was listening, politely, with kindness, with detachment and yet with utterly concerned affection. Ah, so it was someone he knew then. Or someone, at least, who knew him.

He was not confiding by nature, though everyone thought of him as totally candid and outgoing. He always spoke frankly, fearing nothing, for there had been nothing in his life which had ever frightened him or hurt him or judged him or criticized him. His life had been like—a river of cream.

"I don't know why," he said, "but I want to die. That's all I've been thinking about lately. Suicide. It's probably the male climacteric." He laughed gently. "Hormones, or something. I'd go to my doctor except that I'm shamefully healthy.

He knew me all my life, by the way. Only last week he congratulated me on having a 'dream life.'"

He stopped. Then suddenly he cried out, "A dream life! A nightmare! The worst nightmare a man can ever know!"

He listened to his words. He said to himself, "What in hell do I mean? What, in Christ's name, did I *say?*" He said, almost stammering, "I'm an idiot. I had no intention of saying that. No one has ever had a happier life than mine. You must excuse me. You know who I am. You are probably wondering what I mean. I'm wondering, too. It was all subconscious. As you know me, you are well aware that nothing has ever touched me in life. Everything was given me from the very moment I was born. Loving parents, devoted parents. I'm the only child, as you know. The best schools. The best people. The Ivy League university. The girl everyone wanted to marry, Mary Shepherd. The best friends a man could ever have—people I'd known all my life. Travel after I was graduated. All the money I ever wanted. Health. Always escaped a war. A child at the first, influence at the second. Yes, influence. I was a dollar-a-year man in Washington. Steel procurement. Wonderful house in Georgetown. That was a splendid war; never enjoyed anything so much in my life; all that excitement in Washington, and the uniform I wore, and the dances. And my wedding. The President attended. He and I had much in common, you know. Our families had always known each other. We often had intimate chats together.

"And then my children. John Junior, vice-president of the biggest bank here. Prissy, our girl. Wonderful marriage she made, better even than Johnnie's. And Sidney. Carried all the honors of his class at Yale; married a marvelous girl. I have seven grandchildren, as you know. Each one more perfect than the other. No one ever thought about money; it was always there. I inherited ten million dollars, you remember. Mary inherited more than that from her parents and grandparents. Everyone has always wanted me to run for governor, or senator. But too busy, you know? Too busy enjoying life, and my fine family. And Mary—you will remember her— adorable. No one can beat Mary. We never exchanged a bitter word in all these twenty-nine years of marriage. Except that time I mishandled the yacht on the way to Florida—you remember our house in Palm Beach? Right near the Kennedys. I never thought about them. After all, only second generation money. Ours goes back six generations, or even more. There's something about inherited money. It gives you status. Thank God I inherited it and don't have to try to make it now, with taxes! Taxes prevent newcomers from rising to our Rank. 'It was planned that way,' you know? We have to have an aristocracy of family and money sometime. We aren't on the frontier any longer."

He looked with a confident smile at the curtain. Not a deep fold moved. It was a little disconcerting. "Maybe I should have run for office," he said, tentatively. "We need patricians in Washington, not plebeians such as we've had, except for Roosevelt. What do you think?"

There was no answer. But the sense of someone listening was acute.

"If ever a man was blessed—and I'm the first to admit it—it is myself," said John. "I've never known a day's illness or pain. Neither has Mary. Nor my children, nor their children. Health is our greatest blessing, after money. I'm not one of those who deprecate money. It's the greatest power in the world. I have it. I have everything."

The taste of vomit rose in his throat, and again he put his hand to his mouth. Then his hand dropped and he cried out, "I have nothing at all! I have nothing but happiness! And it is nothing! I want to kill myself! I can't go back to that house, where I was born! I'd rather be dead!"

A breath of coldness seemed to project itself from behind the curtain, and yet it was mingled with sadness. John put his face in his hands; he rocked in the chair as if he were overcome by a tremendous physical agony. "Nothing but happiness," he groaned. "Nothing but happiness."

He was suddenly rigid. Had he really heard that voice say, "No, not even that"? He dropped his hands. His pale face, white under the tan, flushed. "Don't be ridiculous," he said. "I'm the happiest man in the world. It's just a matter of middle-age funk. I'm fifty-six. I'm looking at sixty, just over the horizon. Sixty, then seventy, then eighty— No! I can't live forever, and that's the terrible part of it. I can't live forever, and so I want to die now." He paused. "Isn't that the damndest paradox you ever heard? But I'm afraid of growing old, of leaving this world I want to leave with all my heart now."

There was no reply. John muttered, "I won't grow old and senile, and lose all my happiness. It is better to die now, and be done with it, instead of watching all those faded years. Still, my grandfather lived to ninety-five and enjoyed every moment of it." He began to smile brightly. "Good old gent, tough old gent. He didn't mind dying. He said, and I remember it very well, 'As Stevenson said, "Glad did I live and gladly die, And lay me down with a will." ' Crazy, isn't it? Old Fundamentalist bastard, and I mean that fondly, I really do. He believed in something he called God. Never made a dishonest penny in his life."

His voice changed, became rough and harsh. "What are we living for?" he asked the curtain. He did not know his was the frightened voice of a child.

No one answered him. The silence was so profound that he could hear his own breath. There was no clamoring of traffic; he might have been alone on the desert. The desert. He remembered something very dimly: Someone had been in a desert for a long time. Hadn't he eaten honey and wild locusts? Strange how those old myths, surrounding old forgotten names or names not ever known, came back to one at odd moments. But it must be like this in the desert at night. The very thought of a boundless nothing curiously affrighted John Service and made him cringe internally as at the threat of an ancient pain too well remembered. Night and boundlessness; no end to any of it anywhere, no matter how far one might travel. Now terror took his throat, and he swallowed and moved his head.

He spoke in a low tone, "I don't know what the hell's wrong with me. I'll confess something to you. I was never what people call an intellectual, though everyone thinks I am. I belong on a dozen cultural committees in this city; I'm supposed to be an expert on modern art. I am responsible for the historical museum, or at least for its expansion. I'm negotiating, now, to bring the Elgin Marbles here for an exhibition; it's an enormous idea, but not more enormous than the idea of bringing Michelangelo's *Pietá* to New York. Everyone consults me when he has a fine, expensive idea as to how to improve the cultural climate in the city. Expensive. They can rely on me for a large check. And that's where my 'intellect' comes in.

"Oh, I didn't exactly flunk out at Harvard, but I always knew I had been accepted because of the family name, and the fact that my great-grandfather was an honored alumnus, and that my grandfather and father were on the Board. I had had such a happy time at my preparatory school; no one expected me to be more intelligent than I was, and God knows, looking back, I can see that my intelligence has only been average. But all was made delightful for me all my life; it was the money, you know? Then, I was considered handsome, even as a boy, and I was an athete, one of the best. And I could always get along with people. I have the social arts; I inherited them from my mother who was a charming woman." He halted, and frowned. "The most loving parents a man could ever remember. It's peculiar that I should remember, just now, that their deaths didn't disturb me very much. I wonder why. Was it because I had always been so insulated against life from birth? They died within six months of each other. All my friends and relatives spoke of the 'shock' to me. I was relieved; I've never been the best of actors, so I let them think what they wanted to think; yes, I was relieved that they thought me numb with grief, or something. I've always been frank; their deaths hardly touched me at all. Death never did. It was handled so discreetly that it became another social event, a little sadder than most, but always artistic and exactly right. The body was consigned to the grave in a storm, a very quiet storm, of flowers and one continued to live, pleasantly as always, and just as serenely. The lawyers handled everything. I was just twenty-one years old.

"I never gave a thought about what had happened to my parents; even the causes of their death remained nicely mysterious. But now I think my father died of cancer, and my mother also. I don't remember any sign of illness in the house; there was never any talk of hospitals, or any hospitals, either. My parents simply died. A little sad, but there it was. Then I studied law; I wasn't good at that, either, but the river of cream carried me forward and I just stepped into my father's office and was at the head of his firm—six of the best lawyers in the state. They did everything. The river of cream flowed tranquilly on."

He felt his arms pushing him to his feet. The bile was again in his mouth. "My parents' deaths were the only disturbing things in my life, and I wasn't really concerned with them. I don't even remember if I loved them. They made life so comfortable for me." He looked desperately at the blue curtain. "Is that what is wrong?"

As there was no answer he began to walk up and down the room in his favorite courtroom fashion, serious, absorbed, faintly frowning. It inevitably impressed judges and juries; no one, however, could recall that he had ever pleaded a case. There was always a highly competent lawyer, in his employ, or in his partnership, who took care of such sordid matters. He, John Service, applied—what was the word?—the props. But he liked the picture of himself during one of "his" important cases; he liked the image in the eyes of the spectator. But law bored him; only the public spectacle of himself gave him enjoyment. He had so many things to do.

"I had so many other things to do," he said aloud. "So many more interesting things. I was busy all the time, from my very childhood. There was never a moment that wasn't filled with laughter, traveling, sailing, playing games, enjoying myself, visiting people like my own family, dancing, racing cars, buying and selling excellent horses, riding, listening to the best of music—not that I cared too much for that— moving among my own kind, having one hell of a good time. A hell of a good time. A hell—"

He swung about and confronted the curtain and half-lifted his hand as if to halt a question. But there was no question. He let his hand drop. "That's a stupid thing for me to say," he muttered. Then his voice sharpened, "But it's true! It was hell; it is hell. And paradoxically I want to escape it and I am afraid that I will escape it."

He approached the curtain quickly, but stopped when it was within touching distance. He saw the button at the side which informed him that if he wished to see the listener he had only to touch the button. But his hand shrank back as if it had been about to touch something loathsome. He shivered. "What was I saying?" he said.

"Yes. I can't bear living, but I want to live. I can't bear growing older, for that will bring me closer to the end of my life—which I want to end now. Why do I want it to end? My sweet and lovely life, my happy life, my busy life, always filled with pleasure and comforts and ease and serenity. My very busy life!"

He had never felt so old and tired as he did now, and he was alarmed beyond any alarm he had ever known before. He had just had his fall check-up; his doctors assured him that he was, biologically, ten years younger than his chronological age. Mary was still in love with him, and he was as ardent as he had been ten years after their marriage. He was still in love with Mary. Yet he was so tired now, and he felt so old and so broken, as if he had run a long and noisy race and he had fallen on the winning rope, exhausted. Yes, it had been a long and noisy race, always full of cheering and affectionate voices, and there was always the prize waiting for him at the end and he had never been bored by the prizes. Each race had been a joy. If, he thought, it had actually been a race at all, and not merely a staged event with himself the inevitable winner.

"I've never regretted a thing I've ever done," he said to the gleaming blue curtain that confronted him and hid the listener from him. "Wasn't it Spinoza who said it was a double sign of weakness to feel remorse or regret? I love Mary, but I've had my women all my married life, and enjoyed every one of them. I had only to put out my hand—I never once gave it a thought—about Mary, I mean. If she guessed she never told me. She is the most serene woman I've ever known. Did she ever prance, herself? I'll never know that and I really don't care. We have the most satisfying marriage in the world; it's a grand success. Everyone says so.

"It's funny, though, I don't remember Mary and me ever having a long, quiet conversation together, at any time, not even in bed. I don't remember myself ever having a long quiet conversation with anyone, for that matter, not even my parents. And not my children, of course. They are as self-contained, and as busy, as Mary and I always were, and still are. Always busy, always coming and going, always surrounded by other people and voices and music and social events; always happy and serene."

The tiredness was now so heavy on him that he sat again in the chair. "My God," he muttered, "why am I so tired?" He took out his handkerchief and wiped his face, though the room was cool and seemed scented with the fresh fragrance of fern. He remembered the marble tablet in the other wall, and he smiled faintly. "I can do all things in Him Who strengthens me." "Well," he said, "I did, and do, all things in myself and it never occurred to me to need anyone's help. After all, a man must stand on his own. That is what I did— No! I never had any need to stand on my own, not one day in my creamy life!"

Now he began to speak in a rapid and disordered tone. "It first came to me, about a year ago. I remember it now. There is so much talk these days about the 'space age.' People are always getting so excited over an 'age.' I remember the 'air' age, and how we were exhorted to be 'air-conscious.' Then it was the 'jet' age, and before that the 'atomic' age. There's always an age. You'd think people would remember that, but they think every morning or every event is just out of its clean cellophane wrapper.

"Yes, I remember how it all happened to me. The space age. The astronauts. We had a pleasant discussion at the club about it, those young fellows in their capsule. And then when I went to bed I couldn't sleep and I didn't know why. Usually I fall asleep in a minute or two at the most; I've never even had a headache to disturb me in my life, or a pain. And then I saw that 'space' they're always talking about lately. I explored it with my eye. I saw the universes fall and lift, all the colors of the rainbow against the black emptiness of space. My roving eye rushed on and on, past systems and constellations, looking for the boundaries, looking for space to curve, as Einstein said it did. But on what does it curve? Yes, I've seen those demonstrations with a strip of paper; you twist it some way—I never quite understood what it was—and if you went in one direction long enough you'd turn in space and you'd arrive back to where you started, without having taken one backward step. No, I never did quite understand. After all, you can do the same thing in traveling around the world. But beyond the world is space, and other worlds and other systems and constellations and galaxies—

"I found myself sitting up in bed staring at the darkness and my heart was thumping, and I actually felt pain in my chest! There was no end to space, even if it curved. You could rush forever through eternity, through endless universes, and there was no end to it. I tell you, I almost lost my mind! I could feel it totter, and lurch, and a horrible sensation came to me as if I were dying. I knew you'd never come back to the same spot."

He did not know when he had stood up but now he saw that he was once more before the curtain, and he was panting and his shadow trembled on the white wall near him.

"Endless space," he whispered, "endless universes and galaxies and constellations. What is the meaning of it? How did it come into existence? Where is it going, all of it? And why? I never once thought of it before, but since I thought of it I've wanted to die, to kill myself. Chasm after chasm of dark space, spotted with those damned glowing universes spinning on themselves—chasm after chasm—going on forever. Even when I think of it now I could feel my brain staggering and sweating. Why?"

He saw his hand, without its will, hovering over the button and again he shrank.

"Can you understand, you in there? Here I had been living my serene and pleasant life, with no disturbances, my busy, busy life, filled with comfortable or delightful events, and calm talk—always on the surface, you know—and traveling, and visiting the children and the grandchildren, and visiting friends—wonderful busy life. And all at once, my important life, my important city, my important family and wife, my important place in society, and in the country, dwindled down to nothing and was of no importance at all! I lived on a world that was hardly a sparkle even in its own solar system, and was not even a sparkle in its place in the galaxy, and would never be known on the billions of worlds which occupied that damnable, that damnable! endless space. It was the space, you see, the endless space. And none of what filled it was important, either. It was all meaningless, just as my life is meaningless and always was, my busy, busy life."

There was sweat on his forehead and on his cheeks and on his hands. He was wiping it away without knowing what he was doing. His panting was quicker and louder in the utterly silent room. He had forgotten how he had come to be here; he had forgotten everything.

"I—I've tried to talk about this to other people. They just stare at me. They didn't know how frantic I was. I talked to Mary. And she said comfortably, 'Well, it doesn't do, does it, to think a great deal about that? You could really go off your rocker. We'll never know. So we just live as pleasantly and as serenely as we can, every day, and let the scientists think about all those things. That's best, isn't it?' That's what Mary said.

"But now, God help me, it's not 'best' for me at all! I can't stop thinking, and when I think I hate living, and then I am afraid to die and leave everything that I have, which is everything any man would want. Why can't I put it out of my mind, and just go on enjoying myself, with my friends and family and the agreeable amount of work I do? It would be easier if I had any religion; then I'd let some mumble-jumble from a minister fill that spot in my mind. It would be easier if time had a stop, and I'd remain forever where I am. But, you see, I am growing older. In four years I'll be sixty— And then, someday, there will be the end, and I'll go out into the darkness. I won't even see those infernal universes."

He flung up his hands in an acute gesture of despair. "I'll be nothing, just as my busy, teeming life is nothing. And I won't be conscious to know that I am nothing. If only my family, in my childhood, had known any religion. Oh, they took me to church with them, for propriety's sake, when I was very young. And, of course, there were always the proper marriages and confirmations and baptisms and funerals to attend, and a fine smooth minister to say the proper soothing words and congratulate his God on having so well-ordered and polished a congregation to bless.

"There were only words. I remember hardly any of them, if any. I sat soberly with my parents, and then with my wife, and then with the whole family, and friends, on the occasions when it was the thing to go to church. But it was all only words, and boresome. I always counted the minutes until I could go back to my busy life, my orderly and contented and interesting life.

"My life which is now nothing at all, because it was never anything."

Again he flung up his hands and one struck the blue curtain. It trembled as if a wind, a boundless wind, blew behind it, and he was terrified. "Help me!" he cried. "I was never a colorful man, an intellectual. But you must be; you've heard all these stories —But don't console me, for God's sake, as Mary tried to do! Don't tell me to stop thinking, to stop looking at space, and at the stars at night as I do now, and fix my eyes just on this daily round. Don't tell me that! It won't do any good; it won't save my life and what reason I have left. Who was it said, 'Consider the stars'? Isn't that Biblical, or maybe Shakespeare? If someone greater than I urged others to 'consider the stars' then it can't be nonsense, can it? There must be a reason, mustn't there? God, there *must* be a reason! Tell me it's a mystery, and I'll believe in what you say to me, and it'll be some comfort. But, even mysteries have a frame of reference, and before God—before God?—I need a frame of reference!"

Slowly his hand approached the button, and then it rested on the cool silver. But he could not bring himself to press it yet. He was afraid of the calm face he would encounter, the compassionately amused eyes; he was afraid of the placid voice, soothing him, telling him to return to the once-loved toys which were now horrible to him.

"Surely," said John Service in a voice he would have considered craven only a year ago, "I'm not alone. Surely others have asked the same question and have felt the same fear. Surely others have felt—forsaken. Forsaken! That's how I feel. If others feel so, why haven't I found them, so we could talk it out together and forget we are alone? Or, do they feel it, so many of them—all those who commit suicide?"

Now his fingers pressed the button and the curtains silently parted and flew aside. Beaming light fell over his face like a wave of brightness. And in that brightness stood the man who listened, and who listens forever.

John Service looked and at last he was silent. He began to fall back, slow step after slow step; but his eyes never left the face of the man. He could feel the great eyes looking at him and into him, and he saw the tremendous compassion in them. He uttered a faint sharp cry and laid his arms on the top of the chair and buried his face in them. He did not know he was crying; he could not remember that he had ever cried. His lean and disciplined body shuddered over and over, and he shrank in himself as if bitterly cold.

And then at last he remembered some words—or did someone speak them in the room?—"Be still, and know that I am God."

Be still. Be very still. Be removed from all the busyness of life if only for a little space, a little time. Be still enough not to hear all the world's pleasant voices, or even the ugly ones. Just be silent. Still. "Be still, and know that I am God." And in the knowing, know that all is well and on some day you know not of all will be explained.

Be still, and know that you can bear your life, that it has a distinct and unique meaning, belonging only to you, important more to God than even to yourself, and that to God it is of more worth than the sun or a billion suns. With that importance in his heart a man can walk fearless, joyful with a true joy, peaceful with a peace that no pleasure can give, and no busy life satisfy.

"No, no," said John, his head still on his cradling arms. "I can't believe it. Not even though you said it, yourself. For you see, I can't believe you know anything about it, or ever did. It was all such a tragedy—if it ever happened at all."

He turned his head a little and looked at the man with reddened eyes.

"You thought it was important, all of it, didn't you?" he said. "How tragic. It isn't, you know. Did you discover that for yourself, later, or were you really not—"

He was not an imaginative man. But all at once he thought he saw a powerful sentience in those majestic eyes, in that tormented yet truly serene face. He thought the eyes focused on him and saw only him, and that there was actually a voice in his ears which said, "I have not forsaken you, busy child. All your thoughts have been my thoughts, and all your fear of being forsaken was my fear, also, for do I not bear your flesh and your wounds—though you did not know they were wounds? Come to me, and let us speak together, out of our human nature, and let us reason together, and be still, and know that there is God."

Later, he was certain that the man had spoken so to him. He could remember the very tone of that deep grave voice, that manly voice, the voice of a father. But he could never tell anyone of this, for it was his secret alone. He moved around the chair and sat down and as he did so, facing the man, the black cold agony left his mind and the only true serenity he had ever known replaced it. All that he had thought was serenity in his past life was revealed to be what it truly was: Sound that meant nothing, joy that was not joy, delight that was not delight, contentment that was only a luxurious animal's contentment.

He said at last with humility, "It will be very hard for me, you know. It won't come easy to remember what you said, and act on it. How shall I act on it? Will you tell me? Yes, I am sure you will tell me. But how strange my life will be, then! How mysteriously strange. I don't even know if I'll like it!

"But I do know one thing. I've got to find a different way, and a reason. I've got to believe something I've never even dreamed of, not once in my life. But it's going to be exciting." He smiled, as if in apology. "It's going to be the most exciting thing I've ever encountered. An adventure. A wonder. That, at the very least, will make life worth living. At the best, if I come on it, then it will be all the world, and more. I'll have my answer at last, and I won't know fear any longer, or confusion, or despair."

SOUL TEN: *The New Breed*

> "They have taken away my Lord and I do not know
> where they had lain Him."
>
> JOHN 20:13

"Where're you going, Lucy?" asked a young girl of her companion as they moved together to the parking lot of the campus.

"Well, I thought I'd just run around—someplace," said Lucy Marner.

Her friend peered at her inquisitively. "Something wrong? You haven't been looking on the ball for a couple of months." The friend giggled. "Nothing wrong, uh?"

Lucy flushed. "No," she said in a short tone. She did not invite her friend to accompany her. "But I—well, I'm going to the doctor for the early summer check-up. No use waiting until the end of the semester, when things begin. 'Bye now, Sandy." She walked very fast to the parking lot. She was usually proud of her smart white convertible and would glance over it to be sure no hot-rod had marred its bright finish. But today she merely threw herself onto the red leather seat and roared off the campus. Friends, young men and women, hailed her but she did not reply for she did not hear them. The heat of the early summer day poured down on her bare red head and her pale set face and shone in her green eyes. She was a pretty girl, only twenty, but despair had tightened her expression, a despair which had been increasing for over a year as she learned more and more and really knew less and less.

"Stupid, stupid, stupid," she addressed the great arching trees over the road of the campus which led to the street. A squirrel ran across her path and without volition she stepped on the accelerator to run it down. It skipped up a tree, terrified, and Lucy said aloud, but faintly, "Oh, excuse me, I didn't meant to do that. But my God, why did you bother getting out of the way? Why does any of us?"

171

Stupid, stupid, stupid, sang the tires on the street as Lucy recklessly drove. Everything is stupid, stupid, stupid. "Sing, bright Spring!" said Lucy. "Sing yourself to death, you idiot bastard!" Idiot yourself, she remarked inwardly. Why are you doing this, anyway, going to that kookie place?

She came to a busy thoroughfare and stopped for a red light. Her eye fell on the textbooks on the seat beside her. Again without volition, but with violence, she swept the books onto the floor and kicked them with her heel, over and over, with increasing lack of control. Someone sounded an impatient horn behind her, and she screamed a curse over her shoulder. Then she roared on, reckless of traffic and alarmed horns. Her red hair, long and straight, streamed behind her like a flag, and her white profile had the tenseness of a leaning statue. "Oh, stupid, stupid, stupid," she moaned softly, screaming around a corner. "Go home, you imbecile, go home and smile, and smile and smile, and be lovely to Dad and Mom, and answer the telephone messages, and plan and plan and plan for all the exciting activities for the summer."

There was the most taut pain in her slender shoulders and the back of her neck. There was an aching in the small of her back. She fumbled in her purse for the tranquilizers Dr. Morton had given her two months ago. Then she pushed the purse onto the floor also, where it lay on top of the kicked books. No, she thought. I don't want to feel so calm for a while. This thing has to be faced eventually, face to face. But, what is there to face? What's the *matter* with me, anyway? Maybe I need a headshrinker, who'll smile at me urbanely and tell me I don't want to face maturity and just want to be a kid all my life. But what in hell is there to *face*? Maybe it's only excess hormones, after all, but I'm not going to be like Sandy and the others, wrestling and sweating around and worrying whether the Enovid's going to work this month. Maybe I'm maladjusted. Granny, why the hell did you ever tell me all those superstitions? You did this to me— You clot! Why don't you look where you're going?"

She was addressing a sedate elderly man who was driving his car with excessive caution along the noisy street which she had entered. The man stared at the furious young vision in the gay convertible and he thought to himself: No responsibility these days. Everything given 'em without effort. Everything soft and easy for them. No worries. What we need is a good depression again, to shake 'em loose and make them go

172

to work. Look at that girl in her fancy car! Bed of roses, like they used to say.

I could, thought Lucy, whose eyes were smarting dryly, drive this heap down to the river and just keep going. Oh, come off it. That's no answer. Or, is it?

She thought of her devoted and gay youngish parents and involuntarily she swung her car about and started toward the river. Then at the next corner she called herself a vile name, turned the car again and resumed her drive. It's insane, she thought. I can't really be going *there!* But where else is there to go? Who will give me the answers? A clergyman? Dr. Pfeiffer, with his glossy collar and his talks to Dad about golf and the Racial Problem and our Community Responsibilities and our Duties to Those less Privileged? That's all they talk about when he comes to our house and sips a nice little discreet glass of sherry or maybe a weak highball. Sitting there with all the polished antiques around them and the hi-fi going softly, and the pictures shining on the walls in the last sun—just before dinner! What if I told him about me, and this *thing* in my chest and my mind? He'd say, "But dear child, I've been talking about that in my pulpit—" Have you, Dr. Pfeiffer, Reverend Pfeiffer? Have you, damn you, *have* you? No, you haven't! Maybe you think it's all settled so you don't even have to mention it. I have news for you: It's never settled. There's no deposit of knowledge in the younger generation; do you think it's acquired by osmosis, Reverend Pfeiffer, or that we breathe it in, in this lovely, sweet, tolerant, wishy-washy Christian civilization, all full of tenderness and compassion for the Disadvantaged? Dr. Pfeiffer, you're an ass! You've fallen down on the job, Dr. Pfeiffer, clunketty-clunk. We're all so civilized, aren't we? Nowadays the things that preoccupy us are Civil Rights, segregation, desegregation, integration. Dr. Pfeiffer, does it ever occur to you that the Negro doesn't want to "loved" by us, damn it? He just wants to be treated like an ordinary man, Reverend, and the hell with our "love!" The hell with everything, Dr. Pfeiffer, and go back to your sweet and stylish wife and your golf game! Go back to the Sunday recessional, "A Mighty Fortress Is Our God," and know nothing, as usual, either about God or any Fortress at all in this Goddamn, stinking, senseless world! Oh, Granny, I could cut your throat! If it weren't for you I wouldn't be thinking of the river all the time.

She reached the place of the Sanctuary, the name the people of the city had given it over the years. There was a broad

173

path, intersected by narrower paths on the immense green lawns. She turned her car onto the wider path, but an old gardener working nearby came running. "You can't drive your car up there!" he shouted to her. "That's not a drive-way."

She stared at him with her eyes full of green fire, and she had an impulse to strike him down with her car as she had tried with the squirrel. She swallowed. "Where's the parking lot?" she demanded.

"Ain't none." He waved his hoe vaguely. "Park some-wheres on the street."

"You mean I have to *walk* up there?" She pointed incredulously to the shining white building on its gentle rise behind the golden willows and the blossoming crabapple trees and soaring elms.

He grinned at her. "Crippled? That why you got that go-cart of yours? What's the matter with your legs? You kids think walking an eighth of a mile or something is goin' to break you down. On your way, sister. Park on the street, if you can find someplace."

"So that kind of talk is what they teach you up there in that damned little chapel, is it?"

"Ain't never been in it. Just work here on the grounds." He grinned at her again. "Never needed to go in. What for? I ain't got no aches and pains. But you sure look as if you have, girlie! On your way, before I call the cops."

"The hell with you," said Lucy Marner, who had been taught all her life to be courteous to the Deprived. She swung her car around and was pleased that her tires made ruts in the beautifully cultivated grass and made the old man yell an-grily. She drove off. She circled all the adjacent streets for a long time, in that crowded business section which was also full of apartment houses and shops. Then at last she found a parking lot, at least a mile from the Sanctuary, and she whirled into it so fast that she almost collided with a car that was leaving. The attendant came running and shouting. She flung herself out of the car without a word, seized her purse, and ran, heedless of the ticket waved at her back.

"Crazy little bitch," began the attendant sympathetically to the startled matron in the car which Lucy had almost struck. "They get worse and worse," she responded. "Too much money, too much time, too much food, too much fun."

"You said it," replied the attendant, getting into Lucy's abandoned car. "Look at this job! Must've cost at least seven thousand dollars."

Lucy was running down the congested main street, dodging pedestrians who glared at her with umbrage. She had a wild appearance. Eventually, she became aware of laughs about her, and reduced her run to a fast walk. Beads of sweat appeared on her forehead; the glare of the late sun on the buildings blinded her eyes. She fumbled for her sunglasses; when she did not find them immediately she began to sob with dry frustration. At last she had them and she put them on and at once she was soothed. She was hidden; she was no one at all; she was protected. She smoothed her tossed hair with trembling hands, and shifted the light rose linen on her wet shoulders. Slow down, slow down, she told herself. He won't run away. What do they call him? The man who listens. He's always there, day and night. Wonder what his wife thinks of it? And why the hell are you going there, you fathead?

It was a long walk. She did not remember ever having walked so far in the city before. She had no worry about her parents' anxiety because she had not arrived home at the regular time—when she did, anyway. They believed in Respecting the Privacy of Our Children, and never asking any questions. She was twenty years old; but her parents had been Respecting her Privacy since she was ten years old. What did that mean? she asked herself. That they really didn't care a damn for her at all and only wanted not to be bothered? Her parents and their contemporaries and social counterparts believed in respecting the Privacy of everyone except the Culturally Deprived—who apparently neither wanted nor deserved any decent human reticence. Who had degraded them so? Her parents, and their kind. It was her parents and their kind, including Dr. Pfeiffer, who had brought her to this dithering state, and millions of other young people like her. This awful, empty, agonizing state. It would serve her parents right if she came home, sometime, vividly pregnant, or drugged. Or at least dead drunk and with her "clothing disarranged," as the newspapers delicately put it. She wondered if that was part of the reason why the papers reported so much "rising crime" as they did lately. What in God's name had the world really *given* young people like herself? Fun times, the best of food, education, money, cars, wonderful clothes, beauty parlors, refined lectures, "understanding of the adolescent," something they euphorically called "love," and that was about it. Even the so-called poor had all that, too. But, what else was there to "give"? They have really given us

175

nothing at all, thought Lucy, and thought again of the river, the cold dark river which would put a stop to questions.

The summer western sky was a brilliant scarlet when she reached the Sanctuary. The men working on the lawns had left. Now the lawns stretched before her with their flower beds and their trees and their neatly raked gravel paths. The sun lay on the red roof of the building yonder, like a fire itself. Lucy walked up the path; it was really steeper than it seemed. It was wide enough for a car; they should have a parking lot. Or, maybe no one ever came. No; it was rumored that the place was always full of whiners and sick people, to see the doctor or the psychiatrist or the clergyman, who waited to listen to them or hand them out a placebo. I'll be something different for him, thought Lucy with some hard grimness. He's never known anyone like me. I swear to God, if he gives me any of that psychiatric crap about "facing maturity" I'll spit in his face! What's immature about my body or my mind? What is there that I don't know?

I should have gone away to college, she thought, as she panted in the heat and with the effort of walking. That's what Dad and Mom wanted. "New experiences, new outlook. That's What Our Children Deserve in These Days." It was to spite them that I insisted on going to the university here. It occurs to me that I'm always thinking up ways to spite them lately. No, I've been spiting them ever since I was a kid. It was the only pleasure I ever had, spiting them. And they'd look so Hurt and Confused, but never a slam on my face, never that old-fashioned discipline. They never told me anything worthwhile at all!

She looked in her purse for her wallet, the beautiful gold purse her parents had given her on her last birthday. It was full of bills, as usual. She crumpled a ten-dollar bill in her hand, in preparation for the collection. That should please the replica of Dr. Pfieffer in there! I swear, she thought, if he tells me I'm so Advantaged and that I should direct my thoughts and actions to the betterment of "humanity" I'll give him a sample of the talk of The New Breed! That should curl the edges of his nice haircut. She was full of fresh hatred and fresh despair. She did not know whom she actually hated with such ferocity and such desolation. But there was a hunger in her for something she did not know, a ravenous hunger which was like furious starvation.

She pushed open the bronze doors with angry impatience and charged inside the room, terribly anxious only to confront the hypocrite who would lie to her as he had lied to multitudes of others, lie to her as she had been lied to all her life, with such kindness and such sickening "understanding." But she saw only three people in the waiting room, two elderly women and one young man with a face as desolate and intense as her own. It was a nice, quiet room, beautifully furnished. There was a marble tablet sunken in one marble wall: "I can do all things in Him Who Strengthens me." Silly damned thing. Who was "He"?

She sat down in an empty chair. No one looked at her though she looked at the others challengingly, especially the young man who wore a very fine sports coat. His hair was too long, too carefully combed. Lucy was accustomed to having young men stare at her and smile hopefully. She prepared a contemptuous expression, but the young man was not even aware of her presence. This startled her; she looked at him more closely. Why, he was one of her own kind! Funny. Did he feel the way she did, too? No, she was unique. He had another problem. But she smiled bitterly. She couldn't stand, any longer, young men of her generation. She glared at the youth. He, too, perhaps, had never been told anything of value, either. They were two of a kind. It was strange that she hated herself in him, and felt no pity and nothing but a hopefulness. So many of us! Perhaps I'm not unique at all.

She picked up a magazine, expecting only religious matter. But the magazine was a pictorial one, full of people in gay, exciting occupations or engaged in fun. She threw it aside. There was *The Wall Street Journal*. So, people like her father came here, too. She saw a dim nameplate. She looked at the stock-market reports with vague interest. Her father had given her a nice block of stock on her eighteenth birthday. Then a wave of sickness came over her and she threw aside the paper also. She wished she had brought one of her schoolbooks, for she had a final tomorrow. She hadn't studied, really, for nearly a month. What was the use?

She had been vaguely aware of a chiming which had intruded just a little on her thoughts, a soft chiming and then a rustle as people rose and went to that door yonder where the clergyman or the psychiatrist or the doctor or the social worker waited to talk to the intruders. She allowed herself the pleasure of thinking of what she would say to the kook inside. She would shout in his stupid face. Stupid, stupid, stupid. The whole stupid world.

The chime sounded. She ignored it. It chimed again, with gentle insistence. She lifted her fallen head. She was alone in the room. So the chime was for herself. She hesitated. Then she rose, smoothed down her wrinkled rose linen dress and slowly approached the door. It was cool in the room, but she was sweating again. In spite of her delicate deodorants she could smell her own body odor, acrid and insistent. She could smell the cologne she had used this morning after her shower. She was suddenly aware of herself as she had never been aware before, and it was as if she were naked and exposed in all her suffering, a frightened child, a lost child, who had been deprived remorselessly—of what? But, strangely enough, she was herself and all that was herself, something she could not remember ever feeling before. A distinct personality, with responsibility for herself, and with no responsibility for another person, and with no reason to smile and talk gaily.

She pushed open the door and saw within the second room nothing at all but whitely beaming marble walls and shining floor and a large marble chair with blue cushions and an oval blue-curtained alcove. The door closed behind her. She stared at the alcove. Did he prefer to be hidden? Maybe it was Dr. Pfeiffer behind that curtain, the urbane and polished Dr. Pfeiffer with his soft voice urging Social Responsibility. She felt a bilious taste on her tongue. That would be a joke—Dr. Pfeiffer. But no, she had once heard him talk indulgently of the "superstition" of the alcove and of one of his parishioners—a family friend—John Service, who had tried to get the Sanctuary abolished. Dr. Pfeiffer had been in hearty agreement with Johnnie Service. And then Johnnie Service had unaccountably stopped going to Dr. Pfeiffer's church and had seemed changed a little and less loquacious about Social Responsibilities when he talked to Dad. In fact he and Dad had quarreled on the subject once. She wished she could remember what they had said. It seemed very important now.

Lucy moved slowly to the chair, and coughed tentatively to inform the man behind the curtain that she had entered. It was very funny, but she thought that he had become instantly aware of her. He must have a one-way mirror or something. But the walls about the alcove were smooth. However, science could do anything these days, and nothing was what it seemed.

She sat down, her purse primly on her knees. She looked about for a receptacle, but saw none. Well, the collection would come later, or she could lay the bill on his desk. She looked at the curtain. It did not stir, and there was no sound of breathing. Yet the impression of a presence grew stronger.

"Good evening," said Lucy, the well-bred girl to an elder.

The man did not reply.

"I don't know why I'm here," she said, and thought that the man must be astonished for people generally knew why they had come to this place. Lucy smiled. "I don't suppose you get girls like me, privileged girls, of good family, and with everything they ever wanted, love and all that. That's what I am. Do you want my name, or something?"

It was really crazy. She suddenly had the idea that the man knew her name and all about her. She cringed a little. Then, it was a friend of the family, and she blushed with mortification. The curtain remained tranquilly folded in all its lustre and beautiful blueness. She rose and went to it, and saw the button near it which informed her that if she wished to see the man who listened she had only to press the button. She did so. Nothing happened. The curtain did not move. So, he recognized Lucy Marner! So what? Let him listen and write his notes and know, once and for all, that all that she had, and so many like her, was nothing, worse than nothing, less than nothing. It would give him something to think about and maybe talk seriously with his stupid colleagues who were all as "liberal" as himself. Perhaps he would even talk it over with Dad and Mom. She grinned, spitefully. Let someone tell her parents what she really thought about them and perhaps they would be jolted out of their damned complacency. She hoped he would tell her profs, too, with their supercilious smiles and their jocund sense of reality and their rich, indulgent smiles when someone like herself asked "Why?"

"All right," she said angrily. She returned to the chair. "You know me. Who cares? Tell everybody. Tell the whole damned world. I'm sick of your kind, sick of everybody."

The man waited. She received no awareness that he was annoyed. He merely waited.

"I'll make it short and sweet," said Lucy. "I'm what the profs and the sociologists and the clergy admiringly call 'The New Breed.' You know? The young people who ask questions and dissent against everything and insist on facts and intelligent answers. The dissatisfied New Generation who won't be put off with the old clichés and old pat explanations and the old theology and old traditions. The generation which wants to know Why. The generation which wants replies—which will satisfy the New World and the World of the Future."

The taste of bile was sicker on her tongue. She leaned toward the curtain. "Do you know what they answer now? They answer nothing! They merely admire us, God damn them! They merely stand off and say, with nods of their silly heads, 'The New Breed,' and that's supposed to be an answer and we're supposed to admire ourselves and be satisfied!"

It was crazy, really, but she thought she heard the man say, "There is no New Breed, but there is always an answer to the old eternal question."

"What?" she muttered. "I thought you said—something. But I don't think you said anything, did you? I'm just talking to myself. I was thinking of Granny, and I imagined that she was speaking to me again. My father's mother."

The man said nothing. He merely waited. Lucy had the impression that his face was turned to her alertly behind the curtain, and that he was hearing something he had heard thousands of times before. Crazy.

But Lucy's young tense face began to glow softly. "I'd like to tell you about Granny. She wasn't very old when she died. Less than fifty. You couldn't have known her. She lived in Cleveland, and I understand you're a younger man and that you've never been out of this city. Young? No, they say you're old, very, very old. Are you?"

Oh, mad, mad! She thought the man had answered that he was much older than time. She put the back of her hand to her forehead. "I'm sure a mess," she said. "Now I'm imagining things, things I thought you said to me. Insane things."

What was that she had heard? A sigh? No, it was herself who was sighing.

"Granny," she said, in a young and desperate voice. "I was about twelve years old. She lived in Cleveland. That was the year my parents went abroad and everything was so prosperous that they couldn't get anyone to take care of me adequately here at home. I was a big girl, and very mature. But to my parents I was a 'child.' Granny offered to take care of me in her house in Cleveland while Dad and Mom were gone, and so they took me to her. I had seen her only three times before. She wasn't popular with Mom, especially. Mom said she was 'medieval' and that she didn't want me 'exposed' to 'foolish ideas.' Mom's very modern, you know. She's a lot more modern than I am. Mom's right out there in orbit with the astronauts!"

Lucy burst out laughing. She did not know how desperate her young laugh was.

"In fact," she said, when she could control herself, "Mom hates what she calls the 'feminine mystique.' She's forty-one, and about a thousand years younger than I am. She thinks a woman can do 'everything.' If Washington doesn't watch out Mom is going to march on it and demand that she be the first female astronaut. Maybe I'm imagining that and exaggerating, but Mom's like that. She prides herself on being aggressive and right with it. To look at her you'd think she was only about ten years older than I am, and she just loves to have everybody tell her that, and they do. As for Dad, he looks like a juvenile. He's younger than young. He's like a kid. You'd never suspect he was the most prosperous realtor in town. Younger than young. And modern! My God! They're so modern they make me feel as ancient as the hills. And sick to my stomach."

"Yes," said the man. "It is very piteous."

"What?" cried Lucy, moving forward on the chair. " 'Piteous?' Is that what you said, or am I imagining things again?"

The man did not answer her. But Lucy was certain that he had said what she imagined he had said. She leaned back in her chair. She frowned. Piteous? Her vital, young, bouncing parents? Her laughing, gay, serene, healthy parents? What was piteous about them? They "adjusted" to everything. They were tolerant about everything and serious about nothing. They smiled at her when she tried to tell them of her despair. They said it was a "phase." An adolescent turmoil. They did not know that they had taken away— What had they taken away, they who had given her everything, including boundless love?

"Granny," she said again, and now for the first time her young eyes filled with tears. "I did love Granny, though I never saw her again after I was twelve and my parents came back from Europe. Her house was so—tranquil. It's funny that I don't think my own home is tranquil like Granny's, yet our home is really so peaceful. No one ever raises his voice. Everything is good humor and sensible and can be 'discussed reasonably.' Yet, it isn't tranquil the way Granny's house was. There—there seemed a presence in Granny's house, just as there is a presence here. Now, isn't that absolutely mad?"

She pressed her pink young palms together fiercely. The tears were spilling over her pale cheeks. "I—I've talked to Dr. Pfeiffer. He's our clergyman, you know. I've tried to ask him—things. About what Granny told me. And he just touches me gently, and says, 'That was right for your grandmother's time, Lucy. But you are The New Breed. This old gent admires you so much. You refuse to accept the circumscribed answers. You ask wider questions. Yes, I admire you so much. You have given us a great deal.'

"The thing," cried Lucy, "is that they don't give us any answers! They talk about science and 'new discoveries.' And

Social Problems. As if social problems stand out in space and are apart from us! As if we don't have any personal identity at all, and as if we aren't hungry for something that would —that would—make life meaningful to us! Surely people aren't just collectivist animals, like a herd of cattle! Surely we are alive as individuals, aren't we? Surely we have a responsibility to ourselves alone, first of all, before we have a responsibility to other people? Surely we have—have—what did Granny call it? Souls!"

She blushed. That silly, silly word. The man must be laughing silently behind that curtain. She looked at the curtain defiantly. The sweet and fragrant silence about her appeared to move closer, as if not to miss any word she said. Insensibly her taut body relaxed in gratitude. She smiled tremulously, and her face paled again. She began to fumble with her bag, and she fished out a crushed clipping from a newspaper. She held it out to the curtain.

"I've something here that explains better than I can what I mean. It was printed in *Pravda*, the Russian newspaper, and it was reported in our newspapers. This girl, she was named Svetlina, in the paper, and she lives in Moscow. Seventeen years old. She wrote to *Pravda*. I'll read you what she says, for it's exactly what I mean.

"'I consider the world stupidly conceived and irrelevant. We learn and work all our lives and study, and then when we are valuable to humanity and our country we grow old and die. What is the meaning of all that? What is more worthless? All that effort which ends in nothing and extinction. Our scientists should try to develop an immortality pill for us.'

"Now," said Lucy, who did not know she was crying again, "that sounds awfully pathetic to me. But I know what she means! What is the use of our going to school and listening, when there are no answers to the admiration of those idiots who call us 'The New Breed'? Our frantic questions are received only with adulation, as if the question were important in itself and an answer could only be stupid! Stupid, stupid, stupid.

"But Granny had an answer, even if my parents said her answer was medieval." Lucy did not know that she was standing in extreme and desperate agitation. "Those few short months! I can't tell you how wonderful they were. What Granny said may be silly, as my parents said it was, and backward, and superstitious and Victorian and outmoded. But it *meant* something to me! They—they—well, it's like you're hungry, and someone takes you into a wonderful

182

brick-floored kitchen and there is a smell of bread baking there, and wonderful things cooking, and someone gives you a plate and you fill it, and you eat, and you aren't hungry any more. You're filled. You feel satisfied and at peace, and so wonderfully happy.

"So happy," said poor young Lucy. "So satisfied. I don't remember where it was in the Bible, but Granny read it to me. 'The Lord is my Shepherd, I shall not want. He leads my soul—my soul—he leads my soul—Green pastures. Thy Rod and thy Staff, they comfort me. The valley of the shadow of death—I shall fear no evil.' I don't remember it very clearly, you know. But when she read it to me, I felt so peaceful, so filled, as if someone really loved me. As if someone really *listened* to me. As if everything was—explained. I think it was the Old Testament, but I don't know. I never saw a Bible before or since.

"And then," said Lucy, weeping without restraint, "there was something Jesus said. Granny read it to me. It was about children. He said something about permitting little children to go to Him and forbidding them not. And there was something else a woman said after He had been crucified. 'They have taken away my Lord and I do not know where they have lain Him.' Whenever I think of that, I think of me. What have they done with my Lord? Where have they taken Him that I don't know anything about Him? If there is anything to know at all?"

She pressed her clenched hands to her young breast. "Where have they taken Him? Why don't I ever hear about Him? Why do my parents laugh indulgently when I ask? Why do my profs talk only about 'Social Consciousness' and all the other stuff, as if individuals have no existence, and no hope beyond this mere living? Why does Dr. Pfeiffer talk about us 'merging ourselves in humanity and losing our selfish individuality'? But our individuality is all that counts! It's all that we have! We aren't group-souls. We aren't just collectively-striving animals. We know only ourselves and our own thoughts.

"We're hungry! We want something else besides this world and our 'social obligations.' We want to be satisfied as *persons*. If we aren't satisfied as individuals, we aren't going to be good for anyone else, either. We are just going to regard our fellow human beings as biped animals; is that any good? Why, human life doesn't mean anything, then, and I and millions of girls like me are going to be just as desperate as that poor Russian girl, Svetlina! And just as amoral and as meaningless."

Lucy put her hands over her wet face and moaned a little. "Meaningless. Meaningless. Where have they taken my Lord, so that I don't have a sense of being alive, but just part of a group?"

She threw down her hands. "Why do they forbid us to go to Him? Why do they block the way with 'problems' we are supposed to solve in the world, which has always been filled with problems? And if we go to Him, what can He tell us? Where is my Lord? They have driven Him away, from our houses and our churches, from our government and our schools. They have taken Him out to a field and killed Him and have put Him in a grave, and He can never talk to us again or give us a reason for living."

The man did not answer. In utter despair Lucy ran again to the curtain and struck the button. The blue curtains silently drew aside, as if weary and sad, and the light shone out and in that light stood the man who listens.

"Oh!" cried Lucy, sharply, and retreated. "Oh, my God!"

Then she cried over and over, "Oh, my God, my God, my God!"

She had never knelt before in a church, before an altar, or at her bedside. But she knelt now, slowly, painfully, trembling. She clasped her hands together like a little child and not a woman of twenty. She stared at the man in the light, wonderingly.

"I believe!" she whispered. "What was it Granny said? 'I believe, I believe. O God, help Thou my unbelief!' Yes, yes. 'Help Thou my unbelief.' Give me—give me—something that can feed me and that can answer me. You didn't die after all, did you? Granny told me. But no one else ever did, no one else. They never told me that you had not gone away, that you were still here, even if they had driven you out and had laughed at you. They had never told me that you were still in this 'modern' world, even if everything is shut against you now.

"'Help Thou my unbelief.' I know you talked to me, because I never had thoughts like those before. I never had anything but ridicule. I was sufficient unto myself—they thought. They were sufficient to themselves, too. Maybe that's what makes them so frightened when they are a little sick, or they feel they are growing old and life won't be fun any longer. Maybe that's why I was so—hungry, like that girl, Svetlina."

Lucy got to her feet. She went to the man, slow step by step. She reached out and laid her hand on his. She smiled, though she was still crying. There was such a peace in her.

"Help Thou my unbelief." No, just give back to me what Granny gave me, and everybody else took away afterward. Look, I still have my world to face, and college and the profs and my parents— You did call them piteous, didn't you? Oh, how piteous! I see it all now. They are just like children in the dark. Why did they drive you away, and why did they hide me from you? The poor people. Poor Dad; poor Mom. Maybe that's why they are so frantic about staying young and 'modern' and enthusiastic. They seem so—feverish—sometimes. So desperate. Even more desperate than I—was.

"I'm not so desperate any more. There's a little church near our house, with candles. It's always open. It has beautiful statues in it. There's a light, near the altar. I don't know why.

"But every day I'm going to stop there before going to school. I'm going to find out—where they have lain my Lord."

SOUL ELEVEN: *The Dream-Spinner*

> "All which thy child's mistake
> Fancies as lost, I have stored for thee at home . . ."
> THE HOUND OF HEAVEN. Francis Thompson

The golden spring day was no fresher than the air in the white and blue waiting room. The men and women and youths waiting for the chime to sound for them unconsciously relaxed as if, even now, some of their weight and sorrow and despair were already lifting in the sweet air with its hint of fern. The woman entering peeped at them coyly, a half-smile on her widely rouged lips, her painted eyes tilted in a coquettish way, her brazen hair rolling in waves about her coarse cheeks. It was evident that she expected a glance of interest from those already in their chairs, but no one glanced at her, no one appeared aware that she had entered. Her smile faded a little, and she pouted. The door silently closed behind her and she leaned against it, casually, breathlessly, like the young girl she had been some fifty years ago. She sighed, and said appreciatively, "Um." No one looked at her; some were reading, sunken wearily in themselves.

Smiling again, after a moment, she elaborately tiptoed to an empty chair and sat down. She was large and stout, massively stout, but relentlessly girdled. She was dressed like a young girl, in a gay green silk dress with a wide green silk coat over it, and every seam strained. A string of patently false pearls encircled her flushed and deeply lined throat. As she had had the vague idea that she was going to some sort of church she had put on a hat, a rather broad velvet and black straw suitable for a girl fourteen years old. Her white-gloved hands carried a patent-leather purse to match her cheap patent-leather slippers, and her fat nyloned flesh bulged over the arch and the sides. She exuded a scent which had been optimistically named *Turkish Night,* at one dollar the ounce, and smelled, as one of her more ruthless friends

186

had said, like perfumed sweat. It was considered distracting to ladies like Maude Finch.

Some of her kinder friends told her that she looked not a day over forty-nine, but her powdered and colored wrinkles blatantly announced her full sixty-five birthdays, and not one article of her clothing had cost more than twenty-five dollars. She was considered, by friends of her own generation, to be "a card," for she could play poker like a man, could drink beer like a man, and had a hoarse jolly laugh, and she earned sixty dollars a week as a clothing saleswoman in a branch of a downtown store in the little suburb where she lived.

Sadly, she considered herself extremely stylish and believed, most of the time, that she had éclat. (She had read the word in *Harper's Bazaar,* and now used it lavishly though not with the proper pronunciation. She had never learned how to pronounce half the words she used with an air, but at least she knew the meaning to a certain extent.) Her hair was dyed, and not by a professional. Her eyes were small and blue and webbed with tiredness and with her everlasting smiles. Her one good feature was her teeth, without flaw, and big and white, without fillings. She had rarely needed a dentist, which was fortunate for her. When she smiled brightly, as she did almost always, her teeth sparkled, she appeared younger, and yet far more pathetic than ordinarily.

She sat down, carefully rearranging her dress and coat so they would not wrinkle. They were real silk, in a large size, and she had been able to buy them at the shop for half their original price because no customer had called for them. She was very proud of the costume. This was the first wearing. She touched her hat, now, opened her bag, took out a compact and peeped at the glass. She did not see her large-pored skin. She saw the charming sweet girl she had never been, not even once in her life. She smiled widely at the dream-image, snapped the compact closed, replaced it, snapped the gilt fastening of the bag and looked about her, beaming.

But no one turned to give her a brief glance or a smile in return. So she reached for a magazine. She did not wear glasses in public, except furtively behind the cash register in the store, and at home. Therefore, she could read nothing though she pretended to do so, and with deep interest, her head cocked, her pink lips pursed reservedly as if she did not entirely agree with the writer.

Becoming bored by this small touch of acting, she put aside the magazine and stared at her fellow-waiters in the room. Not a bad dress on that woman there; it must have cost at least one hundred dollars. But black, on a lovely day like this! And the woman must have cancer or something, she was so white. Why hadn't she tinted her cheeks and her lips? No one went bare-faced these days, like a farm wife. She must be all of forty-five, too. And so thin! A twelve dress, at the very most. But no style. Maude's eyes, disapproving, went from face to face, but every face was absorbed in its own pain or misery. What a bunch! She was the only person here with any life to her, or any color or bounce. She made her dyed thick hair bounce on her neck and cheeks. It was a wiry bouncing, but nevertheless she felt young and vital at the feel of it. She began to wonder why she had come at all, she, common-sense Maude Finch, with all the wonderful life that she had had and all the wonderful things that had happened to her!

It was just that she was a teeny bit tired, that was all. The shop had been open to nine-thirty last night, and there had been quite a number of customers. She had made five dollars, at least, in commissions. It made up for the days before that when she had barely made her pay. So, she was five ahead of Nancy, her fellow employee and her best friend. Poor Nancy, with that terrible crippled husband of hers to support. She, Maude, was glad she had no one to support except herself, and in a way she didn't need the money. Plenty in the bank, to live as she wanted to the rest of her life. She smiled widely again, and cocked her head complacently and the blue eyes filled with a glaze of dreams and became young again and wistful. After a time, she glanced at her small gold and diamond watch; only six installments left to pay on it. Half-past six! Had she fallen asleep or something? She had left the shop at five, had raced home to dress, had set out for the Sanctuary at half after five, and had arrived here long before six—a fifteen-minute ride on the bus.

She had never been on the lawns or the path before. She had moved from the city to the adjacent suburb twenty years ago when darling Jerry had died and left her so very comfortable. Since then she had been in the city but once or twice a month, to visit friends, and always at night, and though she had been aware of the Sanctuary's existence since she had been much younger, she had felt no curiosity about it. "Some old goat's little church," she had once said. "Methodist or something. No? What then? Oh, 'The man who listens.' Now, isn't that silly? Why should he do that? Yes, I know it's a pretty place; it's been there for ages, ages. I don't

188

even remember when it was built. But ages, really. I heard millions of people've come to it, even from them foreign places. Somebody said the Governor came once, but I don't believe *that*, honestly! Well, there's more than one way to waste money, it seems, and that old man—his name was Goodwin or something—had no kids or wife and he built this because he was a Catholic and he just couldn't *stand* the Roman Catholics any longer, and built his own church! Funny, isn't it? It takes all kinds."

Why had she come? It was because she had been so tired last night. She wanted to ask the man inside if she should quit her job for an easier one. Something part time, just to take up the slack of her comfortable days. Most of her friends worked; gave them something to do now the kids had left home. Every woman should *do* something, for heaven's sake, besides sitting around the house running up new drapes! Shouldn't they? It kept a woman young and on her toes to have a job, though really her job wasn't *that* important. It was fun, though. It was fun because she didn't need it; Jerry had been so good to her. God, she was tired. And there was that funny ache right under her breastbone at night. The company doctor had said she was sound as a dollar, so it wasn't heart or cancer of the lungs which everybody was dying of. Thank God she didn't smoke, so she didn't have to worry. It was just that ache, and the tiredness coming last night. No, she had been tired a long time, a very long time. She had heard the man inside was a psychiatrist and maybe she needed a psychiatrist.

She giggled like a child ten years old. Maude Finch, who had never had an ache or pain in her life, or a minute's depression, needing a psychiatrist! But then, lots of times, she'd heard, something could go wrong in your mind and make you feel sick—no, tired. No, sick. Let's face it, girl. You feel sick, sick at your stomach, and sometimes you can't sleep and you just stare at the black window at night— You— You've got such an ache, right here, right under this wonderful pin that I got at wholesale, only five dollars, and no one who saw it thought it was fake. The blue stones looked real turquoise, and the red ones rubies. It had been on sale for twenty dollars, but it was too big for the teeny little women, and so she had bought it right off the counter in the shop, for five dollars. Trust her to get a bargain, Maude Finch! Though God knows she didn't need bargains, not with her money. But them that has looks for bargains. They do it every time. She chuckled fondly at herself. She was as bad as old Mrs. Schlott, who everybody said had a million dollars. Well, Maude Finch didn't have a million dollars. Not yet, anyway. She chuckled again. If stocks kept rising as they were doing now, she'd make it, she'd make it! Maybe she'd buy one of those villas on the Ree-ve-air-ay, which she had seen pictured in *Harper's*. And invite all her friends. "Come anyway. What do you care what the jets cost? Look, when I live there I'll send you the two-way tickets." She hadn't said that yet; people were so envious, and she was afraid of envious people. Superstitious, that's what Maude was.

An elderly gentleman who had entered after her leaned toward her and said, "I think that chime's for you, lady." She started. There were still a lot of people in the room, but the ones she had seen had already gone. "Thank you," she said with enormous politeness and rose with majesty and a flick of her wrist. She had seen that airy dismissing flick in one of those foreign movies; French or something. The old man smiled faintly and sadly. With a model's sway she went to the farther door, opened it, and entered the stark blue and marble room beyond. Then she gawked. There was no one there at all, nothing but that tall marble chair with the blue velvet cushion and fringe, and a blue rounded drape over an alcove or something. Where was the psychiatrist?

She cleared her throat. There was no sound. Had he gone out on a coffee break? All right, *then!* She could wait. She was honestly awful tired. She sat down in the chair, and admired the blue silk velvet on the arms. Real stuff, not that synthetic. She could tell. She took off her gloves, after a furtive glance at the hidden alcove, and felt the velvet. Just like the chairs at home when she had been a kid, except that some of the chairs had been pink and yellow silk velvet. But the quality was just as good as she remembered, maybe better. No! Nothing could be better than the chairs, and big Empire sofas, that had filled the drawing room of her childhood home. What did people know these days of drawing rooms? Family rooms, for heaven's sake! Just cheap; just folksy. And that big white marble fireplace, exactly like that one in *Harper's* last month, showing the home of one of the Rosenbergs in Paris, no, it wasn't Rosenberg. It was—now, let me think a little, things sometimes slip my mind. Got it! Rockschild! No, not quite right. Rothschild! She felt quite triumphant at remembering. She looked complacently at the huge sparkling stone on her left hand, her engagement ring. How Jerry had laughed and kissed it when he had put it on his finger first to show how tiny the loop really was. It hardly covered the first joint of his little finger. Nothing cheap about Jerry Finch, God rest his extravagant soul. Everybody envied her that ring. "More at home," she would say merrily, tossing her head. She would add, "No, I mean in the bank vault, where I keep all my stock and papers and extra cash. They'll never catch me again like that bank holiday 'way back in Roosevelt's time. I believe in lots of loose cash."

Remembering those remarks, her lined and tinted face beamed radiantly. Sometimes she wished she had had a son or a daughter, to make happy. Well, it goes to show. Some has them, mostly the poor, and some don't, like herself. It all comes out in the wash anyway. You never know.

Then, suddenly, she was aware that all the time there had been a presence in the room with her, that someone was behind that curtain. But why hadn't he spoken? Could he have come in the back door? She cleared her throat musically. "Good evening," she said. "I didn't hear you come. I hope I haven't kept you waiting. They say you have all the time there is. That's awful good of you. I'm Maude Finch, a widow, fifty years old, and young for my age if I admit it myself."

The gentlest sensation came to her, as if someone had smiled understandingly. She was so touched that she said heartily, "Oh, you shouldn't tell the doctor lies! I'm really sixty-five! But, would you believe it?"

No one spoke, but later she could have sworn that some man had said, "No, I don't believe it! You are only a young girl." She would remember that always, always.

Even now there were sudden acrid tears in her eyes. She opened her bag and took out her handkerchief, scented with *Turkish Night*, and blew her nose.

"It says, over the door, the man who listens. That's you." Her voice was subdued. "But there must have been other doctors or such over the years, not just you. How could one man have been here all this time? Of course, that's impossible. There've been different guys—I mean doctors. Excuse me."

Yet she had the incredible impression that the man had dissented, that he had implied to her that he, and only he, had been here over the years and no one else. "Honest?" she said, wonderingly, and now her voice was not raucous but fluting like a girl who was just past puberty. "Honest?" she repeated and did not know why she should feel so relieved.

After a little she said, in a coquettishly awkward tone, "I honestly don't know why I came here. It's just this tiredness;

from last night. No, no, I got to tell the truth. Over a long time, maybe a couple of years. And I'm sort of sick to my stomach, sometimes. Sometimes I can't eat. It's kind of lonely eating by yourself, even if you've got a good cook in your kitchen, serving up them French menus; I get *Realités,* you know, with all them French receipts, and Denise, that's her name, always tries them out. You know what she did a month ago? She sent me looking, on Saturday, a day I had off, to look for saffron! Why, it costs as much as gold! I bought an ounce and Denise says, 'Oh, Mrs. Finch, I only needed a soopsong'—that's French, too. She meant a little. But she needed it for rice to serve with the Chicken Mornie. Yes, it's awful lonesome, eating them fine meals by your own self, with a nice bottle of chilled wine. Chautoo Two, that was the brand. I keep my wines in the cellar, like the way the Rothschilds do. Locked up. There's other tenants in the apartment house where I live, and you never know. Sometimes the ones who look the most rich are the poorest. It makes me laugh sometimes. But I never let them hear me. I was brought up right. Dear Mama and Papa!" She sighed.

"Well, I shouldn't complain," she went on more briskly. "And I really shouldn't be here, taking up your time with all those poor souls waiting to tell you *real* troubles. Not like me. They say you shouldn't brag, knock wood. But I've had everything I ever wanted all my life. Born with a gold spoon in my mouth. Ate on gold plate, too, no, I don't mean *exactly* that, I mean it was Servus china with a gold border, like I saw in *Vogue* once. Not in my nursery, of course, where I had white and blue English bone china. But in the dining room, on holidays, to celebrate my birthdays and Christmas. Mama and Papa, though, used to use it all the time, with Mama's silver, heavy as iron, which her godmother gave her. Did I tell you my parents were English? Came from England before I was born; my father got in some kind of trouble with that English Congress, and they didn't like what he said. No, I guess they don't call it Congress like us; House of Lords.

"Papa wasn't a lord, though he was right there in it. Well, anyway, I'm not bragging. What's gone is gone. We didn't live here in this city, though, when I was a kid, or even afterward. I've been here only thirty years, after Jerry and me got married. He was from New York. But, look, you didn't come in here to listen to me brag, for heaven's sake. You just want to know why I got this tiredness all of a sudden, and this queasy stomach, and why I can't sleep sometimes. I dunno."

She flicked her wrist. "Say la guarr. That means that's how things are. French. I can speak French like a native, and not even the hoy-pol*lie* can speak it as well. Hoy-pol*lie,* you know, means big shots. We get them all the time in our saloon."

Don't he ever say a word? she asked herself. Well, I'm sure he said *something*. I'll remember later, when I'm not so tired.

"I don't know how old you are," she said, "but if you've been here all these years you must be as old as God. And maybe as tired." She laughed apologetically. "They say you're a minister too, as well as a psychiatrist, and I hope I ain't—I mean haven't—insulted you. But sometimes I say just what pops up in my mind; everybody says I always say what I think and mean. Well, you've got to be open, don't you, and not a hypocrite? I don't believe in saying things that aren't true."

Suddenly her face wrinkled in scores of deep lines and squeezed together and tears burst into her eyes again. "Oh!" she cried, "I just get sick, remembering my wonderful wonderful life, with Mama and Papa—that's what they call their parents in England—not Mum or Pop, like American kids do. I keep thinking of my marvelous life with Jerry, too. There was never anybody like Jerry, honest. Gave me everything, though I didn't need it. My parents left me plenty. Plenty! But they died when I was eight, no, seven. And me, and everything I had, was made guardian to my aunt and uncle. Aunt Sim, that's what I called her. I guess her name was Simplicity, those old-fashioned names, you know? And Uncle Ned. He was a big stockbroker in another city, it don't matter where, for I'm living here now.

"I sure would like to tell you all about my childhood! Can I, please?"

Had she heard, "Yes?" She was sure of it. She smiled lovingly at the alcove. She arched her head. "Maybe you're rich, too, so you'll understand. I can remember clear, just like yesterday. Our house had a big lawn all around it, like a park. With gates; I used to swing on them. Kind of like gates of rich houses I see in *Vogue* and *Town & Country* all the time, and *Harper's Bazaar*. I never can get enough, just looking at all those wonderful, wonderful houses and gardens, like I had when I was a kid, before Mama and Papa died. And absolutely fabulous rooms inside, with white walls and gold trimmings, just like the Rothschilds, and drapes! Papa brought them from France and Italy. You know? Those brocade things, bed ropes, I mean bell ropes, brocade too, like the drapes. And we had the funniest little old man for a gardener; I read about his kind once, in an English story in a magazine. 'Madam,' he'd say, 'you just don't touch my roses!' As if I would! Mama would have *killed* me!

"— read a book one time—I don't have much time for books, with my social obligations—and it was called *West Lynne*. Or maybe it was *East Lynne*. Anyhow, the heroine, it says, always smelled so sweet and good, like bath salts. Well, that's the way Mama, and our whole house smelled, and Papa used to smell like the tobacco they advertise in *Esquire*. Manly, and tweeds. Dear Papa! He used to take me out in the dog-cart for rides around the grounds and sometimes to visit Aunt Sim and Uncle Ned. Lovely, lovely. And we'd come back for tea, on Sunday, with all the bells ringing, and I'd eat with my nurse.

"Well, that was a *good* part, but I liked school best. Mama wanted me to go to private school, but Papa was democratic, after all those lords, you know? So I went to the best public school in the city, and were the kids jealous of my wonderful clothes! I didn't mind. Oh, God!" she cried in a desperate, ringing voice, "I didn't mind! Not really, not really! What did it matter? It was just that it hurts so much, all the kids laughing—"

She stopped appalled. She put her fingers to her shaking mouth and stared at the alcove. But nothing stirred behind the curtain. The man listened. She knew he understood, all those jealous kids, because she had such pretty golden hair. Like a princess. Like that little Princess Anne in England, with a ribbon over the smooth front.

She could finally speak in a trembling voice, "My life was just like a fairy tale, you know? No need to talk about it so much, I guess. Nothing but happiness, and sunshine, and such loving parents. Mama was a dainty queen. She'd sit most of the time on her chase-long, with a wrap over her feet, like I read about in a romance when I was a kid. But love! No kid ever had so much love as I did! And such fun! You should have seen our Christmasses! Tree right up to our nine-foot roof, and all spangles and angels and gold balls, like I saw through a hotel window once when they was having a private party for some debbutante. I tell you, I just stood there in the snow and dreamed about how it was when I was a little girl, with all those presents from everybody, a big white rocking-horse, too, and a gold locket with a diamond in it, like I saw in a jewelry store once, and a little white dog. I called him Tim. He was all fuzzy." She sighed. "He got lost one day. Papa offered hundreds and hundreds for him, but he was a high breed dog and they kept him. He wasn't a poodle, like you see in *Harper's*. Something a lot better. He had a collar with rhinestones in it, and it was made of silver.

"Oh!" she exclaimed, her face shining like a child's and with wonder and delight. "You got no idea of what it was like when I was a kid! So peaceful, so loving, so rich, so *right!* Like a dream, like *heaven*. All those kisses I got; Mama and Papa'd just grab me away from each other; they was jealous, you know? Look. I got a scar, a nasty big one, right on the flesh near the elbow, like a burn. They pulled so hard I fell into the fire, and did they scream and kiss it! I had an extra nurse for a month. Sure, it's a burn scar, not what the doctor said, a sort of ragged wound from 'some instrument.' He wasn't very bright. I used to read a lot when I was a kid," she said abruptly. And her face changed. "Mama loved romances, all kinds, she was sentimental, you see? And we had such a big library. All full of romances—and I guess history and poems for Papa. I read all kinds of things, but mostly stories of people like us, rich and loving and kind and smelling nice, and big old green gardens full of flowers, and people in pretty clothes—voiles and China silks and taffetas like they had—just like ours. And great big old furs to wrap around you when you went out in the sleds in winter, and to skate on the little lake nearby.

"Sometimes," she cried despairingly, "I can't bear to think about it. Dear, dear, merciful God, I can't bear to think about it!"

She put her face in her hands and she sobbed as if something had broken in her. She groaned, over and over. "I can't bear to think of it!"

She sobbed until she was exhausted. There were no windows in the room; the light that bathed the white walls became softer and softer and more consoling. Her sobbing slowed; eventually she was able to wipe her swollen eyes. Her face was old, the paint and the powder gone, the lines accentuated, the slack mouth trembling. "I can't bear to think of it!" she said, in a quieter tone. "I was only eight years old. That's when Papa and Mama died. They never told me. I think it was skiing. I never did find out. And then I went to live with Auntie Sim and Uncle Ned.

"I'm not complaining. Of course, I cried a lot at first. But they was just like my own parents to me." She gulped. "And rich, or richer, than Papa. They didn't have no children of their own. They adopted me. And my life became just like my life at home." Her hands clenched on the arms of the chair. "Like my life at home!"

"Yes," said the man sorrowfully—did she hear him, honestly?—"just like your life at home."

She nodded eagerly, and with a fierce and terrible smile. "Yes, yes. Just like my life at home!"

Silence. Profound silence. After a time she put her hand quickly to her temples. "I get a headache, an awful headache, sometimes, when things get mixed up in my mind. A queer kind of headache; I don't mean 'queer' like people say these days." She tried to laugh. "Funny, though. Everything mixed up, running together, and I get scared. I just say to myself, 'Now Maude, cool it. You got to face things. You don't live with Aunt Sim and Uncle Ned any more. You live right here, in your nice, lovely apartment, with all the antiques, and the silver, and you got a lot to be thankful for, even if your job ain't so much. It's a living, isn't it?' "

Again, she flung her hands over her mouth, and dark color ran over her face. "I—I don't know what I say, sometimes. Things pour out; I mean, they never poured out like this before. That's because you're listening. But you've got to excuse me. I'm kind of not talking straight. You got to have patience.

"Well, like I was saying. I didn't go to any school when I lived with Aunt Sim and Uncle Ned. I had private tooters; the very best. Oh, I was like in a convent! Only the best girls came to see me, all girls going to be debbutantes, like me. And the nicest boys. I didn't like the boys very much; they pulled my hair and they laughed at me. I was kinda shy all the time. Awful shy. It got worse and worse." Now the words were tumbling out. "And when I was seventeen I met Jerry Finch. He was a—I mean a lawyer. Good position in a big firm, like Perry Mason, you know? Only more lawyers. He didn't like Aunt Sim and Uncle Ned very much, and they sure didn't like him! He wasn't very rich, not like us, but a wonderful, wonderful family! They had acres and acres! But no one was ever like Jerry. We—we ran away and got married. I was still only seventeen. We lived awhile in that city, and then we come here. That was thirty years ago. A new start, Jerry said. He—he'd made so much money as a partner. Like that old lawyer I read about when I was in my twenties. Clarence Darrow! A mouthpiece. That's what they called it in them days."

She let the brilliant stone shine out into the room. She cried victoriously, "Look at my engagement ring! Jerry paid ten thousand dollars for it, and it was way back before the Depression! That's the kind of man Jerry was, nothing too good for little Maude, he'd say. That's what he called me. Oh, Jerry drank quite a bit. He—he'd had a tragic childhood. I know all about this mental health thing. It's all in your childhood. He was an orphan. He went to a—a—well, it was sort of a private boarding school for orphans, like Prince Charles of England, only Prince Charles isn't an orphan, you know what I mean? But kind of rugged; that's what Jerry said. It made him drink a lot; I didn't mind too much. I was kind of grateful—I mean, I loved him. Nobody was ever like Jerry. I look at other women's husbands, and they're jerks, not like Jerry. Just clods, going to work every day and handing over their pay checks to their wives, and playing with their kids—I mean, all the time, on Sundays and at night. I see them a lot down the street; it's what they call it a garden apartment, but it— I mean, it's very nice like that, but not like my apartment, with Denise."

She bent her head. She could not remember when she had taken off her gloves, both of them. But they were wet and wrinkled on her lap, and a little grimy. She'd have to wash them again, tonight, so they'd be right for tomorrow.

"Jerry," she said, in a dull voice, "was kind of sensitive. He got to drinking more and more; you know, in the drinking department? Oh, it didn't matter about the money part. We had plenty. I had Mama's and Papa's money after I was twenty-one. It wasn't too bad. We didn't have any kids—I was kind of thankful, in a way. Jerry didn't like them, anyways, and Jerry was my life. I almost chewed his food for him. We was so devoted all our rich neighbors were jealous. How I used to laugh." She laughed. "I was forty when he—well, he had a brainstorm, that's what they used to call it. Softening of the brain, or something. And he died, after all those wonderful, wonderful years! Sometimes I can't stand it!"

Her voice shattered. She cringed in her chair. She pulled the hair that now straggled over her ears. She rocked on her massive buttocks. "I can't bear it," she muttered. "I can't bear thinking about it, or anything. I guess I'm going crazy. Maybe I'm going to throw up."

"Be still," said the man. She started violently. "What did you say? 'Be still?' No, I guess I'm imagining things again. Sometimes I imagine too much."

She sighed, and this time the sound came like a long moaning from the depths of her agonized soul. Her lips felt numb and weak when she said, "But Jerry left me well fixed, wonderful. I shouldn't complain. Insurance. It's true I—I mean, I never thought about the insurance. Honest! I just wanted Jerry. He was like a kid to me; so helpless; I even forgave him when he'd—I mean, he'd get in a mood and he'd say cold things to me. But he didn't mean them! Honest!

"And now I'm here, talking about all those things—I mean, I'm sixty-five now, and sometimes things gang up on you, and you can't stop thinking, and you think what's the use, and you can't stop remembering—it wasn't so bad when I was younger, and kind of hoped—but now I look at myself and I—I mean, things should've been so different but I guess they're not for people like me—I just have to stand things."

She jumped to her feet and threw out her arms and almost screamed, "But why did it have to be that way! Why couldn't it have been different! Was I such a bad kid, such a mean, stinking kid, that it had to happen to me that way? What did I *do?* I think about that. I didn't do one damned thing!"

She turned with a violent gesture and flung herself into the chair and turned her head and leaned her cheek against the back and clutched the top and wept as she never wept before, broken, shaking, crushing sobs, as if her body were falling into ruins moment by moment and her heart was exposed and turning in anguish. She was an old woman, older than her years. She was also a desperate and lonely child, a terrified child, a skulking child, a child who lived with terror and pain.

"I came here," she said, with her lips pressed against the chair's back as a child presses its lips against its mother's breast, "because I'm so tired, and I get these headaches, and sick at my stomach—maybe it's the old menopause—and I think and think, and I look at the women in the nice little houses with the nice kids, and the good husbands, and a car—I never had even a bicycle—and I wonder why they have things so good, and I—I never had anything—not anything, in my whole damned life!"

Her lips went deeper into the velvet hungrily, and it was like flesh to her loving flesh. "If just I'd had one single thing, just one! Just one to remember."

She swung about in the chair, fiercely, defiantly, still clutching the arms. She glared at the curtain. "I've never had a single person to talk to, to tell anything to, nobody to care whether I lived or died, nobody just to care or be worried about what would happen to me! Do you know something, you man behind there who never says a word, I've told you a pack of lies! And you know why? Because I made myself believe them when the going got tough, as it always does for me. A person has to have something to believe in, even if they make up lies. You know why? Because we couldn't stand living if we didn't. We can't stand the truth of what we've been living—I mean, people like me.

"The only way I could get people to look at me at all, and see me, a person, who was just a little bit of a *nice* person, and not an orphan slob, was to tell them all these fancy stories. Maybe they didn't believe any of it, or maybe they believed a little, or anyway, maybe they thought some of it might be true, or something like it.

"It's all I've got, what I made myself dream about, reading some books I found, and pretending it was me. And then a long time ago I used to buy magazines, like the ones I told you about, and dream I was born a Rothschild, or maybe a Rockefeller, or maybe an English princess, or some kid, rich, who had parents who loved her, had all those wonderful things and childhood. It wasn't just being rich, at first, but just having a father and mother like I see all around me all the time. A person got to have some self-respect, you know? Like having nice folks sometime.

"Look at me!" she screamed, starting to her feet, and leaning forward from her thick waist in an attitude of absolute despair and lonely rage. "I never knew who my parents was! First thing I knew was the orphan asylum, sixty years ago, a dump! Cold, hungry, never having any decent clothes. Most of the kids had *someone,* somewhere, who sent them some things, even if they was second-hand. I had nobody. But I wore cast-offs that was cast-offs in the beginning. I never was warm a day in my life! You, in there! Was you ever homeless, and ever cold, and never had a house of your own? I bet, I just bet, you rich psychiatrist! Did you ever have people turn away from you because you weren't pretty or something, and because you was frightened, the way I was always frightened? All I had was my teeth. A good thing! If they'd been bad I wouldn't have one in my head now, that's the kind of care we got in that old poor orphan asylum where I was, where Jerry was, though I didn't know he'd been there until I was seventeen.

"Did you ever have anyone laugh at you, and make fun of you, the way they did with me? I betcha they didn't, not you with all your education and money! When I was eight years old my mother's cousin, Aunt Sim, and her husband, came around and said they owned me, and they took me out. Aunt

199

Sim wanted someone to work for her in the kitchen, the lazy old bum! The orphan asylum was glad to get rid of me; they was overcrowded; you don't know what they was like in those days. Anyway, Uncle Ned I called him, was a bartender in a dirty saloon, and I used to scrub it out at night after what little school I went to—and the spittoons and all. And all I got was kicks and scratches and bangs from them. See this arm? Uncle Ned was crazy; he got mad at Aunt Sim one night and he took it out on me, and he had a knife and he ripped my arm with it. I can't hardly raise it even now, and you think that's easy in a shop like where I work? You're nuts if you think it is!

"And I met Jerry in the saloon one night when I was working there. They made me quit school when I was twelve; that's what it was like then, and I worked washing dishes in the kitchen behind the bar, making up the free lunch and cleaning up afterward. Jerry was thirty years old, a grown man, a drummer, that's what they called salesmen then. He went around the towns selling things, like liniment and stockings and thread and pans. I thought he was great, just great. Sometimes he'd make fifteen–eighteen dollars a week, and that was big money then, and he was a nice-looking jerk in a way, with shiny shoes. Oh, hell! They talk about teen-agers being kids, these days, but I was a real kid, not with this sex-stuff and lipstick and high-heels like they got now; I was just a kid. Seventeen.

"And I was an ugly kid, too, and I can just see myself in the old rags I wore, and the button-shoes that was all patched, and my hair hanging down my back. No, it wasn't gold-blonde hair, though I kid myself it was, sometimes. It was just plain mousy, and I curled it in a frizz on Sundays in the front. I was an ugly kid, all right! But Jerry, he liked me, he said. One day he got in a fight with Uncle Ned, who was twisting my arm, and I loved Jerry right off, though he wasn't no Errol Flynn, or one of them movie stars with the funny names you see in the movies now. He tripped up Uncle Ned, and then he says to me, 'Girlie, I been seeing you around and I kind of like you, you're so pitiful. How about you and me getting hitched?' I tell you, I could have died!"

She sobbed with a retching sound which she could not control and now did not even attempt to control. "Seventeen, and a real kid, with no idea of anything. Jerry had a room in a boardinghouse, and he took me there, and a couple of days later we were married. I suppose," she stammered, "I ought to be grateful he did that, for things happened to kids in those days, awful things, when they were in a spot like me. And I ate three meals a day, real meals, for the first time in my life. It got to be heaven after awhile. Jerry—well, he drank a little—No! He was drunk most of the time! I had to get a job, in a little factory, and I made five dollars a week, and I worked twelve hours a day, six days a week. It was still heaven for a little while, after Aunt Sim and Uncle Ned.

"And then," she gulped over and over, her face scarlet with pain and tears, "Jerry began to beat me up when he was drunk, and then even when he wasn't. I guess he got sick of the sight of me, I was still so ugly. But he was all I had, and I mean, well I *clung* to him, and I promised him if he'd stay with me I'd take care of him, and so he quit his job and I worked. I worked Sundays, too, cleaning offices, to make it up to him for marrying me and taking me away. Oh, he worked sometimes, here and there, because I couldn't make enough money, all by myself, for his drink; but not very often. Then I heard of a bigger factory in this town, and we came here and I got so I was making fourteen dollars a week by the time I was twenty-two. Not too bad, but not very good, neither. I didn't eat too regular, if you know what I mean.

"Sometimes I got to dreaming that Jerry was a good sober man, with a good job, and making money, and that we had a nice little house, on a quiet street, with maybe a secondhand car and a couple of kids. Sometimes it was so real that when I'd wake up in the morning, in the couple of dirty rooms we had in this city, I couldn't believe where I was! I could just *hear* my little boy—I called him Tommie in my dreams— calling me. 'Mama, Mama!' Just like that." Her lips trembled in a tender smile and again the dreaming look glazed her eyes. Then she shuddered.

"It got so that the only way I could get along, working all the time, and coming to those awful rooms with Jerry drunk on the bed, was to pretend I was somebody else and had a wonderful life. I'd talk about it at the plant. The girls all were jealous; they began to call me 'tightwad' because of my clothes. 'She puts it all in the bank,' they'd say right where I could hear them, and I'd be so proud of Jerry's and my big bank account and I'd really begin to believe we had it. I'd buy up old magazines, like the *Bazaar* and *Vogue*, and look at all the pictures, and by and by— Oh, yes, and the *Ladies' Home Journal* and other women's magazines—I'd begin to dream of having clothes like that, and jewelry like that, and furs. But mostly, the house, and the kids, and the smooth sheets and the

201

pretty dishes and nice rugs. And sometimes on Saturday afternoons I'd sneak around to the real swell shops in this city, and walk through, looking at all the terrific things in them, and the clothes, and by and by I'd think I was really shopping, me with only three cheap dresses to my name, and a coat so old I'd forgotten what I'd paid for it, and it wasn't any good to begin with."

She laughed at herself, half-groaning, half-sobbing. "I guess that's about all, I think. But about thirty-five years ago, looking at Jerry, I'd wonder how I'd bury him if he died. I still was grateful to him, in spite of everything. He was all I had. So I sobered him up one day, and pressed his only suit—he had one of his jobs then—and sent him to the insurance company, no, I went with him, I've got to be straight on things now. I told him I was the one being insured. Anyway, in those days they didn't mind so much, it was prosperous and everybody was buying insurance, you know, the twenties? They didn't ask too many questions, but they liked the idea that I was paying for the insurance and working every day. They checked up on me, and saw I was paying the rent every Monday night. So, anyway, I got Jerry insured for three thousand dollars, and then I could sleep nights, not wondering if they'd bury him behind a fence or something. He was all I had.

"You see, Doctor, he sort of got to be a kind of kid to me, me taking care of him and washing his clothes at night and feeding him when he couldn't even sit up, after being sick from drinking all that moonshine they had those days, or was it bathtub gin? I don't remember; never touched it, myself. And I'd tell myself how handsome he was, and how he was sick, not drunk, and that I was all he had.

"And then, after ten–fifteen years, after we came here, he died, and I was all alone again; he had the D.T.s And it was the Depression. I still had my job, but they cut my pay; I didn't mind too much; things were getting cheaper. And now I had three thousand dollars! I spent eight hundred on Jerry's funeral; it was real smart, even if only me and the landlady and a couple of girls from the plant came to it. And he had a vault, too, and a grave where the trees are real pretty. Now he was settled down, but I was all alone.

"The rest of the money looked awful good to me! It was real good! Especially when I lost my job, and didn't have another for two years. I lived on it, real close, and it lasted, and there was quite a bit left when I got a job in another plant when Hitler began to come up in the news, and everybody was thinking of war, and the government wanted us to rearm and arm the other countries. And so I got a fine job, thirty dollars a week, and then it was forty, then fifty, then sixty, then seventy, when we got in the war!"

She smiled all over her ravished old face and nodded proudly. "Trust little Maudie! Did she blow it the way the rest of the women and girls did? She did not, no sir! She saved most of it! And that's why I've got me seven thousand dollars in the bank, right now, and a good thing, because with the pay I'm getting now, and the high price of everything, I can't save a cent. You see I've got a teeny apartment in an old building in the suburb, just two rooms, and share a bath with Nancy next door, but I got to pay sixty dollars a month for it, and food!

"And all through those years I'd read all the magazines I told you about, and dream and dream and dream. That's the only way I could stand things. Then Nancy, she says to me, 'The war's over, and why do you have to work in a plant in pants, get yourself a decent job, with all you know about style and clothes and perfumes.' So I looked around and after awhile I got a job in the main store, for thirty-eight dollars a week, not much, but with commissions, and I did so good, with my sense of style and what I know about clothes and what to wear when, that I got raised to fifty, and commissions, and all the ladies, some of them real rich, would ask for me, personally, because I always told them the truth and they liked to hear my stories about my wonderful childhood and all the wonderful life I'd had."

She stopped, and her ruined face paled and she put her hand to her heavy breast and held it there. She sighed deeply, long sighing breaths like tearless sobs. "I even saw some of the houses where the ladies lived, the rich ones I mean. I'd walk around at night, looking at them and I'd pretend I lived there. It got so that I could *see* into the houses, and all the expensive antiques and the pictures and drapes and silver and the Orientals, and sometimes at night I'd go right up to the windows and look, and sure enough, the rooms was like the ones I saw in the magazines! And I'd be living there, with a rich kind husband and have half a dozen kids, teen-agers then, or maybe older and married and with kids of their own. It was terrific."

She dropped her head and then her swollen eyes fell on the brilliant ring on her finger. She lifted her hand and let the soft light strike on it. "This ring," she said, half to herself, and smiling apologetically. "It's just fake, though the ring is real white gold. I paid forty-five dollars for it, on a sale, and you just can't tell that it isn't a diamond, honestly. Only a jeweler could; one of those manmade things, you know? Everybody thinks it's real. I tell them Jerry gave it to me when we got engaged."

Sudden exhaustion took her and she leaned back in the chair and coughed weakly. Her massive body took on the lines of dissolution and collapse, and she became smaller. Her voice was hardly above a whisper. "And that's all. It's all I ever had, a few dreams. Did they hurt anybody? No. Sure, they were lies, though sometimes I'd think they were true. It didn't hurt me. I don't see how I could have lived without them, Doctor.

"But now I'm awful tired, though the company doctors say I'm in good health. I get to thinking. I've got seven thousand dollars, and a job, and I won't have a job much longer. They wanted to retire me this year, but how am I going to live on eighty-five or ninety dollars a month Social Security? So they're letting me stay on awhile, after I explained to them. The company psychiatrist asks me, 'How about an aunt, or cousin, or daughter, or sister or brother you could live with, or a close friend, doubling up?' And I just laugh. I say I want to be independent and I want to keep my nest-egg. My God, suppose I got real sick for a year or something! How would I get along?

"Lots of people say that I should have saved more, but I saved every penny I could, and it isn't enough, and there were all those years before and after the war when I was making only enough to get by with. And the money's drawing interest in the bank. I hope they'll let me go on until it's about nine thousand dollars, but the way money's going down these days that isn't much anyway. Somebody said I could buy an annuity, you know? You put in all your money, and they pay you so much a month, and I think it would be around ninety or maybe a hundred, and it's ten years or life, and I could get along with the Social Security as well, but what if I live ten years more and they drop me? I don't care if I die sooner, for there's no one who'd want any money left, and besides the insurance company would keep what was left.

"It's gotten to the point, Doctor, where I worry all the time. It takes every cent I make just to live these days, and I could use more. And then, after all these years! it keeps coming back to me about how I never really had anyone in my life, and when I do fall asleep I dream I'm back there in the orphan asylum and a kid again, or I dream about Aunt Sim and Uncle Ned, and the way they'd kick me around and starve me, and I dream of Jerry and how he'd beat me up, and that ratty room we lived in, and all the hours in the factory, and how cold and hungry I always was, and when I wake up I'm in sweats and trembling, and I'm afraid all over again. Sometimes it takes me a couple hours before I can pretend I had everything, like I told you, just so I can get through another day.

"And then I'm so tired I can hardly wait to quitting time and I go home and can hardly eat, sometimes, and I'm afraid to go to bed because of the awful dreams.

"Oh, God, if I just had someone I could *talk* to, somebody who gave a damn about me, somebody I didn't have to lie to and pretend to! Somebody who cared a little bit about me! When I get a cold I get scared to death, thinking about a doctor or who'd take care of me if I couldn't work for a while, or bring me something to eat, or just *care*. Just once, just caring once. But I don't have anybody and I never did."

Her voice rose to a thin and lashing cry. "Oh, you can just sit there and you don't care! They say you listen, but what good does it do? I've told you the truth and I bet you're sitting there and laughing to yourself and thinking, 'It takes all kinds.' It sure does, Doctor, it even takes kinds like me, God damn it!"

She pushed herself to her feet and she ran to the curtain and glared at it through streaming eyes. She saw the silver button, and remembered what she had heard, that if you wished to see the man who had listened to you you needed only to press that button. Recklessly, and sobbing deep in her chest, she struck the button with the palm of her hand, as a child would strike at something in its desperate misery.

The blue curtains flowed aside and the soft light lay upon the man who listens, and when Maude Finch saw his face and his great and agonized eyes, his loving and merciful eyes, she sprang back with a choked sound and she covered her mouth with her hands. She stared at him with wide, wet intensity and he regarded her gently, and slowly she let her hands fall and her tears became fewer and fewer. Still keeping her eyes on him she put her hand behind her and groped for the chair. She sat down and let her lids drop. She began to speak in a low voice.

"They never said you were like this— When I heard about you, they said you were a terrible person; it scared me; they said you were the Judge. I only heard about you a few times, so long ago I don't remember, but I thought you'd hate

205

me—all the lies and everything. They said you hated liars and hypocrites, and I guess I've been that all my life, and maybe it don't mean anything to you that it was the only way I could live, lying like that to myself and everybody else, and pretending. After all, you are the Judge, and you're terrible. That's what they said, all those years ago, and it scared me."

She opened her eyes and the man was still regarding her with gentle suffering and love, and she began to weep again, but softly. "I see! You don't hate me for what I did, do you? And all that I went through in my life—it wasn't even all that as bad as one day of yours, was it? And you didn't have anybody to talk to, either, did you? Oh, they listened to you, they sure did, but what good did it do? They didn't believe you, but people believed me a little, and that's something. They don't even believe you now.

"You didn't have anyone to talk to except yourself. And God."

Her eyes suddenly shone with wonder and she sat upright. "That's it, you had God to talk to! And so do I! That's what you mean, isn't it? I can talk to you, any time I want to, anywhere! If only I'd known a little more about you in the beginning. That's what the real depriv—the real not-having—not having you in all those years.

"But now I have you!" The wonder brightened on her face and the years left her and she was a child again, hoping. But this time the hope had verity and truth. "That's what you're trying to tell me, isn't it, that I have you, and that if I have you you'll always listen and help me, and that I mustn't be afraid any longer."

She struck her palms together like a child who has suddenly come upon a delightful and incredible truth that swept its heart with joy.

"I know it's true, I know it's true, like nothing else in my life, real or a dream! And I know, somehow, that what I dreamed about, all the wonderful things, you'll save for me, someplace. Won't you? People to care about me, but mostly you. Lovely things to look at, and some beautiful place to walk. How do I know all that? I just *know!*

"And it's all the world to me, and now I'm not tired, and I can face what's to come, because always you'll be with me, and listening to me, won't you?"

She lumbered to her feet and went to the man and timidly touched his knee. It seemed to her that strength came to her weary flesh and a lightness to her spirit. "I'm just remembering something I heard when I was a kid, when once I heard a minister in the orphan asylum: 'Goodness and mercy shall follow me all the days of my life, and I shall dwell in the house of the Lord forever.' With you, and that's all that I care about now."

SOUL TWELVE: The Adversary and the Man who Listens

"—The least of these"

The waiting room was almost filled when he entered, but no one seemed to see him except for a very young girl with mad eyes. He became aware that she saw him and he stopped, and it was as if a dark shadow had fallen over her distraught face. She most certainly saw him and he half-smiled. He knew at once what troubled her and what had caused that dilated appearance in her pupils, and the long, fixed stare. He knew her very well. There was no pity in him, no regret, but only contempt. Weakling. Wretch. Contemptible animal. She was only eighteen, he recalled, but her soul was shriveled within her like a bud that had withered before it had opened. Anathema, anathema, he thought. It was no triumph to him that he had brought down that meager soul so easily. She had needed little tempting! "Emily?" he said, very softly.

The girl's gray mouth puckered drily and the faintest whimper came from her, so faint that no one heard but himself. It was a mewling sound, like a stricken puppy. "But you did it to yourself, Emily," he said in that soft voice which did not disturb others or even make them look up. "You knew what you were about; you had no innocence, did you? You cannot even claim ignorance; it was everywhere. What! Are you going to complain it was all the fault of your environment? That cheap excuse, that mean excuse, that lying excuse? Emily, go home. The Man cannot help you. Go home—and forget."

He was full of hate for her. It was her kind, her countless kind, who had made him what he was, who had reduced him to what he was so long ago that it sometimes seemed incredible to him. He could see their heaped faces, their heaped bodies. Not even he could count them or even know them all.

"What? Are you not leaving?" he asked her. The others in

the room moved restlessly, disturbed. The girl stared at him, the big black eyes like glass. But she did not move. This was intolerable to him. He wanted to take her by one of her desperately thin arms and drag her from this abominable place and throw her into the gutter. She saw his furious desire. Her eyes fled from him and fastened themselves on the tablet in the wall: "I can do all things in Him Who strengthens me."

"No," he said, "not even He can help you now, Emily. You are sweating and trembling. See how you yawn! In a little while it will be unbearable. I know. Poor Emily. I really pity you. Do you remember what you read in your school, Emily? 'The fault, dear Brutus, is not in our stars— But in ourselves that we are underlings.' You were born an underling, Emily and you will die one. You are wasting your time here. He—He has nothing but disgust for you. Go home."

The girl did not move. She was still staring at the tablet. Great drops of water were falling from her forehead. Her lips stirred. He laughed silently. So, she prayed, did she, the little monster? Let her attempt to escape; he had her fast. She had corrupted two other girls, younger than herself, to satisfy her vile appetite, her craving appetite, her deadening appetite. He tried to force her to look at him again, but her lips were still drily stirring in her incoherent prayer.

He lost interest in her. She was nothing. He moved to the door of the other room and bent his handsome head and listened acutely. Then before any chime could sound he opened the door and entered. He moved quickly; the closing door was only a shadow behind him and no one in the waiting room, except Emily, had seen it open and close.

The white walls and ceiling, and the light, were very still. It was as if someone in the room had caught a breath, and held it. The young man smiled. He nodded at the blue curtain which covered the alcove. And, after a moment it silently moved apart and he saw the Man who waited there, and who listened endlessly.

They looked at each other in silence. The young man inclined his head with gravity. No man before who had entered this room had ever been half so beautiful as he. No one could ever match his vibrancy, his electric energy, and the power of his spirit.

"Are you not very tired now?" asked the young man.

"No," said the Man who Listened. "I am never tired."

"Once you were," said the young man, courteously.

"No. I am incapable of weariness, just as you are incapable. Or, could it be that you are weary at last?"

The young man considered, or he affected to consider. His eyes were merry and amused. Then he shook his head. The eyes of the Man who Listened were full of sadness. He sighed. Hearing that sigh the young man moved as if struck by a pain of his own. "May I sit down?" he asked.

"The chair is waiting for you," said the Man who Listened.

"But not the one I wanted." The young man sat down and folded his white hands on his darkly glistening knee. "I have my own," he added. "It is uniquely my own. I made it with my own hands. You had no part in it."

"No," said the Man, and his gaze at the stranger was heavy with sorrow. "I did not make it for you."

"I am still His son," said the stranger.

"That is true," said the Man. "Forever."

The stranger was silent for a while. The light in the room dimmed as if with his thoughts. Then anger took his face like a convulsion, and it was an anger touched with suffering.

"It is some time since we had one of our endless discussions," said the stranger. "Now that everything here seems to be totally in my hands I thought to visit you again."

"It is not all in your hands," said the Man. "You know that, of a certainty. But speak. I confess that I have never forgotten your voice and that once you loved Him."

"Do you think I do not love Him now?"

The Man was quiet for a moment. At last he said, "You love Him, and that is the worst of your punishment. You cannot refrain from the loving. But you and I know how closely love and hatred are entwined. But never has He hated you."

"I know that. But men hate Him with all their black hearts, and that is our mutual knowledge."

"Not all," said the Man, and he smiled with tenderness. "Listen! Can you not hear those who speak to Him?"

They listened together. Now a confused yet harmonious sound emanated from the walls, from the room, from everywhere, beseeching, praising, loving, piteous, brave—but faithful. Music flowed and twined through the voices like threads of gold and scarlet and silver, palpitating, rising and falling. There were the voices of children, piping simply; there were the voices of young men and women, of holy souls in cloisters, of lonely souls in private wildernesses and in private anguish, of old people, of people in sorrow—but faithful. The voices rose and fell like an advancing and then retreating sea which advanced again and broke on invisible rock in invisible rainbows. But rock and rainbow were not invisible to the Man who Listened, and to the stranger. They saw them clearly.

"Not a multitude," said the stranger.

"But His own," said the Man. "Not ever yours."

"They will soon be silenced," said the stranger. "You and I—we know the future. These innocent voices will be silenced by the silencers, who in their turn will be forever silenced. How peaceful will be the orbit of this world, then! Fragments, catching the light of the moon and the sun, but only fragments, deathful and dark and lifeless."

The Man did not speak. The stranger waited politely, then when there was no sound at all in the room he said, "I did not choose it. They chose it themselves. I did not plan it; they planned it themselves. Are you not proud of your part in it?"

The Man smiled a very little and with grave pain. "That is a question you have always asked me, and you have desired the answer with a desire greater than all else. You do not see the future as I see it, but only as you imagine I see it. You can never know my mind and my thoughts. In that, you are no wiser than any of the tormented you have seduced and destroyed. My brothers."

"They chose not to be your brothers." The stranger rested his elbow on the arm of the chair and he shaded his dark and beautiful face with his hand. "I did not take them from you. They came to me, eagerly. They solicited my help. They poured themselves like vehement snowflakes into my hands. They never came to you like that; they come, the few who do, one by one, almost reluctantly. But my own stormed my very battlements; they storm it hourly. I am deafened by their urgent voices, their demands, their adulation. What they offer me is loathsome."

"I do not find them loathsome," said the Man. "I bled for them, and I bleed for them."

"And sometimes—but not often—in the very midst of their urging, their desire for me, they hear your voice. And sometimes—but so few that they are not worth the counting—they turn from me and fall at your feet."

"One is one, and one is all," said the Man. "What you despise I love. What you would destroy I would save. My ear is never turned aside, never closed."

"But it is closed to me."

The Man did not reply. The tortured eyes gazed at the stranger long and deeply.

"I lie, as always," said the stranger. "Your ear is not closed to me. But how could it be possible for me to repent when I know what I know, when righteous hate is in my heart though you would not call it righteous?" He laughed abruptly, and his laughter was echoed by a thin turmoil of far but tumultuous mockery. "—'All the morning stars sang together and the sons of God shouted for joy!' Do you remember that hour?"

"I have never forgotten."

"It was the hour when He bestowed free will on all His worlds, when angels and men—in all His worlds—were crowned with their kingly responsibility to live or to die, to stand at His side or to retreat from Him. Was that not too terrible a gift?"

"You are all His children. Do you think He wished unreasoning beasts who obeyed because they had no desire to disobey, no choice? The free offering of a soul is more to Him than mechanical creatures who sacrifice at an altar they do not know exists and offer a sacrifice of which they are not aware. Obedience is not desirable when disobedience is impossible. Love is not love if there is not an alternative, hate. Worship is not worship if possibility of denial is not present. What is His essence is the essence of His children; He would that His children be as the angels, who are my brothers also, capable of disobedience and pride but also capable of obedience and humility. As He is Spirit, so are His children spirit also, and shall one be divided from the other as cruel master is divided by slaves who have no choice? But we have spoken of this before through all the centuries."

"It was still the most terrible of gifts. I am what I am because of that offering."

"Would you prefer that you had had no choice?"

The stranger shook his head. "No, for then I should have had no existence."

"True. Then this dialogue was unnecessary."

"Without free will there is no true existence?"

"There is no true existence. You have said it."

"But it should not have been given to humanity. It should have been the prerogative of the angels."

The Man moved his head painfully. "Consider yourself. It was your prerogative. Consider how you have used it. Yet you despise men, who are lesser by nature than yourself, who are lesser in resistance to evil. Detest them if you must. But remember that many repent and come to Him. Those who

212

departed with you do not return to Him and do not say, 'God, have mercy on me, a sinner.'"

"What we chose is our choice," said the stranger, lifting his grand head high.

"And what you chose was your pride. You accepted His gift, but consider it your own alone, and would deny it to the least of His children. Are you greater than He?"

"I never believed that, nor in truth did I truly desire it. I was at His hand and He loved me. I protected His grandeur and His awful majesty, not out of hatred but out of love. I was jealous for Him. I would have none approach Him with unclean hands nor call Him 'Father' as I called Him Father, nor look upon Him with my own eyes. If I was proud, I was proud for him, and detested those who dared, in their arrogance, to know Him also. But you have known this for a long time."

"Yes, for a very long time," said the Man with a sigh.

The stranger contemplated the hands and the brow and the side of the Man. "Did I inflict that agony on you? Was it I who spat upon you and jeered at you? Was it I who mocked your torture?"

"You have forgotten. I chose it for myself."

"Still, it was man who consummated it, and not I. They choose for themselves; I do not make the choice for them."

"But you have heard the voices of those who have come to me at last. They choose for themselves; I do not make the choice for them."

"You have lost. Have you not lost?"

"Ah, you would like to know! But I shall not tell you, little one."

There was silence again in the room. Then slowly the stranger began to beat his clenched fists on the arms of the chair. As his anger rose the light from the walls darkened, but the light in the alcove increased until it almost blinded him.

"I shall conquer!" said the stranger. "Am I not prince of this world? He shall repent again, that He made it! As He has repented other worlds which became but bloody holocausts and drifted away with the suns."

"If you are so certain, why are there tears on your face?"

"It is because I am certain that I weep."

"Ah," said the Man, very gently. "It does not please you, then."

"It pleases me when I prove that He was wrong in the beginning."

"Your pleasure could be mistaken for anguish. Would that men felt such pain in their hearts!"

The stranger stood up, trembling and darkly radiant, a frightful but magnificent presence. "The whimperers, yours, Lord, await you. I regret that I have delayed you for an hour. Shall I leave?"

The Man considered. Then he said, "Call whom you will. And let us see what will come about, in our presence."

The stranger smiled. "There is a woman-creature, young in years, in that room. She is past all redemption. She is mine. I will call her."

He lifted his hand and pointed with a threatening and commanding gesture at the door. Immediately the chime sounded. The door opened a moment later and Emily, the girl with the mad eyes and the dampened face entered, breathing with a ragged and audible sound.

"Come, Emily," said the stranger in a voice of mock kindness. "You see me, do you not?"

"Yes, I see you," she said. She seemed fascinated by his appearance, by his forbidding splendor, for neither angel nor man had ever possessed his beauty. He was fire and marble midnight, flashing and burning and darkening—and his shadow flowed and ebbed on the white walls, and struck the ceiling in alternating bands of flame and blackness.

"Who am I, Emily?"

She pressed her trembling hands along her cheeks, then slowly pushed back her disordered brown hair. She licked her dry lips. The sweat shone on her forehead, on her upper lip. "I don't know," she said. "But I think I know your voice." Her own had become weak and uncertain.

"Yes, you know my voice. You have known it since you were a child. But—do you know him, Emily?"

She obeyed his pointed finger and looked at the Man who Listens. She started violently. She shrank back until the seat of the chair struck the back of her knees, and she fell involuntarily into the chair. But now she could only look at the Man in the alcove.

"Do not be afraid," said the stranger in his mocking kindness. "As you see, it is only an Image. It was always only an Image to people like you, Emily, and so always it will be, a dream, a myth, or a subject for scorn and contempt, for denial and rejection, for heaped derision and accusation, to all men. Do you understand what I am saying, you uncouth and wicked young wretch, or are you lost again in your drugged fantasies?"

"I understand," she whispered. But still she did not look at him. She gazed only at the Man in the alcove. "That is why I came here, in the first place."

"And you knew what you would see?"

"No. Not really." Was that disappointment in her voice, or suffering? "I—I thought perhaps he was—"

"A doctor whom you could persuade to give you more of your drugs?"

She was small and desperately emaciated, with a narrow face blotched at the cheekbones with a raw and unhealthy color. The eyes were enormous in that sunken oval, the nostrils distended. Her lips appeared of no tint at all, but only a dry line of half-opened torment. However, her clothing was good and her small hands were delicate and well-kept. Her disordered brown hair flowed long and straight over her thin shoulders and had no lustre.

"I," she said, and swallowed, "I don't know what I expected. Help, perhaps." The mad eyes shifted, dulled, fell.

"Help in what way?" His voice was harsh now and she shrank. "Answer me, Emily, and answer truly. You cannot lie to me, for I know lies at once. You see, I invented them."

"I—I thought things—could be different for me, if somebody listened and told me what to do."

"But your parents, and your teachers, have been telling you all your life. Have they not?"

She wrung her fingers together and stared at them.

"They did not hate you, Emily. They loved you. Nothing of any importance was denied to you, though your parents are not rich and are only kind and simple people. Your teachers believed you were extraordinarily intelligent; they, too, gave you all they had to give. What excuse have you, Emily, for what you have done to your body, your mind and your soul?"

She continued to wring her fingers, over and over, until they reddened.

"You have no excuse, no excuse that you were orphaned or abandoned or unloved, or rejected, that you were deprived of simple necessities, that you were the object of cruelty and hate. You were given too much, until you were surfeited, until you believed you were important and deserved even more. You became discontented, and discontent leads to arrogance and to demand. Your father went into debt to give you foolish toys. Your mother denied herself to give you the clothing you desired. Your teachers strained their tired bodies to polish that fine mind of yours. But always, you wanted

215

more and more, and were frustrated when it was not possible for anyone to give you more. What did you consider yourself, Emily? A princess with a world at her feet, as so many stupid millions of your generation, your pampered and worthless generation, also think of themselves?"

She did not speak, but slowly her head nodded, over and over.

"It was bad enough for you to destroy yourself, Emily. But you have destroyed two other girls, younger than you are. Why?"

"I—it's hard to explain," she whispered. "You have to know what it's like. After awhile—they—want more money from you. And you begin to steal from your mother's purse; you take little things and sell them; you steal from the shops, too. Then there never is enough money for—for— So, they ask you—" She swallowed desperately. "You've got to have it, that's all. It's like something eating you; you've got to feed it, or you'll die. You don't know what it's like."

"I know only too well," said the stranger. "I was the first to feel it. I was the one to whom you came, Emily, for your first pleasure. The first pleasure which finally became not pleasure only but a wild necessity. Was life so frightful for you that you were driven to it?"

Her face slyly lit up. She lifted her head eagerly, assent ready in her eyes, on her lips. But her glance struck, not on the stranger, but on the Man in the alcove. The malicious radiance receded abruptly from her face; she dropped her eyes again.

"It is only an Image," said the stranger. "Only you and I are real, Emily. Speak."

"No, my life was all right," she muttered. "It—I mean, I only wanted some fun. Everybody talked about it; it was fun; something I hadn't tried yet. I'd tried about everything else. You know?"

"Yes, I know. Did I not suggest all of it to you from the very beginning, you unloving, undisciplined, selfish, pampered, degraded wretch! Life had palled on you; it was so effortless, so easeful, so sheltered. Have you, in truth, not a legitimate accusation to hurl at your parents? I believe you have, Emily. They gave you all they could, and that should be accounted against them, as a blasphemy. They should have withheld; they should have demanded in return. They should have said to you, 'This far shall you go and no further.' But they did not say that to you. They thought that to deprive you of anything, even for the salvation of your soul,

216

was unjust to you. Tell me, Emily. Were they stupid or were they cruel?"

The girl pondered on his words. Her face had become wizened, haglike, the hair fallen about it. She shook her head like an animated toy, and did not answer.

"Were there no realities in your world that you had to buy dreams, to steal for them, to corrupt for them?"

She frowned vaguely, as a sleeper frowns when his body notifies him that it is disturbed. "I think," she murmured, "that it was because—because it was something different. Something to heighten sensation, something to make you free—?"

"Of what did you desire to be free, Emily?"

Her lips moved over and over, soundlessly, and sucked in and out. The light in the alcove glowed on her stunned face and in her lifeless eyes. Then she whimpered, "I guess—of myself. There wasn't anything in me. I don't know. I didn't have anything to fight for—I guess. But I wanted a lot of other things, you know? I can't explain it; I was restless all the time. Everything was dull as death. School; home; fun. I had to have something better."

"Even sexual encounters bored you finally, did they not?"

She shivered. "My parents never knew about that. They don't know about this, either."

"No. You were very clever. But they will soon know."

She gave a shrill cry, and let her head fall.

"How banal is evil!" said the stranger. "How ordinary. How undistinguished, colorless, commonplace! How low, base, silly. It has no splendor; it is not even frightful, for if it possessed frightfulness it would also possess terror, and terror increases in proportion to its abundance. Evil dulls all the senses and reduces man to less than beasthood, for beasts lack the capacity to be evil. It finally deprives man of His awful gift of free will."

"True," said the Man who Listens. "But not always. You will recall David the King, for instance. And he was only one."

"Look on this woman, this degenerate, debased woman who has no valid excuse for her crimes against herself or others, except ennui. No pain drove her to this pass, no sorrow, no extremity of despair. She is the embodiment of the banality which is evil. Therefore, she is beyond your salvation. She cannot even declare that love brought her to this place in her existence, as love brought the Magdalene. She is not even worthy to be stoned. She is a nothingness."

"She is a soul," said the Man.

The girl had heard this exchange in the throbbing of her drug-induced madness. She had slowly lifted her head and listened, her faded lips parted, her eyes moving from one to the other. Finally her gaze fixed itself on the Man in the alcove.

"I heard you!" she said. "You aren't just an Image, are you? You really are, aren't you?"

"Yes, dear child."

"You hear only your imagination, Emily," said the stranger. "It is truly only an Image, a dream, fashioned by man of the stuff made by man or grown by earth."

Emily stared at the Man.

She saw a great alcove, twice the height of a man, and as wide as the stature of a tall human being. It arched like a shell of light—and in that shell reared a tremendous Crucifix of smooth carved wood, faintly trembling with radiance. On the Cross was nailed the God-Man, carved of ivory, white as the moon, vaster than any man who had ever lived, more muscular, more masculine, and perfect in every sinew and line and curve. He lived; He appeared to move in His agony. From the heroic and serene forehead dripped drops of bright blood, and from the hands and the wounded side and the crossed Herculean feet. But above all was the majesty of the mighty face, the face of youth imbued with humanity and yet with the aloof, impersonal and remote splendor of divinity.

Pity and mercy, contemplation and force, seemed to pour like the rays of the sun upon the shriveled girl who looked upon that face, and power and fortitude. The self-willed Sacrifice hung upon the Cross, straining yet resigned, offered up by Himself, at once a King and a Lamb. Government lay on His shoulder, and humiliation strained from His body.

But it was upon His eyes that the girl lingered most fully, the great and tender eyes, glowing in their sockets, the just and tormented yet smiling eyes.

The stranger moved closer to the girl and there were two vast and crepuscular shadows rising from his shoulders, and they stirred like wings, for he was an archangel, the most puissant of all the angels, the most grand, though the glistening robes he wore were blackly shining and the sword at his side pulsed like lightning. Only his face and his hands were white, as white as death and as cold. In the folds of his garments there appeared to be glints of fire. His face was beautiful and stern and implicit with a misery and sorrow and anger beyond the understanding of man, and rage and hatred sparkled in his eyes.

"It does not live," said Lucifer. "It is an Image. Man obliterated Him long ago and drove Him from his imaginings and from the filthy little alleys of his existence. You will observe that it is fashioned only of wood and ivory and paint. It has no verity. You and I, Emily, are the only reality. In truth, you have no reality of your own. I am all that is and all that ever will be."

"I heard His voice," the girl said. "I heard what you said to each other."

"You heard only my voice, not His, for has not your generation declared that He has no voice, and that He never lived? If He endures at all it is in hidden places where the fearful pray or in the sickly brains of poets. What has He to do with your world, and mine?"

For the first time the girl felt an utter terror, beyond anything she had ever known in her short existence. She grasped the arms of the chair; she turned her feverish eyes upon Lucifer. Her mouth opened and closed, and she saw all he was, and her fogged soul crouched in dread and loathing.

"Yes," she said. "You do exist. You aren't a fable, a lie. You do have reality."

"I am the reality you have made, woman, and the countless myriads of those like you, through the uncountable centuries, from the beginning of time."

One word caught her frantic thoughts, which were hurrying through her skull like frantic mice. "I—I am not a woman, an adult. I am only eighteen years old; that's all I am."

"You have the body and the soul of a woman; you can marry and conceive and bear children. It is I who told your mentors that you were a 'child,' and not responsible for your actions and your desires and your perversions and your degradation. How eagerly they listened to me! How eagerly they all listen, the betrayers of men. But, above all, how delightedly you have listened, woman."

She shrank from him, naked and alone, abandoned and shivering in a cold she had never felt before.

"My child," said the Man on the Cross, "why did you come to Me?"

She had heard Lucifer's voice, like the clashing of steel. Now she heard a Voice like the voice of a father, not the weak father at home whom she knew gave her gifts in craving for an affection she did not possess to give to anyone.

"He spoke!" she cried, and pointed to the Cross. "He spoke! I heard Him!"

"You hear Me because you sought Me," said the Man.

She pushed herself to her feet for an awful terror of Lucifer had fallen on her like a curse again, and she did not know where to run. She looked at the Man, then she tottered to Him and fell in a small heap below Him.

"You are mad," said Lucifer, and he stood behind her and the murky shadow of his wings lay on her body. "You have been mad for over a year, and the only relief is your drug, the drug of dreams and fantasy and far and beautiful places and strange voices. That is the only heaven you will ever know. Come with me."

But the girl reached out and grasped the feet of the Man above her and it seemed to her distracted mind that they were not ivory but pulsing flesh.

"Save me," she groaned. "Oh, God, save me!"

"It does not exist," said Lucifer. "Only I exist."

"Tell me, My child," said the Man. "Speak."

She laid her head on His feet. Her whisper was shrill in the room. "Everything was so empty. Just one day after another, of fun and food and money and clothes and—doing what I shouldn't. It made me dirty, but everybody was doing it. For kicks, for laughs, for a ball. Why not? I said to myself. What else is there but what I've got? Just growing older, out of my teens, and being like my mother, and marrying like my mother. And," she murmured, "having kids like me, and living in a flat house like ours full of gadgets, and having a new car every year. Just—nothing. And then I'd be old, like my grandmother, and there wouldn't be any fun any longer. How could I stand it?"

"And no one ever told you there was anything else?"

"There wasn't anything else. Oh, some of my teachers told me that I had to 'advance the cause of humanity,' but why? I had to think of myself, didn't I? I wasn't just living for other people. I didn't want what they wanted!" Her cry was a scream of despair. "So, there was a way; it was fun and wonderful and when you had it you were beautiful and ten feet tall and you walked on clouds and everybody admired you and thought you—were glamorous. Nothing mattered but that."

"Look at Me, My child. Lift your eyes to Me."

The girl's face was dripping with sweat and tears. Slowly she raised her head and encountered again the living eyes of the Man.

"You heard nothing," said Lucifer, "but only your madness and your own thoughts."

"Long have I known you," said the Man. "Long have I followed you, and saw your emptiness and saw those who gave you that emptiness and not the bread of life. You are one of My little ones, betrayed by a plentitude of worthless gifts, by false tongues who told you you were important, more than any other generation, and that you were more valuable than all else that lived. I saw the degradation heaped on your immortal soul by those who should have been your protectors, who should have shown you the way of life and not the way of a materialistic ruin. I saw the fine buildings built for you, where no discipline was imposed upon you, and where your mind was not truly polished but darkened with sophistries.

"Above all, I saw your pain."

"You have never had a pain; you do not know sorrow or despair; you have not been honed on any stone," said Lucifer. "You have your pleasure, and your pleasure still awaits you. Cease this lying to yourself and thinking your own thoughts, for they have no reality."

But Emily looked up imploringly at the Man's tender face. "I did not look for anything else," she said. "I won't lie to you. I felt there was something else, but everybody said it was superstitious. I—became sick. I had to have someplace where I could be more than just Emily Hoyt, looking for fun all the time."

"And you came to Me, and I am He you sought."

She nodded her head with despairing eagerness. "I didn't know just—who, or what. No one ever told me. But yesterday, one of my instructors— Everybody laughs at him. They call him the Mess, because he isn't like the others. He stopped me in the hall, and he said, 'Emily, I don't know what's wrong with you, but you're very sick. Why don't you go to the Man who Listens, on the hill downtown?'

"I thought he was kidding," said the girl, holding tighter to the Man's feet. "But I began to think. Here I was, getting 'way down in my life, such as it was, and killing myself. And then," she faltered, "there was Charlotte and Bette, younger than me. It was like I'd just seen them for the first time, and that they were human beings like me, and sick like me. But the worst thing is that I—I had done that to them. It was like having sunglasses taken off and you saw everything in a big glare, and it burned your eyes. And I remembered all the dreams I'd been having this last week or so. Not the beautiful, romantic dreams, and the fun and feeling important. The terrible dreams."

She laid her head on His feet again. "Save me," she said. "Help me save Charlotte and Bette, too, more than me."

"Lying and contemptible fool!" said Lucifer. "Weak fool, who must run to insensate wood and bone to whimper out your sins!"

"Save me," Emily beseeched, and her shaking hands rose upon the body of the Man and touched His knees. She looked over her shoulder at Lucifer and she screamed and shuddered.

"Tell me he isn't really there, that I'm dreaming it!" she cried to the Man.

"He exists," said the Man, sadly. "He will always exist. It is not a dream."

"Then tell me what I must do, to get away from him!" the girl said.

"Think in your heart what you must do," said the Man.

She pondered, thinking, and the light was on her face but her shoulders and body lay in the shadow of evil. She began to tremble. She said, "No, how can I do that? The police, and telling my parents. They—they might put me in jail. They'll tell everybody. I'll be expelled, maybe. I'm a criminal; everybody will know what I've done to myself and the other girls. There won't be any place to go—"

"You have confessed your sins," said the Man. "You know your sins. The way will be bitter and terrible, but it is the way you must go. For you are not a child; you are a human soul, a woman, and you have brought your responsibilities upon your head. If you have no bravery now, no fortitude, then you are utterly lost and delivered forever to evil and death and agony."

The girl whimpered like a wounded child. "They'll take the—they'll take what I need away from me. They say it's awful. You can't stand it."

"There are horrors worse than that," said the Man. "You have already experienced them. That is why you came to Me."

"Maundering fool!" said Lucifer. "Why do you babble to yourself? There is none speaking to you but me."

"He lies?" said the girl to the Man.

"Yes. He is the father of lies. Child, will you take the way of pain and penance and repentance?"

She implored him with all her strength.

"You will help me?"

"You have only to call and I will hear you, and stand with you, for I am your Guardian who neither slumbers nor sleeps. But you must call Me in the worst of hours, in the most hopeless of hours, for they will be many."

"They will laugh at me," said the girl, "even when things are awfully bad."

"They laughed at Me also, but I endured."

"Yes," said the girl. "I—I heard of you, at Christmas and Easter. But I didn't know very much; I didn't want to know. My parents tried to take me to church, or a guidance counselor—they knew something was the matter with me. But I wouldn't go. I was afraid."

"But you will do as you know you must do?"

The girl laid her head on His feet and crouched before Him. "Yes, I will go," she said. "I will honestly go."

"It is your own choice?"

"Yes, it's my choice."

The Man looked at Lucifer and said, "You are rejected again, by this poor child. Does it wound you so greatly?"

Lucifer smiled. "What do tradition and rumor and ancient men say of me? That I have fallen but when men reject me, any man at all, I rise one step toward Heaven. Must I regret that?"

The Man's mighty face was full of musing. "You are His son, and you stood at His Hand and He called you 'Star of the Morning.'"

Lucifer retreated from Him and he lifted his hand as if to shade his face from the glory of the light. And as he retreated he became fainter and fainter and at last there was nothing of him at all in the room, where the walls were bathed in radiance.

The suffering girl was not aware of Lucifer's departure except that some appalling weight left her body and her shoulders. She said to the Man, "I can do all things in Him Who strengthens me."

She fell into a dazed dream for a little while. When she awakened she saw that she lay at the foot of the Crucifix. She was refreshed; the sweat still rolled from her face but there was a calmness and stillness in her in spite of her pain and her great trembling and the twitching of her deprived muscles.

"I had a dream," she said to the silent Man. "But it was a wonderful dream! I dreamed that You spoke to me." She quivered. "And I dreamed that—someone—else was here. I was so frightened."

She pushed herself to her feet. But she was crushingly weak; her knees shook under her.

"If it was a dream it was the best dream I ever had. I must believe in it. I'm going now. I'm going to tell Mom and Pop—everything. It'll be terrible. But I must do it.

"And I know You will help me."

The madness was gone from her eyes. There was a peace in her wretched body she had never known before. She went out into the summer night and lifted her eyes and for the first time she saw the stars.